THE WRONG MOTHER

Charlotte Duckworth is the author of five psychological thrillers, including *USA Today* bestseller *The Perfect Father*. She lives in Surrey with her partner and their daughter. You can find out more on her website: charlotteduckworth.com.

Also by Charlotte Duckworth

The Rival
Unfollow Me
The Perfect Father
The Sanctuary

THE
WRONG
MOTHER

CHARLOTTE
DUCKWORTH

QUERCUS

First published in Great Britain in 2022 by

QUERCUS

Quercus Editions Ltd
Carmelite House
50 Victoria Embankment
London EC4Y 0DZ

An Hachette UK company

A CIP catalogue record for this book is available
from the British Library

PB ISBN 978 1 52942 300 6
EB ISBN 978 1 52942 301 3

10 9 8 7 6 5 4 3 2 1

Typeset by CC Book Production
Printed and bound in Great Britain by Clays Ltd, Elcograf S.p.A.

Papers used by Quercus are from well-managed forests and other responsible sources.

PROLOGUE

No matter how much I clean, I still see the blood everywhere I look.

The fragments of his skull and pieces of his brain, spattered across every surface. Even the walls. It is the dominant image in my mind at all times. An image that has become my reality.

Who knew a shattered human skull could make such a mess?

No matter how hard I try – and I have, I have tried so hard – I can never clean the blood away. It springs back as soon as I have finished. And so I start again.

It is always there, visible only to me, fixed behind my eyes whenever I close them. Imprinted for life.

But still I clean. In desperate hope that one day the picture will fade.

Throughout our lives, we clean up after ourselves, over and over again.

But we can never truly escape what we have done.

NOW

FAYE

Jake is screaming and everyone in this Tube carriage is staring at us.

Of course they are. I would be staring too, if I wasn't the one with the screaming baby.

'Shh, shh,' I whisper, cradling him to me. Why won't he stop crying? I've made him a makeshift sling from my scarf, and have tucked him inside so that he's close to my chest. I read somewhere that the sound of your heartbeat is meant to soothe them. It's supposed to be familiar, as it's what they heard in the womb.

But it's not working. He's not happy and won't stop screaming.

'It's OK, little one,' I say, glancing up at the Tube map. Four more stops to Morden. But then what? My heart isn't beating, it's racing – no wonder it isn't calming him. 'It's OK. Not much longer, I promise.'

'Sounds hungry.'

I turn to see a middle-aged woman peering up at us from the disabled seat.

I nod. Of course. Of course he's hungry.

'Here,' she says, standing up. 'Have my seat. Poor thing. You both look worn out.'

I smile without meeting her eyes, and sink down into the seat. I don't like talking to strangers. I don't much like talking to anyone.

It quietens him a little. Perhaps he didn't like the vibrations of the train while I was standing. Or the noise.

'What's his name?' she says, leaning down as she holds on to the handrail. The train hurtles through the tunnel.

'Oh,' I say, pausing. I look up, but I can only focus on her chin. 'Jake. His name's Jake.'

'He's a little cutie,' she says. She's smiling. 'Is he your first?'

I nod.

'Don't worry, it gets easier. Mine are now sixteen and eighteen and don't want anything to do with me! I know it can feel all-consuming at this age though.'

I smile again because I know that's what she expects, and I look down at Jake. He yawns, his cries finally quieting. I exhale slowly. My heartbeat starts to slow. The relief.

'How old is he?'

'Oh,' I say, racking my brains. 'Um, three weeks. He's three weeks old.'

'Oh gosh, he really is box-fresh, then. Bless his heart.'

I nod. *Box-fresh.* As though you could just buy a baby and have it delivered the next day.

Jake yawns again in my arms. Has he worn himself out?

'Are you . . .' the woman continues. 'Sorry to ask, but are you OK? You seem a little jumpy. I wouldn't normally ask, it's just I'm a mental health nurse, and . . .'

'What?' I say, staring up at her. I feel like everyone in the carriage is looking at me again.

8

Look at her. What a terrible mother. She doesn't even have a proper sling for her baby. Can't even remember how old he is.

'Sorry,' she says, sliding into the now empty seat next to me. With alarm, I see her reach out a hand, as though she might pat me on the arm, but then she thinks better of it. 'I don't want to pry. It's just such a difficult time, having a newborn. It can be a real shell shock. But there's lots of help and support out there, if only you ask for it. I know that it can feel like everyone else is on top of things and you're falling behind, but honestly, everyone feels this way . . .'

She won't stop talking. Why won't she stop talking? I want to cover my ears with my hands, but I can't because I'm holding Jake.

She puts a hand on my shoulder.

'So really, my question is: are *you* OK?' she says. 'He'll be fine, you know. He *is* fine.'

I find myself staring at her. My eyes struggle to focus on her face. I can tell by the way she's looking at me that her thoughts about me aren't good. Distrust. Suspicion. She's thinking, *that baby deserves better than this woman.* I don't like it. My heart is hammering in my chest again and I feel sick.

Slowly, I shake my head.

'No,' I say, 'I'm . . .'

I glance down at Jake, his tiny red face now sealed shut, as though he's given up, accepted his fate.

'I'm sorry,' I say. 'It's been a difficult time.'

I swallow. Her eyes are wide now. She's looking at me the same way Hannah does sometimes.

9

'We're . . . we're on the run from his father,' I say, closing my eyes. I take a gulp of the musty air inside the Tube. 'He's . . . he's a very bad man and we need to get away from him.'

FAYE

Jake starts screaming again the second we get out of the Underground. He must be starving. What have I done? How could I be so stupid, not to think about his feeding routine?

I didn't have time to think. I just had to take him and go. I was terrified Louis would come back.

I'm still terrified now. I can't stop glancing behind me as I march towards the tiny supermarket opposite the station, in case I'm being followed.

Inside, I make my way to the baby aisle. I grab some ready-mixed milk and take it to the counter. I took Jake's changing bag when I ran but didn't realise the only bottle inside was empty. Jake screams the entire time and I find myself keeping my head down, terrified that if I look up and see anyone staring at us, I'll start to cry.

The woman from the Tube gave me her number and told me to call any time. She also gave me a leaflet about a domestic abuse charity. But I won't be needing that. It's too late now.

The man behind the counter looks at me suspiciously as he scans my items. Jake's piercing screams ring out across the shop.

'He's just hungry,' I say, trying to smile, make light of

it. What would Hannah say? 'I was a bit disorganised this morning.'

The man raises his eyebrows. He doesn't care. I wish he would hurry up.

People don't care about you as much as you think they do – that's what I learnt ages ago. But I keep forgetting. I keep worrying about what people think of me. But they're all wrapped up in their own lives.

'That will be £11.79,' he says, pushing my groceries towards me. I try to shove them in my rucksack, but it's difficult with Jake still screaming in my ear, and I'm worried he'll fall out of the sling.

The woman in the queue behind me tuts.

'Um, sorry,' I say. My cheeks are burning now, but I hurriedly yank my purse out from the front pocket of my rucksack and tap my card against the reader.

'Thanks,' I say, but the man doesn't even acknowledge me, handing me my receipt without saying a word.

Jake sounds as though he's about to pass out from the screaming. A word drifts into my mind. *Puce*. A colour I never thought I'd see a child go.

I'm failing him already.

'It's OK,' I say, as soothingly as possible. It's difficult to calm him down when I'm feeling just as stressed as he is. But that's my job, as his mother. What would Hannah do? 'It's OK, sweetheart. Really. Not much longer.' I kiss the top of his little head.

It's an eight-minute walk home and I practically sprint back, slamming the door behind us. We should be safe now, thank God.

It wasn't meant to be like this. Somehow I always end up making a mess out of everything.

'It's OK,' I say, feeling a little calmer now as I settle myself on my sofa and take the exhausted baby out from my sling. 'It's OK, Jake, I've got some milk for you.'

I unscrew the top of the bottle and peel the seal off the teat, screwing it onto the bottle.

He slurps gratefully, the scarlet colour draining from his face as quickly as the milk from the bottle.

'That's better, isn't it, sweetheart?' I coo, stroking him on the head. His eyes remain closed while he drinks, and eventually he falls asleep, his lips no longer sucking hungrily on the bottle. He's drunk nearly the entire thing.

I sit for a few minutes, just gazing at his wrinkled little face, the tiny trickle of milk that has dribbled down his chin. He's so beautiful. So precious. A gift.

It wasn't meant to be like this. But this is how it is now. And I'll have to make the most of it.

RACHEL

I'll miss Kylie.

Of course, some of her habits grated on me in the end, as they all do. She was never off her phone, for a start. If not tapping and tapping at the bloody thing, then screeching nonsense down it to her various friends. She often complained about the Wi-Fi speed – *oh, Rach, you really should upgrade, they have fibre in the village now, you know!*

I only had the internet installed a few years ago – so that I can keep in touch with Brian in Australia – and for all its convenience, it still leaves me a little uneasy. We shouldn't be so readily contactable. It's not necessary.

Even so, Kylie baked a good cake. And she amused me with all her stories.

I look down at my nails. The last manicure she did for me has seen better days. But I don't have any of the things I need to remove it.

'Rach,' she said, as she filed each nail into a perfect 'squoval' – a square-oval apparently, the most suitable shape for someone of my age. Kylie had talons. Secretly, I coveted them. 'Your nails are amazing. So strong!'

I had smiled at the compliment. I have always kept myself

fit and healthy. Strong hair, strong nails, strong bones, strong constitution.

But Kylie's gone now.

I stand there for a few moments, listening to the silence.

Never mind.

I wipe the windowsill with a damp cloth. When I lift the cloth up again, it's black with grime. Clearly, Kylie didn't clean her room once the whole time she was living here. I sigh. I'll have to steam-clean the carpet too.

And then, when that's done, I'll get the new advert up. The sooner the room is rented again, the better. And this time, I'll try to find someone who's a bit older. Someone who doesn't make me feel quite so out of touch.

I don't much like being in here, even though it's the bigger of the two bedrooms, so I work as quickly as possible. It'll always be Mother and Father's bedroom to me.

I take down the curtains and fold them neatly into the washing machine, and then I spend the rest of the afternoon moving the furniture into the middle of the room, so that I can thoroughly clean the carpet.

It's the best invention, my SmartWash vacuum cleaner. Part vacuum, part mop, it kills up to 99 per cent of bacteria, automatically dispensing the perfect amount of water and cleaning solution as you go. So clever.

Not all modern technology is bad.

By the time I'm finished, the room is sparkling and I am exhausted. But I feel as though a weight has been lifted.

I cut myself a slice of Battenberg and make a cup of

Yorkshire tea, then sit in the armchair in the bay window downstairs, looking out across the village green.

Not much going on today. It's nearly Halloween. I'll sit with the lights off, as usual, to make sure no kids try it on.

In my day, trick-or-treating was seen as a disgusting American custom. But it seems to have caught on over here, lately.

Don't we have enough of our own traditions, without taking on theirs too?

I shake my head. The world is an annoying place. It was annoying when I was young, and it seems to get more annoying with every year that passes.

I make my way over to the small desk in the alcove and switch on the big black tower underneath.

It takes my computer a good ten minutes to gee itself up these days. Kylie had laughed at it, called it an ancient relic.

I didn't like that. When she laughed at me.

'It's perfectly serviceable,' I snapped. 'It does everything I need it to do.'

'You could spend some of my rent getting yourself a laptop, you know,' she replied, but I turned away from her, resisting the urge to tell her that I didn't appreciate her lip.

Eventually, the yellowing screen on my desk flickers into life and I log on to the World Wide Web, checking my emails first. Nothing of interest there. Just lots of tempting marketing emails from chocolate companies. My one vice.

I move them to the little bin icon methodically, then I bring up the page for rentaroom.com.

Nigel told me about this site. I'd always put up an ad in the local newsagents before, but at one of our meetings, he told me about advertising online.

'You'll get a much greater variety of lodgers to pick from that way,' he said.

Annoyingly, he was right.

I log into my account, copying the password from the Post-it note stuck on the screen, and pull up my previous advert. There's a big button that says 'Duplicate', so I click on that, wait for the screen to load itself again, and then check over the ad carefully.

Bright and spacious double bedroom now available in my immaculate cottage in the centre of Helston village. You will be sharing with me, a 64-year-old female and the homeowner. Looking for someone clean and tidy.
Non-smoker.
Shared kitchen and luxury bathroom (recently refitted).
All bills included. Bus stop five minutes away.
No students. No time-wasters.
£450 per month. Available immediately.

I pause at the last bit. Obviously, Kylie's departure was unexpected. I hope that doesn't look suspicious.

I sit back in my chair. I suppose if anyone asks, I can just say she ran out of money and had to move out in a hurry.

It'll be fine. No one from the village has asked after her yet. The ambulance came late at night – I don't think many people even noticed.

And anyway, people have short-term memories. They're all so busy, wrapped up in their own lives.

I publish the advert, and then move to the dining table to work on my jigsaw.

It'll be interesting to see who I get this time.

FAYE

It's only a matter of time before Louis will be here, hammering on my door, demanding I hand Jake back.

I won't let him. I can't do it. Jake belongs with me.

I lay him down on my bed and search the wardrobe until I eventually unearth my suitcase, covered in dust.

A change is as good as a rest. That's what they say.

I've never liked change.

I cram things into the suitcase, unthinking. I grab my passport from the drawer in my bedside table before realising it's out of date. Never mind. I sling it in anyway, along with the wedding photo I keep beside my bed, and my medication.

I pause, one hand on the blue velvet dress hanging in my wardrobe. I can't bear to leave it, so, even though it will take up too much space, I carefully fold it in half and put it on top of everything else in the suitcase.

Then I lie down on the floor and grapple around in the dust underneath the bed, drawing out the metal safe with difficulty. I tap in the combination and wait for it to open.

Here's all the money I have saved from years of being paid cash-in-hand. My father was big on having cash in the house. He didn't like the idea of using a card to pay for things.

'You don't want people tracking your every move, Faye,' he said. 'It's none of their business.'

It was also illegal, I knew. To take this cash and not declare it. I have no idea how much there is – I wasn't intent on tax-evading, I just never quite got around to paying it into a bank.

Perhaps I'm more like my father than I want to admit.

But even so, I'm grateful now. For this. My life's savings. Here, when I need it most. I count it quickly and tuck it into my pouch.

I pull out all the baby clothes and bits I bought for Jake and shove them in the lid of the suitcase, zipping the whole thing shut and pulling it onto its side.

A quick glance at the clock on the wall tells me that it's 11.45am. I have a lesson at 12pm – one of my adult students. I have to be gone before they arrive.

I take one last look around, whispering a pathetic apology to my houseplants.

My flat. It's a sorry state of affairs. All I have to show for myself after forty years of life. One grotty, dark basement, that doesn't even belong to me.

I'm reminded of my childhood home. The stench, the mess. I swore I would do better, that I wouldn't end up living like that, but I have.

I imagine someone breaking in in a few weeks' time. My neighbour perhaps. Or my landlord. Wondering what's become of me. They might expect to find me curled up on the sofa, dead. Flies buzzing and feasting on my remains.

But instead, they'll find an empty apartment. Breakfast

dishes in the sink. Dirty washing in the basket. A home frozen in time.

How long before anyone realises I've gone? Will anyone even care?

I feel a stab of guilt about Jonas. He will care. He will wonder. But I can't risk sharing my plan with him.

And Hannah. I can't think about her yet.

I go over to the piano. It's too much, the thought of leaving it. But what choice do I have? It's that or baby Jake.

I stroke the lid one last time. It's a John Broadwood upright. The case is rosewood with inlaid marquetry. It's the most valuable thing I own and I never thought we would be parted.

'I'll come back for you one day, I promise,' I whisper to it, but I know it's a promise I can't keep.

How could Louis do this to me? How could he put me in this situation?

I feel tears threatening to emerge and I pull myself together. I have to be strong. For Jake. It's too late to go back now. Jake squirms in my arms, opening his eyes briefly and looking up at me.

I can get another piano. I can't get another baby.

And anyway, I have no choice. I have to go, before Louis finds me. Because God knows what he would do to me if he did.

My stomach is turning over.

I have no choice.

'You have no choice,' I say out loud to myself. 'No going back.'

But even so, as I close the door on my little flat – my life, my whole world up until now – I find myself looking back at the piano one last time, and I feel like my heart might break.

Outside the station, I withdraw as much money as I'm allowed from my current account. Then, I take the Tube back into town. Jake is well fed now, and happy. He sleeps soundly against my chest, tucked in my makeshift sling.

If anyone looked over at us, they might think I was a bit of a hippy, given my slightly disordered state, and the fact I'm wearing sunglasses and a beanie, but they wouldn't suspect a thing.

They wouldn't suspect that I was on the run from his father, or that I have just left behind everything I've ever known.

The beanie isn't much of a disguise, but it covers my hair, and will hopefully make it more difficult to spot me on CCTV.

For the first time ever, I'm grateful to be anonymous-looking, invisible. My whole life it's felt as though people have looked through me, rather than at me.

I need a plan now. I acted so hastily this morning – on impulse, driven by heart, not head. Now is the time for calm and clear thinking. The most important thing is that I get as far out of London as possible. Somewhere – anywhere – that he wouldn't think of.

I remember a great-aunt on my father's side. She had a little cottage in a tiny village in Norfolk. Perhaps I could go there, for now.

What was the village called? Hel-something. Helston? Yes, that was it.

I'll go to Helston.

A tingle of something like excitement rushes through me as I queue in Boots at King's Cross station, waiting to pay for nappies and more ready-mixed milk. But then I see someone out of the corner of my eye that stops me short. That slick of blond hair, the same Roman nose.

It can't be him, can it? He can't have found me already? *Please no.*

I feel sick with nerves, unable to risk looking round in case it is him and he spots me. I keep my head bent low, hoping the beanie is providing some camouflage, and look down at Jake. My darling son. He looks so sweet and peaceful, tucked up against me.

I kiss him on the top of his head. I feel a wave of what feels like love. Oxytocin, that's what they call it. The bonding hormone.

The shop fills with more people and I risk a glance to my side. But there's no sign of Louis, or even the blond man I thought I'd seen.

It wasn't him.

I feel my breath slacken.

'We're going to be just fine, you and me,' I say to his tiny pink head, trying to make myself believe it. His eyelids flicker in his sleep.

I'm going to have to be careful with money though. With the cash I withdrew and the money from my cash box, I have nearly ten thousand pounds in my pouch, but I'm not sure how long that will last.

The train ticket up to Norfolk is more expensive than I expected. The woman behind the Perspex screen in the

23

ticket office frowns at me when I ask how much Jake's ticket costs.

'It's a baby,' she says, looking at me as though I'm insane. 'They get free travel until they turn five. Which looks like a bit of a way off.'

'Oh, right, yes,' I say, giving a fake laugh. 'Of course. Silly me. It's the sleep deprivation, you know . . .'

She rolls her eyes at me and I feel stupid. But it doesn't matter.

I get onto the train as soon as it comes in, walking the full length of the platform to the final carriage. I'm desperate to get away from the busy concourse to somewhere quiet. Hopefully, fewer people will notice us here.

I feed Jake again as the train rolls out of the station. He's awake for a few minutes, gazing without focus as the train travels through a tunnel. Thankfully, it's early afternoon and the train is almost empty, so I don't have to deal with anyone commenting on my parenting skills, or lack of.

I have never felt so little confidence in my life. But I know one thing for certain: I love this little boy with all my heart, and I will do anything to keep him safe.

It's dark by the time the train pulls into King's Lynn. What was I thinking? I'll never get to Helston today. I'll have to check into a hotel here, and then make my way there in the morning.

I left my mobile phone at home. I couldn't risk the police tracing it. I watched a documentary once, about missing people. The first twenty-four hours are critical. After that, it gets more and more difficult to find them.

I have twenty-four hours to disappear with my baby.

24

I haven't been to King's Lynn since I was a small child, and I have no idea where anything is. So I leave the station and cross the road and go into the first hotel I see.

Thankfully, they have space. I'm exhausted from carrying Jake and pulling my heavy suitcase behind me.

'Would you like a cot in the room?' the receptionist asks me, smiling at the bundle against my chest.

'Yes, please,' I say, 'that would be great. Thank you.'

'Not a problem. I'll send someone up with one.'

Once I'm checked in, I take a deep breath and draw back the heavy curtains, looking out across the town. The lights from the buildings twinkle at me.

I feel hopeful, and most importantly of all, safe.

I lay Jake down on the bed and change his nappy. He's awake now, and staring at something above me. The shadows on the ceiling.

'Do you like them?' I coo. 'Are you practising your eyesight, little one?'

He looks like a little alien, his face scrunched up and snuffly.

I tickle his chin and beam at him, but he doesn't smile. He's still too young for that, of course. But over the next few weeks he should start to smile when he sees me. I can't wait.

I've read all the baby books. I did everything I could to prepare myself for becoming a mother. For us to become a proper family.

It hurts so much that we won't be.

'I love you,' I say to him. 'And I'm sorry your daddy has let us both down. I hope you understand that I didn't have a choice. I had to make sure you were safe.'

I scoop him up and sit on the bed, propping him up against my knees.

'I thought he was the answer to all my dreams, your daddy,' I say. 'But it turns out he wasn't. It turns out he was a nightmare. But don't you worry. It's just you and me now. You and me against the world.'

FAYE

I wake up to the sound of a baby crying. It takes me a second to work out where I am, and where the noise is coming from. And then it comes flooding back to me.

Jake. My tiny Jake. I've run away with him. Because of Louis.

'It's OK, sweetheart,' I say, scrambling out of bed to scoop Jake up. His cry is plaintive, repetitive, a call for something specific: food. I've watched all the YouTube videos about interpreting your baby's cries. How different sounds mean different things.

This sound means he's hungry. I grab another bottle from the six-pack I bought and screw on the teat. I only have one ready-made milk left now. I have so much to buy, so much to organise. It's not easy, running away from your whole life with a baby in tow.

'Here you go, my darling,' I say, and he slurps gratefully on the bottle. I stroke his head, watching him drink, the way his breathing stutters and starts as he sucks contentedly.

I wonder what time it is.

I reach for my phone, but then remember that I left it behind. I'll have to buy a new one today. What do they call them on TV? Burner phones.

There's no clock in the hotel room so I switch on the television and find a news channel. It's 3.07am. Jake has slept for hours. I'm so proud of him.

I'm about to turn the television off when it occurs to me that there might be mention of a baby being taken in London. I watch the headlines, but there's nothing. What is Louis doing, right now? Is he pacing the corridors of his Kensington flat, wondering where Jake has gone?

It doesn't matter. No amount of speculating on my part is going to make any difference. I need to focus on action. The future. Building a new life for us both, away from that man.

Somehow.

I settle Jake back down in the cot – *feet to foot* for safety – and stroke his head. He's grizzly though, squirming this way and that, his voice trying out a new sound: an angry, uncomfortable cry for help.

Then I realise what's wrong.

'Oh, of course,' I say. 'I'm so sorry, my darling. You need winding! I'm a silly mummy.'

Silly mummy.

I still can't believe I am his mummy.

I pick him up again and place him carefully over my shoulder, tapping him gently on the back and jiggling him up and down a little. Eventually I hear it – the most impressive burp from this tiny person – and once I'm sure he's comfortable, I place him back in the cot again, and watch as he falls asleep.

Then, I climb back into my own bed and try to ignore the hammering of my heart. We're safe. Nearly.

*

28

I have so much to buy.

More clothes for Jake. Bottles. More nappies. Muslins. It's like starting my life all over again.

My head swims. But first of all, I need to find somewhere for us to live.

The hotel has a bank of computers available for guests in the reception area, and so, with Jake tucked up against me in the scarf-sling, I sit down and search for rooms to rent in Helston. I can't take on a proper rental agreement, because then I run the risk of them taking out a credit check on me, but there must be some people wanting lodgers, cash in hand.

Within a few minutes I've found an advert for a room in a cottage that overlooks the village green.

It's probably a bit risky, choosing to go somewhere where I had links previously, but my great-aunt died years ago, so surely no one would be able to work out the connection.

I send a message through the site, saying that I'm interested in the room, but that I also have a young baby, and would that be OK?

I keep scrolling. There's another place that looks amazing – a whole annexe of a bigger home – but it's £150 per month more. I pause, imagining us in it. It would be perfect, but it's too expensive. I need to be careful with money. Because who knows when I'll next be able to earn any.

I log off the computer. My next task is shopping. First for a new phone – but one without a contract – and then, to buy all the baby things I need for Jake.

This is the most alive – the most purposeful – I have felt in years. I've spent my life fitting around other people's wants and needs, adjusting to their behaviour, trying to make sure I do and say the right thing.

Finally, I'm putting myself and my child first, and it feels good.

RACHEL

'Don't you want a break, Rachel?' Moira says, looking me up and down. 'You've given a whole life's service. You really do deserve to, well, retire.'

'I am already retired,' I say, my nostrils flaring. 'I retired from the school five years ago.'

'I know, but . . .' Moira stares off somewhere behind me.

I am furious, but I am hiding it well. Years of working with children has taught me to control my temper. Control your temper or it will control you, that's what I always say to the kids.

'But what?' I say, as calmly as I can manage. 'I'm not an idiot. I know what this is about. That girl, Lissa Martin.'

Moira sighs, sitting down at the small desk. We're in the room at the back of the hall. If it wasn't for my tireless fund-raising over the years, she wouldn't even have that desk to sit at. Who does she think she is?

'It's very difficult, Rachel.' Moira sighs. 'She insists that you hit her.'

'It's ridiculous!' I thunder. Too late – I can't contain myself any longer. 'I've never touched the girl. She's a spoilt brat, used to getting her own way. They're all the same these days . . . entitled little . . .'

31

Moira raises her hand.

'Rachel, please,' she says. She shakes her head. 'This isn't the attitude or the behaviour we expect from a Brown Owl. You must understand that. As district commissioner, it's my duty to . . .'

'What? Sack me? Technically, I'm not sure you can, given that it's a voluntary position.'

'Rachel,' she says, breathing out slowly, as though I'm one of the tiresome children. 'I think the time has come for you to leave Girlguiding. We're so thankful for your many, many years of selfless service to the organisation, but it's clear that the role has become too much for you. Understandably.'

'I was the first Queen's Guide this district ever had. You do know that, don't you? You do understand that you're throwing away a literal lifetime's worth of experience?'

Moira closes her eyes. I considered applying for her post, when the previous woman moved on. But I decided that admin wasn't my strong point. Being with the children was. That was where my talents lay.

And now. Look what I've done! I've allowed this snake into the pit and she's eating me alive.

Girlguiding has been my life. When I was young, it saved me. And now . . . this.

Tears spring to my eyes.

'Her parents are threatening to make a formal complaint,' Moira says. 'I really don't have any choice. I'm sorry, Rachel. You know that you'd have to retire next year anyway, when you turn sixty-five. It's policy.'

'I didn't touch her,' I say. 'But fine. If that's your decision, then so be it.'

'Oh Rachel, it's not . . .' Moira calls after me as I march from the room. 'Like I said, I don't have any choice.'

I pause for a few minutes, the blood rushing to my head, and I look around at the tiny, scruffy hall, thinking of all the hours I have spent here. All the work I've put in. For nothing! And this is how they repay me. Not even a proper send-off!

It's gone to the dogs, Girlguiding. Not what it used to be. First of all, they introduced that hideous uniform. More comfortable for the girls, they said. But so scruffy. Half of them look like they've been dragged through a hedge backwards. And then they wanted *us* to wear blue trousers and white polo shirts, like we were plumbers, instead of the smart skirts and blouses.

I should have got out then. I could have done anything with my time. But no, I stayed, like a loyal dog. I should have known I was in for a kicking eventually.

Well, forget it. It's their loss.

I blink away the tears as I march out of the hall for the last time. I won't cry about it. I refuse to.

By the time I've walked home, I feel a little calmer.

It was becoming stressful, still being Brown Owl. The rules kept changing, and there was all that extra training they kept making us do – three hours of health and safety last time around! I nearly fell asleep.

And now, I'll have more time to work on all the other projects I've been putting off. The crochet kit that June sent me last year is still in its box.

And I'll get in touch with the hospital again, see if the neonatal unit want me to knit some more octopuses for the newborns.

And of course, there's the bonfire. Just over a week left and so much still to do.

I'll have plenty to keep me busy. Good luck to them and their newfangled ways.

Once I'm home, I switch the kettle on and go upstairs to my bedroom to change out of my uniform. I try not to be sentimental about it but can't help but feel a pang as I take off the stupid white polo top for the last time. I run my fingers over the embroidered logo.

I should burn it. Stick it on the bonfire next Friday night. Perhaps this year's Guy can wear it. That would show them!

Daisy miaows at me. She's been sleeping on my bed again. I must have left the door open.

'Oh, for goodness' sake,' I snap – at her, but really at myself.

Now I'll have to wash the duvet. Daisy deftly leaps off the bed and rubs herself against my ankles.

'You really are the most frustrating creature,' I say, but it's impossible to stay angry with her for long. 'I buy you all the beds in the world and yet you still want mine. Have you left all your mucky fur all over my beautiful duvet cover? Have you? Yes, yes, you have. Come on, out you go.'

I shoo her out and close the door behind her. She scratches at the carpet, her miaows louder now, but I ignore her and turn back instead to the wardrobe, rummaging around for a new blouse.

I find one – a peach-coloured affair from M&S – and put it

on, doing up the buttons as I stare down at my Guiding polo top.

Daisy continues to miaow.

I open the door. She sits, looking up at me. I know what she wants. She wants to go outside.

I left the window open in here once and she managed to climb out of it – I found her wailing on the flat roof above the kitchen. Stupid thing. She was terrified. I had to lure her back in with tuna.

After that, she got a taste for it. She's an adventurous sort, unfortunately, but I can't let her out. It's just not worth the risk.

She follows me downstairs, rubbing against my legs all the way. We both step over the patch of carpet at the bottom. It has never been right since. I've tried everything to get the stain out, but there's still the faintest trace of a mark.

Daisy walks to the back door, miaowing and looking up at me.

'Oh, for goodness' sake, Daisy, no,' I say. 'I've told you a million times.'

I draw the curtain against the back door so that she can no longer look out through the glass, and she slinks away grumpily. I don't like to look out myself. The plants have taken over the entire garden, and the weeds at the back are almost as tall as me now.

I turn the radio on, and look over at my jigsaw, but it's no use. I'm not in the mood for it.

I'm not used to the house being so quiet. Kylie never stopped making noise. I didn't like it, but I don't like this either.

And then I remember: I haven't checked on the room advert.

I sigh in irritation at the thought of starting up the computer again, but there's no other option. We have all become so lazy, so impatient, myself included. Expecting everything immediately. I must remember that patience is a virtue.

While my computer is waking up, I start soaking some oats for the morning.

Without Guiding, I'll have time to cook more too, now. I go back upstairs and strip my bed. I was going to just wash the duvet, but before I realise I'm doing it, I've removed the bottom sheet and the pillowcase too. Never mind. It's been two days since they were clean on, and they're starting to smell a little musty.

Lissa Martin is an awful child.

No, I mustn't think about her. I have to try to put it all behind me. I'll get in touch with Janet. She left Guiding last year. We can have a good moan about it all together.

By the time the washing machine is switched on, my computer is ready to go. I log into the rentaroom website. Two messages.

I sigh. I was hoping for more choice, but it's a funny time of year, I suppose. I'm keen to rent the room as quickly as possible, so I can't be too fussy. The silence is almost unbearable, and I haven't slept well since Kylie left.

I read the first message, written in barely comprehensible English, and from a man, I assume, given his name. I've never rented the room to a man before. Not since . . . well, that incident was enough to put me off for life.

But I can't say that I only want women on the advert. Not these days. The sexism police would come after me with their pitchforks.

I hold my breath before clicking on the next message.

Hello,

I'd love to come and view your room, please. My name's Fiona, and I'm a single mother. My baby is just a few weeks old. I hope that wouldn't be a problem? He's good as gold, I promise. We are in a bit of a tricky situation but I'd be able to pay you six months' rent up front, if that would help?

Please do let me know how to arrange a viewing?

Thanks,

Fiona

I lean back in my chair, wishing I hadn't upset Daisy, so that I could share my excitement with her.

A baby! In Laleham Cottage.

I can hardly imagine it.

Of course, a newborn here – well, that would be stressful. Far from ideal. But even so . . . I can't help but feel thrilled by the prospect. That would give old Moira something to talk about! And Nigel down the road.

And this poor Fiona. Well, she sounds quite desperate.

Fiona. A good, traditional name. Yes, I can see that working out.

I lace my fingers together, stretching my palms out and away from me, hearing the knuckles crack, and then I type her a reply.

FAYE

I spent far too long in the mobile phone shop, but now I have a prepaid phone which can access the internet, and I feel relieved. If a little nervous. Even though I paid with cash, I'm still worried someone might be able to track me down because of it.

We're back in the hotel room, Jake newly changed after an incident with a leaky nappy, his soiled babygrow soaking in the bathtub, and I've finally got the internet to work.

Please, please let the woman in Helston have replied to my message. We need to feel settled. We need to start making a proper plan for our new life.

It's painfully slow but eventually the website loads and I see that 'Fiona' has a new message. My heart lifts as I click on it to read it.

Please.

Hello, Fiona,

Thank you for your message. I was really looking for a single occupant for the room, but having said that, I could make an exception for the right candidate and I understand that your baby is very young.

Would you be available to view the room tomorrow, at 3pm? It would be helpful if you could provide a contact number so that I can get in touch with you more easily if necessary. I'm afraid that I do not check my computer messages all that often.

The address is:

Laleham Cottage

Helston

And my name is Rachel Morris and I am the homeowner. You can contact me on 07000 345984.

Best regards,

Rachel

My hands are shaking. I can't believe it. I tap again to look at the picture on the advert. The room looks so lovely. Clean and bright. The exact opposite of my damp, dark flat in London.

It's too good to be true, surely?

Whatever. I can't let this opportunity pass me by.

My hands are shaking as I type a message to the phone number Rachel has given me, saying thank you and that I'd love to come and view the flat tomorrow, and that I'll see her there.

I look over at Jake, tucked up asleep in his cot.

'It's going to be OK, sweetie,' I say. 'Mummy's found us somewhere new to live.'

I shower and wash my hair the next morning while Jake lies on the bathmat, sleeping with a towel under his head. In a funny way, I'm going to miss this hotel room. My first place of refuge away from Louis.

I manage to blow-dry my hair just before he wakes up, and take out the make-up I bought yesterday. I do my best with it.

It's important to make a good first impression. I can't

imagine it will be easy to find someone who's happy to take in Jake and me.

We take the bus and Jake is good as gold the entire way, sleeping soundly against my chest. I bought him a proper sling yesterday but I know soon I'll have to get him a pram. He'll be too heavy for me to carry eventually.

I can't bear the thought of it. I want to freeze time. Every second with him is precious. He easily makes up for all of the agony of the past year.

Even though it's October, it's a bright, sunny day, and despite the distinct chill in the air, I'm grateful for the sunshine on my face as I clamber off the bus, rucksack on my back, Jake tucked up in the sling.

I stand for a few minutes, looking out across the village. Trying to remember where my great-aunt's house was. In the middle of the picture-perfect village green is a great pile of branches and sticks. It's as tall as a building. I frown, trying to work out why it's there, and then I remember: it's Bonfire Night soon. Of course, this is the kind of village where people gather on such occasions, and enjoy the celebrations together. Where kids play safely in the streets, and traffic and pollution are minimal.

The kind of place I'd love Jake to grow up.

Certain things feel familiar to me – the tiny stone church, the pub with its black boarding. I can't remember where my great-aunt lived though. Her house was set back from the main street a little, down a narrow road.

Anyway, there will be plenty of time to rediscover it. What's important now is that I find the cottage.

I know from the picture and the tiny map attached to the advert that Laleham Cottage is set against the green, so it should be quite easy to find. I cross the grass, glancing up at the pile of branches in the centre.

There's a row of cute cottages across this side, all painted different pastel shades. I walk past them, slowly, my heart beating faster as I read the names of each. 'Honeysuckle Cottage', 'Rose Cottage', 'The Gables', 'Treetops'. And then, there it is, the smallest of them all, sitting squat and wonky in the centre: 'Laleham Cottage'.

I take a deep breath, look down at Jake. He's awake but drowsy, giving long, slow blinks. I fed him on the bus. Hopefully, I've timed it right and he'll fall asleep now, and stay quiet throughout the visit.

I look around for a doorbell, but there isn't one. Just an old-fashioned black knocker.

She answers the door before I have the chance to knock, and I have the creeping feeling that she was watching me arrive from behind the net curtains in the front bay window.

'Hello,' I say. 'Are you Rachel? I'm Fa . . . Fiona.'

My nerves are getting the better of me. I have never liked meeting new people.

She looks at me. She's short and plump, dull grey hair cropped tightly against her head. She's wearing black flannel trousers and a maroon blouse that gapes slightly across her generous chest.

She's holding a large white cat in one arm.

The expression on her face isn't exactly friendly, or

welcoming, and I swallow nervously, flicking my hair away from my face so that she can see my eye.

'Fiona,' she says, extending her free hand. I shake it, although it seems rather formal. 'Pleased to meet you. Come in.'

The cat stares at me. Its ears are squashed flat to its head. I've never much cared for cats, but I plaster a smile on and lean towards it.

'Hello, kitty,' I say, but just as I reach over to stroke it, it hisses at me. I stand straighter, surprised.

'This is Daisy,' Rachel says. 'Don't mind her. She's a little possessive. She's an indoor cat, and isn't allowed out.'

I nod, smile. Rachel closes the front door behind me and sets the cat down on the floor. Then I look around the room.

The ceilings are low and every surface is crammed with knick-knacks. There's a floral sofa facing the window, too large for the space. The most striking thing about it is that it is covered in plastic, as though it's just been delivered and is waiting to be unpacked. Perhaps the cat is prone to accidents.

But the sunlight is pouring in the front bay, and the room is immaculately tidy. I look down at the polished parquet floor – like something you'd find in a ballroom. There's a faded Chinese rug covering the section in front of the sofa, two large brass dogs sitting either side of the fireplace.

'You're tall,' Rachel says, appraising me. 'You'll have to mind your head on the beams upstairs. The last girl that I had here, well, she knocked herself on them a few times. Once, quite badly. She ended up bleeding all over the carpet.' She pauses, and motions towards the stairs. 'Hence the stain at the bottom of the steps. Blood is very difficult to shift.'

I look down at an orange patch on the cream carpet. You can see where someone has scrubbed at it, trying to remove the mark.

'Oh,' I say. 'Right. Yes. I'll be careful.'

She's staring at my eye. How long until she mentions it, I wonder?

'And is that the baby?' Rachel asks, taking a step towards me. I had almost forgotten about Jake. He's sound asleep, as I'd hoped.

'Yes,' I say, beaming, and pulling down the side of his sling slightly so she can see his tiny face. 'Jake.'

'Well,' Rachel says, smiling for the first time. 'He is certainly lovely.'

'He is,' I say. 'I'm biased, of course, but I think he's the most beautiful baby I've ever seen.'

I meet Rachel's eyes. They are full of warmth. Despite her slightly brusque attitude, it makes me relax a little.

'The living area looks lovely,' I say. 'Can I see the room?'

I haven't seen the kitchen yet, but I can see a step down at the back of the sitting room, and what looks like a butler's sink against the back window. There's a door out to the garden too, although the view is almost entirely obscured by greenery. I can't tell from here, but they look like weeds to me, and I'm surprised. Rachel seems like the sort of woman who would be obsessed with gardening.

'Yes,' Rachel says. 'No shoes upstairs though.'

'Oh,' I say, looking down at my laced-up boots. 'Of course.'

43

Clumsily, I sit on the bottom stair, shifting Jake slightly to one side as I undo each of my boots. I leave them neatly on the doormat, and follow Rachel up the stairs.

She was right, the beams are low, and at one point I have to crouch to avoid hitting my head.

But upstairs, the landing opens up, a lantern light above us brightening the space. There are three doors leading off the hall, all closed.

'This would be your room,' Rachel says, pushing open the one on my left.

I follow her through it. The room is large – directly above the living room at the front of the property, overlooking the green. There's a small double bed in the middle, a white-painted wardrobe and a chest of drawers. The walls are papered in a tiny flower pattern and the whole thing smells of cleaning products.

'Oh, it's lovely,' I say honestly. 'It really is.'

'It's the bigger of the two rooms, and the views are decent,' Rachel says, sniffing slightly. 'My bedroom is at the back of the house.'

'I mean . . . it's everything I . . . we wanted. If you would be happy to let it to us?'

I look up at her, hopeful. She still hasn't said anything about my eye.

'The problem is, I don't have any references. I was . . . living with my partner before. My baby's father. But . . . things didn't work out. I had to get away.'

I turn my face slightly, to make the bruise under my eye even more visible.

She nods, her eyes narrowing.

'I can offer you six months' rent up front? I have it in cash.'

From nowhere, my voice begins to tremble. And before I realise what's happening, I am on the verge of tears. The pressure of the last year has mounted up, a mountain of water against a dam, and I can't contain it any longer.

'I'm sorry,' I say, blinking furiously. I can't believe I've come this close, and now I'm messing everything up. 'I'm so sorry . . .'

But then I feel an arm around my shoulder, and Rachel pulls me towards her in a hug.

'You poor thing. It's all right,' she says, her voice completely different. Soothing and motherly. 'It's all right, Fiona. You'll both be safe now.'

As though agreeing with her, Jake gives a gentle sigh.

RACHEL

I tell Fiona to bring her things back that evening, that she's welcome to move in straight away, but she seems worn out, so she decides to go back to the city for the night, pack up and bring everything over in the morning.

When she leaves, after two slices of cake and several cups of strong tea, I turn on my computer and delete the advert from the website.

Room now let. That was the fastest ever. I do a silly little dance in the kitchen in celebration.

'Can you imagine, Daisy?! A baby at Laleham Cottage, after all these years!'

But Daisy just sits and licks her paw.

I've been renting the front room out ever since Mother died. Despite my solitary nature, I don't like living alone. And for the most part, it's worked out well. I've always been very circumspect about who I let into my home.

After all, you never know what people are capable of.

But despite being careful with my choices, I've had some bad experiences.

I've got a good feeling about Fiona though. Clearly, the girl has been through something terrible. I didn't like to mention her black eye in case it upset her, but there's no doubting that it was a fist that caused it.

And as for baby Jake, well . . . he was utterly adorable.

I look forward to learning more about them. It's lucky she found me. Clearly, we need one another.

Fate has a funny way of making things work.

I microwave some macaroni cheese and sit next to the fire to eat it, looking out over the green. It takes almost a month to build the bonfire – starting with the frame that supports the whole thing. It used to be built almost entirely from hedge clippings, but these days the organisers take branches from tree surgeons, as well as asking everyone to leave out their own cuttings for collection.

Helston is known for its Bonfire Night celebrations. People come from villages far and wide to watch the torchlight procession and the pig roast.

Daisy, of course, hates it. She sits in the front window shaking as the green fills with people.

I'll shut her in the understairs cupboard this time, so that she doesn't get too distressed.

I've been involved with the bonfire committee for as long as I can remember. Along with Nigel, I'm the longest-standing member. I think it's important I remain on the committee, to make sure that our traditions are upheld. Every year more people move to the village from the city and try to change things. Try to impose their modern ways and ideas, full of superiority and judgemental looks. It's important that people like me and Nigel are there to push back, otherwise the village's heritage would be completely lost.

I finish my supper and wash up the plate while Daisy wraps herself round my legs, begging for scraps. I take two Dreamies out of the packet and hold them out to her in turn. She purrs her thanks.

Then I open the cupboard beneath the sink and take out the small metal box that lives behind the cleaning products. The lid is inlaid with mother-of-pearl and enamel – a pastoral scene, with a swan swimming on the river. When my Auntie Vi gave it to me, she told me it was very valuable, but I'm not sure it is. I expect it was mass-produced in India or somewhere.

Even so, it's my most treasured possession.

I open it carefully and then reach into the back pocket of my trousers. I left Fiona upstairs to look around the bathroom but she was very quick, and so I didn't have much time.

It was the first thing I could find. Something I knew she wouldn't immediately miss.

A small white cotton hat. Nothing fancy. I turn it over in my hand, looking for a label, but there isn't one. Baby Jake deserves better than this. I smile, imagining all the hats I will knit him. And cardigans and more! It will be so lovely to watch him grow. I'll have to call the hospital again, explain that I won't be able to make those octopuses for them after all.

I'll be too busy knitting for my new baby. Won't that be lovely?

Who needs Girlguiding when you have your own children, your own family, to spend time with?

I smile to myself. I've never had much call for Him, given the hand He's dealt me over the years, but I suppose every now and then God does pull out the goods.

I sniff the little cotton baby hat but it smells of chemicals – the way clothes do when you bring them home from the shops. I hope Jake won't be cold without it. He was wearing an all-in-one snowsuit-type thing, his head underneath a hood, so hopefully he'll be all right for now. It doesn't look as though he's even worn this hat anyway. It's more of a summer-type affair – wafer-thin.

I'll start knitting him a new one tonight. That way he'll have one for tomorrow.

I look down at the contents of my metal box.

Kylie's scissors are still crusty with blood. She was a silly, silly girl. Such a disappointment.

And then, there are the mementos from all the others. They seemed so important at the time, but now, despite these relics from our time together, I can barely remember their faces.

I don't want to put baby Jake's hat in here just yet. I don't want it contaminated with the poison from all the waifs and strays who have gone before. Women who have all let me down.

No. It doesn't belong in this box of darkness. I close the lid and shove it back behind the bottles of bleach and limescale remover.

And then I take baby Jake's hat and smooth it between my fingers. I'll sleep with it under my pillow tonight.

FAYE

I can't believe my luck. To have found someone – someone as kind and caring as Rachel – so easily.

I take the bus back to King's Lynn feeling like a new woman. Feeling as though all my Christmases have come at once. Clearly, I did the right thing in coming here. Fate is on my side.

It's been more than twenty-four hours since I ran away with Jake. And nothing. No police hammering on my door. Is it possible that I have got away with it?

I'm safe now. Or I will be tomorrow, when I'm out of the city and tucked away somewhere no one will ever find me.

I think of Jonas and Hannah, and swallow. Jonas will be all right. As for Hannah . . . well, I'll have to get in touch with her in a few weeks, when things are settled down.

When Rachel left me upstairs to take a look in the bathroom – 'it's quite cramped up here, take your time' – I was pleased to see that the room, though plain in its decoration, nothing fancy at all, was clean and smelt of bleach. The utilitarian white tiles gleamed white. There was a knitted toilet-roll doll on the cistern, but other than that, the room had a functional, hygienic feel. Not like you might imagine from one of those ancient cottages. There wasn't even a speck of damp to be seen.

Even though I knew I shouldn't, I tried pushing open the third door – her bedroom, I presumed – but it was locked. It seemed a bit strange, to have locked the door to the bedroom in her own house, but perhaps she wanted to keep the cat out. She had made a passing comment about how it liked to try to sleep on her bed, even though it was forbidden.

In any case, I shouldn't have been prying. Laleham Cottage is small, and I haven't lived with anyone since I was a child, but I just have a good feeling. Rachel seems like the kind of woman that will keep to herself.

Perhaps we're actually quite similar.

My good mood doesn't last. I wake in the night, after dreaming of the way Louis looked at me the last time I saw him. The snarl with which he spoke to me. I'm drenched in sweat and my heart is pounding.

As soon as I realise that it's just a dream, Jake starts to cry and I'm plunged into yet another painful reality: that of the sleep-deprived new mother, alone in the night, trying to console their child.

The next morning, even though I'm exhausted, I waste no time in packing up our things and checking out of the hotel. My bag is stuffed full with all the extras I bought for Jake, and weighs a ton. I briefly consider getting a taxi to Helston, rather than trying to deal with the bus. But it would be too expensive, and too risky.

I'm a memorable sight – a single mother with a young baby and a huge suitcase.

Wherever we go, Jake is like a tiny firework, catching

everyone's eyes. People constantly stop to comment, even when I keep my head down and make it obvious I'm not up for a chat.

I zip up my bag, throwing my medication down on top of my clothes. I've got enough left for about a month and I haven't quite worked out what I'm going to do about getting a repeat prescription.

It'll be fine. Maybe I'll just go cold turkey, deal with the consequences. As I leave my hotel room, I glance at my reflection in the mirror. The black eye is a little fainter today.

The bus to Helston is empty and I sit at the front and feed Jake again. It's fascinating to watch him – I swear he changes by the hour. He seems more alert this morning, his eyes swivelling around suspiciously as he drinks his milk.

He's asleep by the time we reach the village. There's a crisp frost across the grass on the green that leaves my boots slick with moisture as I traipse across it, dragging my wheeled suitcase behind me.

Before I reach the cottage, the front door opens and Rachel is there, standing and smiling at me.

If I believed in guardian angels, she's not exactly what I would have pictured, but even so, it feels as though someone somewhere is bestowing their blessing on me by pairing us up. I'm so grateful.

I exhale, and look up at Rachel. She's softened from yesterday. Her cheeks are almost rosy, and she smiles at me.

'Welcome home,' Rachel says, and I take a deep breath and step inside the warm, welcoming doorway, and into safety.

ONE YEAR EARLIER

FAYE

Anya has a line of bruises on her arm, just above her wrist. I notice it when she pulls up her sleeves to play. I'm no expert, but it looks like three fingermarks.

I picture it briefly: a moment of violence, strong fingers digging into her soft young skin. I close my eyes at the thought of it.

When I open them again, she is staring straight ahead at the music in front of her. Beethoven's Ecossaise in E flat. She's preparing for her Grade 3.

'Ouch,' I say softly, laying a hand on her arm. 'That looks nasty.'

She glances at me out of the corner of her eye. There's a pause.

'It's OK,' she says, shrugging. But her voice is quiet.

'Rough and tumble with your brother?' I ask. I don't know a huge amount about Anya, but I used to teach her older brother – he passed his Grade 8 when he was just fifteen. A prodigy, his mother said proudly. He wasn't, in my mind. But he was good – talented for sure – and dedicated, which is often the most important thing.

But Anya shakes her head at me. She doesn't want to talk about it. And it's not my place to pry.

It's difficult not to. In every child I teach, I see a little bit of myself, of the girl who found the world so confusing.

I shake my head. I search for the logic, tell it to myself.

Anya is a kid – just nine – and kids get into scrapes all the time. Anyone could have grabbed her arm at any time. It doesn't mean it was an adult. It doesn't mean it was abuse.

She starts to play. She's good, and has picked up this piece in just two weeks. But there's something robotic in her playing. Technically she's brilliant, but there's no feeling there. No expression.

'Remember to keep it light,' I say. 'An ecossaise is a lively dance, so we want our fingers to dance across the notes.'

I stop her and adjust some of the fingering on the music.

'Try this,' I say. 'It will stop your right hand from being so heavy.'

By any measure, Anya is a model pupil. She practises without complaint, she listens to my instructions. She concentrates. No messing about or distracting me with cheeky but cute questions, like some of them who clearly don't want to be here.

But still, there's something sad about her. Something in her eyes that makes it look as though she wishes she was far away. I know that feeling. I feel it myself.

Before too long, the half hour is over and the doorbell rings. It'll be her mother, come to collect her. I no longer teach her brother. He now goes to see someone in Chelsea. Piano teacher to the stars, apparently. Whatever that means.

Her mother sees me as little more than staff. So many of them do. Most of them have never even heard me play. But

I'm used to it, and they don't know how I see them. They don't care.

Anya lingers for a while on the piano stool, looking at me as I gather her music together.

'I think we're ready to book you in for your Grade 3, Anya,' I say, beaming at her. 'That was really good today. Just keep practising your G minor scale. Remember not to rush it, slow and steady is better, and concentrate on keeping an even rhythm.'

She nods.

'What's that, Miss Miller?' she says, pointing to the corner of the room, by the piano.

I turn in the direction of her finger.

'Oh,' I say, looking at the dark patch on the wall. 'It's just . . . I need to redecorate.'

She sniffs. I stare at the damp. I've complained three times to my landlord but he never gets back to me, and I don't really know what else I can do.

'Is it mud?' she says, incredulous now. I have never been to Anya's house, but I can only imagine the opulence. They live opposite Wimbledon Common. She told me they have a Yamaha baby grand. 'It's black!'

'Not exactly,' I say brusquely. 'Now, let's not keep your mum waiting.'

I take a deep breath before I open the door. I find dealing with people exhausting, and this is the part of teaching I hate the most – the parents.

'Hello, Mrs Taylor,' I say, smiling broadly. I glance in her eyes for a second – just long enough that I don't seem completely

57

rude. 'Anya did brilliantly today. I'll be booking her in for her Grade 3 later on.'

Mrs Taylor is pencil-thin and immaculate, wearing a pair of dark blue jeans and what look like leather riding boots.

'Good,' she says, giving me what might actually be the beginning of a smile. 'About time too. Jeffrey had already done his Grade 3 by the time he was eight, you know, Anya.'

'Yes, Mama.'

'One thing,' I say, wondering if Anya even wants to learn piano. Her parents are the definition of pushy. She once shared with me her schedule: an hour of swimming before school twice a week, tennis lessons three times a week, extra maths and English tuition, and piano and clarinet too. I jokingly asked her when she gets to have fun and she looked at me as though I was stupid.

'Yes?' her mother replies, pulling on Anya's coat. I'm still holding her music. She has a leather folder to keep it in, her initials inscribed on the front in gold letters.

'She has a nasty bruise on her arm,' I say. 'Just above her wrist. It looked quite sore. I'm sure it's nothing, but just wanted to make you aware that I need to be informed of any injuries before a child is dropped off in my care.'

Safeguarding is a minefield and I don't want anyone accusing me of hurting my pupils.

Mrs Taylor's cheeks turn ever so slightly pink.

'Oh,' she says. 'That. She nearly burnt herself on the stove the other day. I had to grab her wrist to stop her.'

'Right,' I say, glancing at Anya. Her head is back down, staring at her shoes. 'Even so, next time, please do let me know

58

before you drop her off.' I try to smile again, but my mouth won't behave. 'Just so there's no confusion.'

Mrs Taylor nods at me.

'Come on, Anya,' she says. 'Say goodbye and thank you to Miss Miller.'

'Thank you, Miss Miller,' Anya whispers, without looking up.

'Have a good week, Anya,' I say. 'Great work today.'

When I close the door behind them, I feel exhausted. Wrung out by the toxicity of their energy.

Poor Anya. It's always the same. I am angry on her behalf – with all of them, these parents. So stressed and concerned with appearances and success all the time, they leave no room for love or warmth. And their children are the ones who suffer.

I turn around in my mind what Mrs Taylor said about Anya's wrist. I can't tell if she is lying or not. I've never seen any other sign that her mother is anything more than cold and preoccupied. They're desperate for Anya to get a music scholarship to the expensive girls' school in Wimbledon.

'And she's hopeless at sport,' Mrs Taylor once said, shaking her head as though it was the biggest disappointment of her life. 'Absolutely hopeless.'

I didn't want to say that, while technically outstanding, her musicality left a lot to be desired, so instead I smiled confidently and said that Anya was one of the most gifted pupils I had ever taught. It made Anya smile, at least.

I sometimes wonder why these women have these children they find so inconvenient and disappointing.

And then, people like me . . .

I lean against the front door of my cramped, mouldy basement flat, taking a deep breath.

It's my birthday today.

Thirty-nine.

I can't really believe it.

I had never pictured the way my life might pan out, but now I think if I had, it would not have looked like this.

It would not have been this empty.

There is only one thing I've ever wanted: a child of my own. And I don't even have that.

Jonas drags me to the pub on the corner and even though it's chilly, we sit outside so he can smoke. They do good pizzas here, apparently – what he calls 'proper stone-baked ones' – and so we order one each and wait for them while drinking beer. Jonas has a pint. I have a Corona, squeezing the lime before pushing it through the bottle's neck.

'Happy birthday to you,' he says, clinking his glass against my drink.

'Thank you,' I say.

He rolls up some tobacco and sets light to it.

'Had a fucker of a day,' he says, breathing deeply. 'How about you?'

I shrug.

'Not much to report.'

'Get any nice presents?'

I smile. The answer to that question is too depressing to share. Only one card, from Hannah and her family. She'll probably give me a scented candle when I next see her.

'Why was today so bad for you then?' I say instead. I much prefer talking about other people.

He shrugs, sucking on his roll-up.

'Landlord's given me notice. Arsehole. But today's about you, Faye,' he says. His eyebrow twitches – an involuntary tic. He has many of these, and although the first time they can seem quite alarming, to me they are now part of Jonas' charm.

I've known him since we were at music college together. He is my best – and probably only – friend. He doesn't ask too much of me. He knows I don't have much to give.

I take a long glug of my beer.

'I feel a bit down, if I'm honest,' I say, suddenly confessional. 'I don't know. Thirty-nine. I thought by now . . . I'd be doing more than just teaching.'

'You could still perform professionally if you wanted to,' he says, clucking his tongue at me. 'You just need to be a bit more ballsy. It's not the talented ones who make it, you know. It's the ones who won't give up, or take no for an answer.'

I shake my head. He's right, but I don't want to perform any longer anyway.

'My performing days are long gone,' I say. 'But thanks. It's not that . . . it's . . .'

From somewhere inside me, a laugh erupts.

'What?'

'I always thought,' I say, my heart hammering in my chest, 'I always thought that by now I'd have a child. I know it's stupid. But you know – we work with so many children. And so many of them seem . . . unwanted. It's like their parents treat them as inconveniences or something. Just another chore they have to deal with. Not something that they love or cherish. And . . . I guess it feels wrong. That they have children and I don't. When really, it's all I've ever longed for.'

'Fuck me, Faye,' Jonas says. He gives a cackle, revealing his uneven teeth. I love him for that – for the fact he doesn't care, that it would never occur to him to have them fixed. 'You always surprise me.'

I feel my cheeks heat up.

'Well, it's embarrassing.'

He pauses, stubbing out his roll-up.

'No, it's not,' he says, staring at me for a little bit too long. 'If you want a kid, then you should have one. Why not?'

'Well, for one thing, I couldn't afford it.'

'Not on your own, you idiot,' he says.

Another strange sound escapes me. Not exactly a laugh this time.

'Oh, I . . .'

'Jesus!' he says, throwing back his head and howling. 'Not with me. With someone else.'

I pull my lip in, annoyed.

'It's not that simple,' I say. 'I mean, it is for you. Because you're male and you can just . . . I don't know . . . meet people . . .' I tail off, thinking of the sheer number of encounters Jonas has told me about. I don't get it, I really don't. I love him, but he's certainly not conventionally attractive, and yet women flock to him. I guess it's his confidence, the fact he behaves as though he doesn't give a toss and loves to be the centre of attention. Something I've never been able to manage. I can't stand it.

'Ack,' Jonas says, rolling his eyes at me. 'Actually, it is that simple.'

He leans in closer.

'Look,' he mutters. 'Over there.'

I turn in the direction he indicates. A bunch of middle-aged men are huddled around a table behind us, snorting and laughing.

'Any of them,' he says. 'You could have any of them.'

I flick a hand at him across the table. My cheeks are burning.

'No, thank you.'

He chuckles again.

'The time has come to join the twenty-first century, Miller. You need to get yourself online.'

FAYE

It's gone midnight and I've drunk four beers by the time I get back to my flat. I'll regret this tomorrow. I usually let my birthday pass by without any fuss, but there's something about thirty-nine. A demand that it be marked, somehow.

One year left before any semblance of youth is officially over.

One year left before . . . what feels like the beginning of the end. Of it all. My hopes and dreams. The future I had pictured on my wedding day, all those years ago.

I look around at my living room. I've lived here for sixteen years now. It's in the basement of a large Victorian villa, so it's permanently dark. When I rented it, I thought it would be nice to have direct access to the shared garden, but it's such a tip I never go out there. It's full of weeds, and the people living above me store all their junk out there – rusting bicycles, an old fridge, a washing line that no longer works.

One night, when I was washing up in the kitchen, I saw a rat run across the windowsill, right at my eyeline.

I know I should move – and I could probably afford to, as I save most of my earnings. But moving house feels like a colossal undertaking. So much paperwork and admin and things to sort out. I'm not good at that kind of thing, and I hate always having to ask Hannah for help.

I find it hard to do things by myself.

I pinch my nose, feeling the tears loom. I don't want to cry.

My head swims as I switch on the light and go through to the cluttered kitchen. I pour a glass of water and drink it while leaning over the sink. Every surface in here is crammed with houseplants. They love it. The damp makes them very happy.

'It's like a greenhouse or something in here,' Jonas said, when I once invited him over for a coffee. He took off his jacket, then his jumper.

'I don't like being cold,' I said, shrugging, and he laughed at me. I'm not really sure what he found funny.

Online. That's what he said. You need to get online.

But I don't want to date anyone. I had a husband, and I lost him. I've adjusted to my solitude. The truth is, I like it. I think I was probably made for it. The thought of sharing my life with someone again terrifies me. It isn't worth the risk.

I sink onto the sofa, pulling out my phone. The man in the Vodafone shop talked me into upgrading to an iPhone about a month ago – he couldn't believe I still had a Blackberry – and I've still not really got to grips with the thing.

But I know how to search the internet.

What would I search for?

I read an article in a magazine once, explaining that Google liked it when people phrased their searches as questions.

I rub my forehead with my fingers.

What would my question be? What is it I want?

A baby.

I shake my head a little at how ridiculous it is, but then I type:

How can I have a baby on my own?

Immediately, the tiny screen is flooded with answers to my question.

Donor insemination.

Sperm banks UK.

Becoming a single mum.

How to get pregnant without a man.

My heart is thudding in my chest, but I click on the answer that calls loudest to me.

Single and wanting a baby? Here are your options.

An hour later, I have sobered up, and am well and truly down the rabbit hole.

Who knew? Who knew such things existed?

Not me.

But here it is, seemingly the answer to my prayers: a match-making app – of all things! – specifically for people who want to become parents, but who don't want to do it alone.

ACORNS

Following the instructions, I download the app, my hands shaking. Within seconds, I'm staring at the home screen's welcoming message, reading the words.

- Are you single? Do you long to become a parent?
- Is your biological clock ticking?

66

- Have you just not met 'the one' yet?
- Do you feel angry that your chance to have a child is being snatched away by your lack of luck in love?
- Acorns is for you!
- We're a *mating* app. Not a *dating* app.
- We connect people who want to have a baby with other people who want to have a baby.
- Our users are united in this goal.
- No messing around. No confusion.
- No hiding your true intentions, or feeling embarrassed to admit what you really want from a partnership. All our users want to become parents, first and foremost.

SIGN UP AND TAKE CHARGE OF YOUR FUTURE TODAY!

Beneath this, there's a picture of an incredibly cute baby, its eyes wide and staring, above a button that says 'SIGN UP NOW'.

I sit for a few minutes, staring at my phone's screen. Then I look up, glancing around at the soggy walls and general lack of charm. There are piles of books everywhere, sheet music stacked messily on every surface. Dotted across the room are mugs of half-drunk tea – I have a tendency to forget I've made them and then forget I've left them – and a pile of dusty, ancient CDs remains scattered across the floor, where they tumbled over weeks ago.

I am a slob. Because what's the point of tidying up when there's no one there to see it? My students don't care, and their parents never actually come in.

I have lived here too long. I have lived alone for too long. Something needs to change.

Before I have a chance to think about it any longer, I tap the button on the app, and start to fill in my details.

FAYE

I don't teach on Sundays.

When I wake up, my iPhone is squashed underneath my cheek, digging into my face.

I open my eyes a crack and look around at the room, wondering why I have a headache. Then it comes back to me – one too many beers with Jonas to celebrate my birthday last night. The ridiculous suggestion that I try to live out my dream by having a baby on my own.

And then . . . this.

I pick up my iPhone.

I knew I shouldn't have Googled it.

I mean, whoever heard of anything so ridiculous? An app, to match you up with other people – men, in my case – who want to have a baby?

It's insane. The modern world gone mad.

Jonas is right, I should just dress up a bit and go out one night and get blind drunk and sleep with the first person I see.

But I've only ever slept with one person. Marshall.

'Ugh,' I say to my fiddle-leaf fig. One of the bottom leaves in the corner is turning brown. It won't be long before it falls off. It's grown nearly a foot since I got it, and soon it will reach the ceiling.

I climb out of bed and stretch my arms above my head, looking out of the window. It's a nondescript, grey day. I find Sundays hard. I usually play the piano for a couple of hours and then go out for groceries, and perhaps a long walk, then spend the rest of the day reading.

I rarely speak to anyone.

I have spent so many Sundays like this. Totally alone.

It comes back: that sinking feeling in the pit of my stomach, that my life is pointless and empty. It makes me want to die.

Thirty-nine and totally alone.

No, that's not true. I have Jonas. And Hannah. She called me yesterday to wish me a happy birthday, but I haven't seen her in a while. That's my fault. I should make more effort. She tries to get me to come over at least once a month, but I find it so humiliating. She has everything I ever wanted and, even though she tries to hide it, I know she pities me.

She's family though. My half-sister – we had different mothers and hers is still alive – but she's the closest family I have left. I'll text her now, see if she's free for a coffee any time this week. I work most evenings, so dinners are difficult, but hopefully she'll have some free time in the day.

I pick up my phone and am just about to open the messages app when I see a little red 'three' above the icon for my email.

I hardly ever get emails. I tap to see who they are from.

Acorns App: You have a new message!

Acorns App: You have a new message!

Acorns App: You have a new message!

I stare at my phone, stunned. I can't believe it. It's only 8am. I must have finished uploading my profile at about one in the morning, and yet three people have seen it and already got in touch.

My fingers tremble as I open the first email, but it just has a link to redirect me to the app. Terrified, I tap it.

The app loads, showing me, first of all, my own profile. I can hardly remember what I wrote. I only remember that I uploaded the photo of myself from the concert I gave last year at Cadogan Hall. I'm wearing my blue velvet dress, and had had my hair and make-up done professionally. It's the nicest photo of me that I have.

I look at it now, tiny me on my tiny phone screen. I look quite pretty, really. My bony shoulders notwithstanding.

I swipe, and there's another picture, from further back, of me playing that epic Steinway grand, my head bent low across the keys.

It's a shock. I look quite impressive.

I glance down at the real me, the real me who is sitting here in grey pyjamas with faded knees. I look nothing like this piano aficionado in my phone. It's true what they say about the internet – about everything being fake.

But no, that's not fair. That photo *is* of me. I haven't edited it. Or filtered it. The PR woman for the venue paid a professional photographer to capture the evening, and these were in the set that she sent over afterwards.

I pull my shoulders back slightly, allow myself a moment of pride.

There's a tiny envelope icon at the bottom of the app, not dissimilar to the main one for my email.

Messages.

I click on it, and settle back on the bed, pulling my pillows up behind me.

Dear Chopin4Life,

I was very interested to read your profile. I've always longed to play the piano. It's most impressive that you've made a career out of it . . .

I pause, heart thundering. What did I say? That I was a concert pianist? Oh God!

I'm afraid my own career is not nearly so interesting. I work in insurance. But I've done well for myself over the years. I have a pension worth just over half a million, and I own a lovely mews house in south-east London. Outright, no mortgage. You would be able to rely on me financially, as well as emotionally. My friends say I'm a wonderful man. Just never found the right lady to settle down and have a family with. I'd love to meet up with you and perhaps we could see if we're compatible?

Please take a look at my profile and see what you think.

Best wishes,

Colin

I click on the little thumbnail by his name. My jaw hangs open as his picture loads on my screen.

He looks ancient. He must be at least sixty. He should be retiring, not having a baby.

I feel a bit sick. Do I have to reply? Say thanks but no thanks? What's the etiquette here, exactly?

I swallow as I click on the next message.

Dear Chopin4Life,

My name is Julian and your profile caught my eye.

Let's chat.

x

Cocky, I think. But perhaps he has reason to be. I click on his thumbnail to see more of his profile.

He's much younger than Colin, and not entirely unattractive, thank goodness, but he's got a smarmy look on his face. I instinctively don't trust him.

This is depressing. There's a reason that all these men are on this app. And it's that they are clearly all awful.

Mind you, what does that make me?

It feels hopeless, but I click on the last message anyway. I'll delete this stupid app afterwards. What was I thinking? As if you could meet the future father of your baby in such a contrived way.

Dear Chopin4Life,

Lovely to 'meet' you. My mother always told me never to turn down the opportunity to pay someone a compliment, so please let me just say I think you're beautiful.

Hope it's not creepy to say that I recognise the venue in your second picture – Cadogan Hall. It's just down the road from me, and I've been to lots of concerts there over the years. Not yours, alas.

So, what brings you onto this weird and wonderful app? A little bit about me – I'm forty-three years old. I married very young to my childhood sweetheart, but sadly things didn't work out as I'd hoped. Since then, I've dated and done the London life, but for various reasons have yet to find the right person to have a family with.

I know they say that men don't have biological clocks, but personally I don't think it's true. I've wanted to be a father my whole life, and don't want to put it off for much longer. I want to have enough energy to do fun things with my child(ren).

I work as the MD for my father's business, so am very fortunate to have financial and long-term job security. I won't name and shame the firm, but we're listed on the stock exchange, and have been going strong for more than fifty years now.

I'm sure you've been inundated with interested parties, but if not, then I'd love to perhaps meet for a coffee?

Louis x

PS My favourite Chopin piece is Fantaisie-Impromptu *– what's yours?*

I realise I've been holding my breath as I come to the end of his message. I bite my top lip, a warm feeling flowing over my body.

What a lovely, lovely message.

And *Fantaisie-Impromptu*! He knows about Chopin. I mean, it's a bit of an obvious choice, and personally I think Chopin's least impressive *Impromptu*, but still . . .

I take a deep breath. Perhaps I was too quick to write off this app. Perhaps I'll reply to Louis at least, and give him a chance.

And after all, what else do I have to do today? I have literally nothing to lose.

FAYE

I redraft my reply to Louis three times before I'm happy. The first version of my message is too long, ponderous and detailed. I need to strike a similar tone to him: light-hearted, not too serious.

I find it really hard. Somehow, my message never seems to come across the way I intended.

Eventually, I decide that less is more, and the reply I do send is short and to the point, and excruciatingly personal. But it feels good, to be taking these risks finally. To be opening myself up to things, even a little.

Dear Louis,

Thank you so much for your message. This is my first time using a site like this and I'm finding it all a little overwhelming! So I was very encouraged by your kind words.

I have a similar story to yours. But really it boils down to the fact that I've reached the age of thirty-nine without having children, something I have always desperately wanted, and that it feels a little 'now or never'.

It would be great to meet for a coffee sometime. Perhaps, if nothing else, I'll be able to convince you to take a listen to Chopin's other

Impromptus! *Though not as famous as the* Fantaisie, *I think you'll find they are greater works.*

Best,

Faye

I can't decide if the last few sentences sound pompous or flirtatious. I briefly consider running the message past Jonas, but I'm too shy. He'd tease me – and quite rightly. The whole thing is a little ridiculous. Insane.

But it's made me feel more alive than I have done in ages. I understand now! Why people do this kind of thing. To feel something. Anything other than the monotony of their daily lives.

It's midday by the time I send the message, my heart still hammering away as I press the button.

A notification pops up immediately, telling me I have a new message.

I frown. He can't possibly reply that quickly, can he?

But when I check my message box on the app, I see that I have an email from the app itself.

I tap to read it.

Hello, Chopin4Life,

Great stuff! You've made a connection. We're so happy and hope that this will be the start of a life-changing co-parenting journey for you.

We just wanted to draw your attention to a few important things that might help you with your co-parenting adventure. You'll find a wealth of advice and information on our <u>blog</u>, and we encourage you to read through it carefully.

One of the most important things to consider is drawing up a co-parenting agreement. This should cover anything and everything related to the care and well-being of your child, and you should make sure you have an open and honest conversation with your co-parent about every facet of your child's life before you embark on any attempt to conceive.

You can find more about co-parenting agreements by clicking the <u>link here</u>.

And please do take time to read through our blog.

Sorry to hit you with the heavy stuff, but we take our responsibilities at Acorns very seriously.

Happy parenting!

The Acorns team

PS Acorns cannot be held responsible for any situation arising from the meeting of people using this app. You should carry out your own background checks on other users if you require them, as we do not do so and we do not have access to your messages with other users.

My head is spinning by the time I reach the end of this. It's all too much.

I giggle like a teenager and close the app, throwing my phone onto the bed.

I feel a burst of energy, so I take a shower and scrub my hair until it squeaks, then blow-dry it for the first time in weeks and head out for a walk.

It's October, and still uncharacteristically mild. We've had a miserable summer this year, and though this is no compensation, really, I'm grateful for the sun on my face as I march towards Morden Hall Park.

I feel elated – ecstatic, even – but then something occurs to me. Hitting me in the tummy, like a punch.

Louis.

I was so blown away by his lovely message that I never clicked on his profile. Never even bothered to find out more about him. What he looks like.

I feel sick with stupidity. It shouldn't matter – it's not as though we're going to be dating – but even so. He's a literal stranger. He could be here, right now, in this park, and I wouldn't recognise him.

I try to remember what his tiny thumbnail picture looked like, but it's tricky. He had fair hair, I think. It was so teeny, it was impossible to make out any distinguishing features.

What an idiot I am. Really! Hannah is right. I shouldn't be left alone with myself, I really shouldn't.

Once I'm settled in the corner of the cafe, I shrug off my coat and tap on the app, hands shaking.

No new messages. Thank God. Hopefully that means Louis hasn't seen mine yet. Surely there must be a way of deleting them?

I tap on various buttons on the app, and eventually I find myself staring down at Louis' profile.

His username is ChelseaLou.

But the thing that catches my eye is his profile picture. I can hardly believe it.

I blink twice, and a hand flies to my face.

He is perfect. Blond hair, cropped close to his head. A wide, open baby face, eyes glinting beneath circular glasses that I know are considered the height of trendy. And a smile that instantly enchants.

How can he be this handsome? And charming? And . . . interested in me?

78

It's too much, to be this lucky surely? There must be something wrong with him.

I tear myself away from his face and instead force myself to read the words under his profile.

Name	*ChelseaLou*
Location	*London*
Age	*40–45*
Interests	*Music and the arts. Hopeless golfer. Non-fiction and biography fan.*
Religion	*None*
Occupation	*Business*

About ChelseaLou

Hi there! Nice to meet you. I live alone in West London and work for my family's firm. I always imagined that I'd have children of my own one day. Sadly, life hasn't worked out like I'd hoped and so I find myself in my early forties with a life that's a bit, well, empty. I'm fortunate to have many wonderful friends that bring me joy and laughter, but although I'm a godparent to many of their offspring, I realise that I want the same for myself.

My father has been a huge influence on me throughout my life – has literally taught me everything I know – and so I'm keen to have someone to pass that all down to. It'd also be good to be able to leave the business that my father started in my own child's hands one day. But no pressure. Just if they were interested!

What ChelseaLou is looking for

A cultured, intelligent, independent woman, who has a caring and nurturing side. It'd be great if they had a particular passion

in life – I'm a huge admirer of people who follow their dreams.
Someone who's not afraid to be firm, but who also knows how
to have fun. But most of all, someone calm, who is ready to take
on a new responsibility in their life.

I sniff at the last two paragraphs, measuring myself against his list of requirements. What would Jonas say? I'm intelligent for sure – straight As across the board at school, despite my childhood – but I'm not sure I'm particularly nurturing. Although my houseplants are well cared for . . .

But I'm not particularly well cared for myself. I've kept myself alive, fed and watered, just about, but I never exercise and I haven't been to a hairdresser in three years. I hardly ever buy myself new clothes.

Well, I can remedy those last two things, at least.

I finish up my lunch and take the bus into Wimbledon, heading straight for the smart department store, Elys. I can't remember the last time I bought anything from an actual shop, rather than online. It was probably the blue velvet dress from the concert. I went into town for that though – a shop that Hannah had recommended just off Oxford Street. The whole experience left me red-faced and panicky.

Up on the first floor, in the womenswear department, I walk around the racks of clothing, trying to act nonchalant, as though I do this sort of thing all the time.

What does one wear on a first date with a man you might end up sharing a child with? I mean, really? Where's the rule book for that?

In the end I decide not to go overboard. Less is more.

Something smart but casual, nothing that looks too over the top. Louis mentioned that he lives in West London so I'm sure all the women he knows are frighteningly sophisticated, but I'll be nervous enough at our meeting as it is. I don't want to feel uncomfortable in my clothing as well.

I head to Mint Velvet, which I vaguely remember as one of Hannah's favourite shops, and I pick up a pair of dark blue jeans and a nice red jumper that has a star decal on the front, sewn on with tiny silver thread.

It's maybe a bit Christmassy, but when I try it on in the fitting room, I'm impressed. Somehow, like magic, it makes me look younger. I should dress like this all the time, rather than in my nineties boot-cut jeans, white vest tops and bobbled cardigans.

There's only one problem though: my boots. They look awful with these smart jeans. I'll have to buy some new ones.

I take the clothes to the till and try not to react when the lady behind it tells me that my two purchases will cost me £152. I feel slightly sick as I hand over my debit card. But it's an investment in my future. I have to see it that way.

Once I've paid, I walk over to the shoe department. I feel even more out of my depth here. I've had the same pair of flat-heeled boots for years. They were expensive when I bought them and I've had them reheeled twice. But they are clumpy and unfeminine. I think about the photo of me that Louis has seen – in that blue dress, onstage – and imagine what that version of me would wear with the smart blue jeans.

I pick up a black boot with a pointy toe and a slight heel. It's not that high. I'm sure I could manage to walk in them.

At the end of this excursion, I'm more than £200 down, but I feel more alive than I have done in years and years. It's the sense of a future: something changing, something exciting waiting in store.

I should have done this years ago.

FAYE

When I get home, I sit on my bed with a cup of ginger tea and tap on the app again.

I have eight new messages.

I frown in surprise. How can I have? Why would he have sent me eight messages?

Suddenly, I feel sick. Of course it wasn't going to be this easy. Of course he was going to be nothing like he seemed.

But then, when I tap to look at my inbox, I realise that they are from other men. Six new men, and one woman, confusingly, all wanting to have babies with me. I gurgle a strange laugh. The idea of it is so insane, it's hilarious.

But I don't care about these seven other people. I only care about Louis.

And thankfully, his name is in there too. I tap on his reply, my heart thumping the way it did when Marshall first held my hand.

Dear Faye,

What a beautiful name. It's lovely to make your acquaintance properly – and thank you so much for your reply.

I have to confess to feeling rather pessimistic when I sent my message. Without wanting to sound rude, I've been a little disappointed by some

of the women on this site and I couldn't believe it when I found you.
I was so hoping that you would reply. I can only imagine you've been
inundated with approaches from other men.

So, if you'll allow me to take you for coffee then I will promise to
listen to Chopin's other Impromptus. *I look forward to learning more,*
with you hopefully as my teacher.

How is your week shaping up? Is there a time of day that works
better for you?

If it's easier, please feel free to text me – my number is 07000 526738.
Yours,
Louis

For the first time in as long as I can remember, I feel desperately sad that I live alone. I wish I had someone here right now – Jonas, or even Hannah – who I could share this with. Share my excitement with. Someone who could listen to me squeal, and hug me and say how happy they were for me.

I can't believe this. Louis is *perfect*. And he likes me!

It was meant to be.

With surprise, I realise that there are tears in my eyes. I sniff, blink, look up at the ceiling and shake my head in irritation. I have to pull myself together. For goodness' sake!

I look back down at my phone, but something else catches the corner of my eye.

The photo on the side table, next to my bed.

Marshall and me, on our wedding day.

Guilt slaps me around the face.

I drop the phone on the bed and stand up, walking towards the photograph. There we are, outside the town hall. I'm wearing a white lace dress that I found in a vintage shop.

Marshall is in his good suit – the one he wore when he did gigs. We are laughing, but faced away from one another, our faces partly obscured by the multicoloured confetti that rains down on us.

Marshall is drunk. More drunk than I'd ever seen him.

After he died, I slept with the photograph under my pillow for nearly a month, hardly believing what had happened. Then, when Jonas wrestled me out of my gloom and told me to start taking care of myself again, I bought an expensive frame for it and put it on the side table.

But it's faded in the sunlight now, the intensity of the colours in the picture muted. Almost sepia.

Almost as though the picture itself is trying to tell me something.

This is the past. Your past. It's over.

I have to move on. Hannah would kill me if she knew I had this photo out on display.

I place the frame back on the table and turn back to the bed and my phone.

It's time to look forward.

FAYE

We arrange to meet at a coffee shop in South Kensington.

It's called Pain. But I presume this refers to bread rather than actual pain.

Which is ironic, because it doesn't seem to sell bread. Just lots of croissants and huge meringues, and a coffee menu that's so extensive it leaves my head spinning. I can't remember the last time I bought a coffee in a shop like this.

'Just an Americano, please,' I say.

'Milk?' she says, and I nod.

'What type?' She sighs.

'Oh, just normal milk. From a cow?'

She laughs and turns to make it. I'm not sure what I've said that's funny.

I'm tempted by the extremely large almond and chocolate croissants heaped in a pile in front of me but decide it wouldn't do well for Louis to turn up and find me stuffing my face with pastry. Not to mention the icing sugar which would undoubtedly go all over my nose and cheeks.

I had wanted to be early for our meeting but now I'm kicking myself at the thought of sitting here for another – oh God – twenty-five minutes, waiting for Louis to arrive. The coffee will be long gone, flowing through my bloodstream and making me a hyperactive idiot.

Oh God, oh God.

The barista has made my coffee in a takeaway cup even though I'm sure I said I was eating in, and I'm tempted to make a run for it. But something stops me. Perhaps the sight of my incredibly expensive and shiny new boots. Or perhaps I'm just not as cowardly as I thought I was.

What do I really have to lose, after all?

I sit at a table in the window of the artisan cafe, having taken my coat off and hung it up on the hooks provided. I hope Louis doesn't notice that it's old and faded and smells slightly of damp.

Once I'm sitting back down in my red star jumper, I feel much calmer. The coffee is deathly hot and so I take tiny sips, hoping to eke it out until Louis arrives.

I hope I recognise him. I hope he recognises me.

It's another ten minutes before I see a man striding towards the cafe. He has a purposeful, charismatic energy, and even before I can make out the details of his face, I feel sure that this is him. Louis.

The future father of my child. I'm about to stand up as he walks through the door but he marches straight past my table and up to the counter. The barista's face twists into a reluctant smile as he approaches her.

'Hi Louis,' she says.

He must be a regular. But she doesn't look very pleased to see him.

'Hello, Margot,' he says, and I am further stunned by his voice. I suppose I should have known he would be posh, but he sounds positively aristocratic. 'You're looking well. Just a macchiato for me, please. Those croissants look immense, but no, no, definitely not for me today.'

He pats his non-existent stomach through his smart black coat. He has a red checked scarf tied around his neck, and for some inexplicable reason he makes me think of Rupert Bear.

His hair is even fairer in real life than in the photographs.

My stomach turns over. I'm almost sick with fear.

He has turned up early too, the same as me. Clearly hoping he could settle at a table and then be ready for when I entered. Me, the glamorous and mysterious classical musician.

Oh God. What will he think when he sees me? When he realises I'm not glamorous or mysterious at all?

I watch him as he pays for his coffee, then rummages in his pocket for some coins which he drops into the cup on the counter. It hadn't occurred to me to tip! She didn't even bring the coffee over to the table.

Too late now.

I'm frozen with fear as he turns away from the counter and looks around for somewhere to sit. What should I do? Stand and wave at him?

I want to cry.

He's looking in the direction of the other side of the cafe now, but it's only a second, I can tell, before he looks over at my window spot.

There.

I give a weak smile, try to stand up, but the table blocks me, my thighs thumping against it. One of my hands shoots out in a kind of wave that's more like a Nazi salute.

I have never felt so humiliated. I can hardly bear to look at his face as he notices me. Realises that it is me he is meant to be meeting.

That I am Chopin4Life.

But if he feels disappointed at all, he hides it well. He responds to my pathetic signal with a broad smile, and marches straight over to my table.

'Faye!' he says, and I stand again, pushing my chair back properly this time.

He leans over and kisses me on both cheeks. He smells of expensive cologne.

'Hello,' I say awkwardly. My neck is burning. 'It's lovely to meet you.'

'You beat me,' he says, smiling, revealing one gold tooth right at the back of his mouth. 'I thought I'd get here early and try to relax and calm the nerves a bit, but . . . well, looks like you had the same idea. Great minds.'

I smile at him as he unwraps his scarf and hangs it and his coat up next to mine by the door. He looks younger than in his photographs.

'That's better,' he says, sitting down opposite me. 'I was getting rather hot and bothered in all that get-up. Such a mild day for October, isn't it? I hope I haven't dragged you far?'

'Oh, no . . . I . . . I'm in Wimbledon. Not too far at all.'

'That's right, you said,' he says, plucking a sachet of sugar out from the pack and stirring it into his coffee. 'Lovely part of the world. I have an aunt who lives just by the common – Lauriston Road, if you're familiar.'

'Oh,' I say. 'I'm from the other bit. The scruffier bit.'

Not Wimbledon at all, but Morden, to be precise.

I had known he would be wealthy, of course, but I didn't expect him to be this wealthy. I'm not sure I've ever felt so intimidated, and I've taught some very moneyed people.

'Hmm,' he says, eyeing me. 'Between you and me, I'm not sure that my flat isn't technically in Earl's Court, but don't tell anyone, will you? Anyway, how are you today? Hope you're having a good week?'

'Yes,' I say. He has so much energy. How could the barista not like him? Maybe she's jealous. Perhaps he rejected her once – that would make sense. He's obviously a catch. 'Thank you. I'm . . .' I pause, deciding I have nothing to lose. 'Well, truth be told, I'm quite nervous. About today. Meeting you. It's all rather unfamiliar territory.'

He leans back in his chair and smiles.

'I feel exactly the same way,' he says. 'I can't tell you how badly I slept last night. But . . . well, we've broken the ice now, haven't we?'

I nod, smile. I feel reassured by the fact that he's a little plumper than he looked in his pictures, that they were clearly taken a few years ago. His teeth, however, are so white they are almost glowing.

I wonder what he's thinking as he looks at me.

'So, tell me about your work. I'm fascinated. I've never met a professional musician before. And, I mean, what a thing to do with your life. What a gift.'

'Well, I mostly teach now,' I say, looking down at the coffee of doom. 'I used to perform a lot but . . .' I tail off. He doesn't want to hear this. My sob story. 'Well, there's just a lot of work out there for teachers, and it's such a joy to introduce a child to an instrument.'

He's nodding vigorously, but there's a faraway look in his eyes, as though he's not really listening to me.

'I'm sure, I'm sure. And you make a good living from that, do you?'

I feel my cheeks colour.

'It's enough,' I say. 'I mean, you'll never get rich teaching, but . . .'

'But you are rich in your soul,' he says, staring at me intensely. 'I can imagine. And what about boyfriends? Never been married? I find it hard to believe someone so attractive – and so clearly talented too – wouldn't have been snapped up.'

I swallow, embarrassed.

'Actually, I was married once, yes. But unfortunately, my husband . . . passed away.'

His reaction is instant. So confident and careful that it feels almost choreographed.

He is so . . . *good* at this.

'Oh Faye, I'm so very, very sorry. Me and my big mouth. Say no more. Let's move on. Now, what kind of food do you like? I know it's not twelve yet, but I'm feeling peckish and those croissants are toying with me. Are you a fan of Italian? Only there's a great little independent place just round the corner from here – we could finish these up and move on there? How does that sound?'

91

FAYE

It's a good thing I don't have any lessons to teach this afternoon, because I'm actually drunk. Even more drunk than I was after my birthday evening in the pub with Jonas.

I sit on the Tube, gripping the armrest as the train rocks from side to side, and I relive the last few hours. They feel like a dream.

Louis kept pouring me wine. More and more wine. It was red and delicious. I've never been a huge fan before, but I realise now that that's because all the red wine I've had has been cheap and nasty. Not smooth like velvet.

Louis chose the bottle. I was too scared to look at how much it cost.

After the first couple of glasses, I began to feel far more relaxed. Being with Louis was like being in the company of a professional . . . I don't know . . . *person*. He was so good at making me feel at ease.

I felt so relaxed in his company that I ordered spaghetti and meatballs, which arrived in a sloppy tomato sauce just destined to end up all over my new jumper, but thankfully I managed to avoid it.

A miracle in itself.

The Italian restaurant was tiny – in the basement beneath what looked like a strange old apothecary shop – and Louis called it a 'hidden gem' that only the locals knew about.

What a life he must live, I thought. So different from mine.

He talked and I listened, and we drank and ate for what felt like hours in the dark, atmospheric restaurant, but was in fact only an hour and a half.

'Tell me about your piano playing,' he said at one point, and I didn't quite understand what he meant, but then he smiled and clarified. 'I mean, how did you start? Are you from a musical family?'

I felt my cheeks redden slightly.

'Not exactly,' I said. 'We did have a piano – I never really found out where it came from, if I'm honest. My father worked in house clearances, and I think he picked it up and brought it home and thought perhaps he could do it up and sell it on. It was in pretty bad condition. But in the end he never got around to it, and I just started to play . . . There was a teacher at school who could tell I had an . . . aptitude for it, and he encouraged me . . .'

I tailed off. I had a speech prepared on just this topic, long ago, when I was applying to music colleges, but I couldn't remember it. In any case, it felt boastful to tell him the truth. That, somehow, music made sense to me. It was like a language I could speak without effort. A language I was born knowing. Even as a young child, I preferred the company of notes on staves to the company of my peers.

Sometimes it frustrated me. That I was so good at this thing, but so bad at everything else. So bad at understanding other people. But most of the time I was happy about it. When I was playing, all the bad things in the world went away.

'Fascinating,' Louis said, nodding vigorously, his eyes intense. 'A child prodigy, then.'

I smiled, looked down at my napkin. People had said that about me when I was young.

They said other things too.

'I'm not sure about that.'

'And to make a career from it,' Louis said, and I could tell that he was trying to encourage me to open up more. 'Well, that's truly spectacular. Can you imagine how many people try and fail? And look at you. You must be so proud of what you've achieved.'

I shook my head. I don't like compliments, and the truth is that I haven't achieved what I might have done. I make a living teaching children, like the majority of music graduates.

'Do you play any instruments?' I asked.

'Sadly no,' he said, dipping a piece of bread into a tiny dish of olive oil. 'But my mother . . . my mother, God rest her soul. She was a pianist.'

He said the word as though it was some kind of title of honour, like an OBE. There was a respect there which took me by surprise.

But 'God rest her soul'? I didn't like to ask for the details, but she was clearly no longer with us.

'Oh,' I said, smiling. 'Did she play professionally?'

'No,' he said, shaking his head. 'No, nothing like that. She was wonderful – truly talented – but . . . she . . .'

His eyes began to water. I felt my heart start to pound. Poor Louis.

'I'm so sorry,' I said. 'You don't have to tell me . . . anything.'

What I really meant was, *please don't tell me because I won't know what to say*.

He glanced up at the ceiling, took a sharp inhalation of breath.

'Sorry,' he said.

'It's fine,' I said. 'Please don't apologise.'

'It's just, well, you only get one mother, don't you? And I miss her every day,' he said, looking back at me. A single solitary tear trickled down his cheek. 'She had a difficult life. We were very close.'

I didn't know what to say to that, so I just nodded, and thankfully the waiter came over to clear our plates and saved me the awkwardness.

At the end, after a shared dessert of tiramisu and him insisting he pay the entire bill, we stood outside the restaurant and he kissed me on the cheek.

'Thank you,' he said, squeezing my hand. 'I'm very happy to have met you, Faye.'

I blushed.

'It was lovely to meet you too,' I said.

He stared at me, holding my hand. I wanted to look away but it might have seemed rude.

'You know,' he said, his eyes looking intently into mine, 'you're not the sort of girl I thought I would end up doing this with, but now . . . now I can see that it's perfect. You're perfect.

A pianist too. It's almost like – if you'll indulge me – you've been sent by my mother.'

I didn't really know what to say to that. My heart was fluttering so much I felt a little faint.

'I'll be in touch soon,' he said, and then he turned and disappeared down the street.

I stood there for a few minutes, staring at the space where he had been standing just a few moments before. I couldn't believe it. Fate had never dealt me many good hands, but finally, it felt like my time had come.

By the time I get to Morden station, I'm feeling a little more sober, but my head is aching. The comedown from the adrenalin of the day, I suppose. Plus, of course, the wine.

As I step outside the Tube, my phone buzzes and I reach for it and see that it is a message from him. Louis.

It was a real pleasure to lunch with you today. I hope very much we can embark on this journey together. Louis x

The intensity of his words would usually unnerve me, but I find myself beaming with joy, and I type a reply and send it quickly. He sent his message more than half an hour ago when I was underground and I don't want him to think that I'm ignoring him.

Thank you so much for lunch. I can't wait to see you again, Fx

Once I'm back in my miserable basement flat, I strip off the jumper and hang it up in my wardrobe, and change into my jogging bottoms and an old sweatshirt. I would normally be working this afternoon, but it's half-term and many of my pupils are away on lovely holidays, their parents keen to catch the last of the good weather in Europe.

I grab my iPhone and sit on the sofa with a pint glass of tap water. The first thing I do is switch my Acorns profile to offline. I've accumulated at least six messages a day since I signed up last weekend, and it's become a little bit strange. So many men out there, it seems, desperate for children. Except that more than a handful of them clearly don't want children at all – they just want sex. One man even offered to send me a picture of his penis, joking that he hoped I could conceive 'as God intended'.

It made me feel sick.

And now Louis and I have met in the flesh, I'm confident I won't need to speak to any of the other men who are lined up, ready to impregnate me.

It's a relief. First time lucky. Who would have believed it?

But it wasn't a date. I have to remember that.

We didn't talk much about the process – how it was all going to happen. I was too shy to bring it up, and he seemed to be having too good a time to want to talk about anything so serious. I suppose that's normal – we have to get to know each other a bit better first. And I know there are no guarantees. No promises.

Still, I feel sure that it's going to work out.

I drink some more water. And then my phone rings.

I practically throw the glass over myself as I scrabble to pick it back up again. But it's not Louis.

It's Hannah.

'Hello,' I say, trying to hide my disappointment.

'Hi Faye,' she says, and I wince. 'How are you?'

She's worried about me again, I can tell by her tone.

'Fine, thanks,' I say. 'How about you? And the kids?'

'Do you want the truth? I'm exhausted,' she says. 'Utterly bloody exhausted. And Marcus is away for work for the week and it's the fucking neighbourhood watch meeting and the babysitter next door has bloody flu and . . .'

'You want me to babysit?'

'Would you? You'd be saving my life.'

'Of course,' I say. 'When?'

'Tonight?'

'Oh,' I say, sighing. The thought of dealing with my nephews right now . . . when I'm practically intoxicated. 'OK. Sure. What time?'

'I need to be there at seven, so come just before? I'll get you a takeaway on my Deliveroo as a thank you. Max will be asleep, so it's only Arthur you'll need to deal with.'

I won't be able to manage a takeaway after all that lunch, but I suppose it's good practice. And I'm sure the wine will have worn off by the time I get there.

'OK, I'll see you soon,' I say.

'Thank you. You are a lifesaver and I owe you.'

She always says that. She thinks she does owe me. After all, her mother had the strength and sense to escape from our father, whereas mine . . .

I swallow the rest of the water and set an alarm on my phone for 6pm. Then I lie back on my sofa and do what I always do when I need to kill time: sleep.

FAYE

Arthur is in a particularly rambunctious mood.

'He's full of Halloween sweets,' Hannah says as she shrugs on her coat. 'Little shit found where I'd hidden them and decided he was going to tuck in.'

Arthur pokes his tongue out at Hannah. She rolls her eyes.

'Where's Albie?' I ask, looking around for my second-eldest nephew, who turned twelve a month ago.

I can't believe Hannah got four kids, and I didn't even get one.

Well, yet. I think of Louis, and my heart lifts.

'God knows,' she says. 'In his bedroom on the Switch probably. Don't worry about him.'

Hannah's favourite child is her eldest son, Reuben. She's always been really protective of him, given what happened to his father. But he's at university now. We don't talk about him very often.

'I won't be long,' she says, 'hopefully. I should be back by nine and then we can have a catch-up. If you can wrestle Arthur into bed by eight, that would be great. Max shouldn't wake up, but the baby monitor is on the side in the kitchen. Thank God I got one that sleeps through! Right, I'll see you. Arthur, be good for your auntie Faye.'

'Bye,' I say, closing the front door behind her and turning to Arthur. 'Right, you, what do you want to do?'

We spend the next hour playing with Lego and then he eventually yawns and I persuade him to make his way to bed. I read him three stories – *The Gruffalo*, *Tabby McTat* and *The Princess and the Wizard*, which he declares is his favourite – and then kiss him softly on the head. He has a red night light next to his head and I pause for a few moments, looking around at all his things as he snuggles down under his duvet. Mostly hand-me-downs from his older brothers, but still, I imagine myself buying all the same bits for my child one day. The books, the cuddly toys, the night lights and hanging mobiles. I've learnt one thing from Hannah's incessant breeding – babies are expensive.

Thankfully, Marcus has a good job doing something in sales and, although he's away a lot, the boys want for nothing. They really are living the childhood I used to dream of.

I'm so lucky that I'll be sharing a child with Louis. He's not only solvent but, actually, well, rich. Marshall didn't have two pennies to rub together.

Hannah comes home at 9.20pm.

'How have they been?' she says.

'Good as gold,' I reply. 'Well, I haven't seen Albie at all. I didn't want to disturb him – his door was shut. But Max has been asleep and Arthur went down just after eight.'

'Great, thanks, Faye,' she says, calmer now. 'Did you get a takeaway?'

I shake my head.

'I had a big lunch. I wasn't hungry.'

She shakes her head, looking me up and down.

'Faye, you need a big lunch *and* a big dinner.'

'My weight's fine at the moment, honest. Stable.'

She blinks slowly, unconvinced.

'How are you really, though?' she says.

'Good! Really good. It's funny you should ask, actually, because . . .'

'What?'

'Well, let's just say that one day soon you might be able to repay the babysitting favour.'

She laughs, jerking her head back.

'Don't tell me you're finally getting a dog?'

'What?' I say, frowning. Then I remember – I once told her that I really wanted a dog, but I couldn't get one as I teach so many different kids at my flat, and it was too risky. 'No! I mean . . .'

I tail off. It's stupid. Too soon.

'Nothing,' I say. 'Never mind.'

She stares at me.

'No, go on,' she says. 'Tell me!'

I shake my head, walk towards the sofa where my coat is waiting for me, slung across the back.

'It doesn't matter,' I say.

'I'm sorry, I didn't mean to laugh at you. It's been a long day, but that was mean of me. Is everything . . . OK?'

She looks genuinely terrified now. I feel bad for her sometimes. I've read articles on survivor's guilt, and I wonder if that's what she has. Even though things were very different for her growing up, she knew what our father was capable of. She knew how lucky she was to have escaped him.

'Everything's fine, Han, honestly,' I reply. 'It doesn't matter.'

'Wait,' she says, her demeanour shifting. 'You're not . . . you can't be.'

I don't say anything.

'Pregnant?' she says eventually. Incredulous, as though the word is foreign to her.

'No,' I say. 'It's just . . .'

'What?'

'I met someone,' I say eventually. It seems the safest. I don't want to tarnish what Louis and I have. It's so very new.

Hannah stares at me. Her mouth breaks out into a smile, but I can see her eyes are filled with concern. She still doesn't trust me, she still thinks I'm a gullible idiot, and it's infuriating.

'Oh Faye,' she says. 'That's . . . great. Good for you.'

'Don't be like that. I really have,' I say angrily. 'And he's lovely.'

'I believe you,' she says, and now her expression is unreadable, and my head starts to hurt. What is she thinking?

'Well,' I say. 'It's early days. But he's keen to start a family. Neither of us are exactly young. Let's see. It might not go anywhere.'

'But starting a family . . .' Hannah says, surprised. 'I didn't know that was something you . . . wanted.'

She hesitates for a few seconds before moving to the fridge and pulling out a bottle of white wine from the door.

'Come on, sit down,' she says, her voice lower now.

102

Sympathetic, almost. 'Let's have a drink and you can tell me all about him.'

'Oh,' I say, flailing around for an excuse. But of course, I don't have one. I don't have anywhere to be, or anyone waiting for me. 'I don't . . .'

'I'm happy for you,' she says, ignoring me as she sloshes wine in my glass. I have sobered up from earlier, thankfully, but this is still the most alcohol I've drunk in one day for years.

'Well, like I said, it's not . . .'

'How did you meet him?' she interrupts, perching herself on a bar stool at the kitchen island and motioning for me to sit next to her. 'What's his name? What does he do?'

I pick up my glass, clutching it by the stem.

'Um, let me see . . . his name is Louis and he works for his father's firm. Fire Leisure? They run a chain of leisure centres . . . well, gyms, I suppose you'd call them now . . .' I pause, trying to remember the details. Louis hadn't wanted to talk about it in too much detail.

'What!' Hannah practically shrieks. 'Fire Leisure? But they're massive. Are you telling me that this guy's father owns them?'

'Yes, I believe so.' I nod.

'Wow,' Hannah says. 'Marcus will be impressed.'

'Well, Louis is the MD, so you know, he's just an employee, really.'

'Even so, if his dad owns them, then that means one day he'll inherit and . . . you're telling me you're in a relationship with him? He's not just a friend? How old is he?'

My cheeks burn.

'Well, like I said, we've only just met,' I say, trying to play

103

it down. 'But no, of course he's not just a friend. And he's forty-three.'

'Where did you meet?' she asks, looking at me over the rim of her wine glass. 'You never go anywhere.'

'Oh,' I say. 'It was ... well, online. Jonas' idea. He talked me into it.'

'Makes sense,' she says. 'Everyone does everything online these days. Which website?'

I pause, take a glug of the wine. It's so cold it hurts my teeth.

'It was an app,' I say.

'Not Tinder?' Hannah says. The red lipstick she put on to go to the neighbourhood watch meeting has smudged at the corners of her mouth. 'You have to be careful of those things, Faye, honestly. There are some right shits on those apps. I don't want you to get hurt.'

I shake my head.

Am I going to tell her this? Am I going to tell her the truth? I can only imagine what she will say. But somehow, I find myself telling her anyway. I can never keep things from Hannah. She's my big sister, I crave her approval.

If I'm truthful, I crave her life. I want nothing more than to be just like her.

'No, it's ...' My stomach turns over as I look at her. 'It's actually an app for ... people who want to have children.'

She frowns, puzzled.

'It's a co-parenting app,' I say. 'It ...'

I'm flustered now. I shouldn't have said anything. She won't understand. She'll judge me. She always judges me, even though she does it with kindness.

'I don't understand. What do you mean?'

'It's just an app, where people who want to have children –
but haven't managed it yet . . . they can come together and,
you know . . . well, see how it goes, I guess.'

She doesn't react. Doesn't seem quite as horrified as I had
expected.

'What, so it's like a dating app for people who are running
out of time?'

I think of the words on the app's home screen.

We're a *mating* app, not a *dating* app.

It couldn't have been more clear: don't expect to find your
lifelong partner here. Instead, hope to find someone to co-
parent with.

Don't get carried away.

But still, it went so well today with Louis. And he kissed
me before he said goodbye. And then he texted me straight
away. Surely . . .

'Yes,' I say, looking back at Hannah. 'That's exactly what
it is.'

NOW

RACHEL

It feels so good to have a lodger back in the front bedroom again. However, it's past 9am and Fiona still hasn't come downstairs. She hasn't even come out of her room.

I hope she's all right.

I heard Jake crying in the night. Heard her whispering softly to him, telling him to shush, not to wake me up.

But I don't mind. I've never slept particularly well. And I'm always too excited the first few nights I have someone new in the house. It takes us a while to get into a rhythm.

But now, I wonder if I should take her up a cup of tea. I made my own porridge nearly two hours ago, but I could always make more. She certainly looks as though she needs a good meal.

I hope she's not nervous to come down and face me. Some of the lodgers take longer to warm up than others. But it'll happen.

I'll take her some tea.

I pad upstairs holding a tray with Mother's best teapot and a mug on it, a jug of milk at the side. No sugar. I can't be doing with people who put sugar in their tea.

I've added some biscuits, in case she doesn't like porridge. I only had Rich Tea left in the tin, but everyone likes those.

I knock lightly on Mother and Father's . . . I mean, Fiona's room.

All these years later, and I still think of it as their room.

'Fiona?' I say gently. 'I've just . . .'

The door opens and she peers out. I'm taken aback by her appearance. She's clearly been crying.

'Are you all right?' I say. My hands are full with the tray. 'What's happened? Is it the baby?'

She blinks, and fresh tears appear.

'No,' she says. 'I'm sorry. He's fine. I'm so sorry, did we wake you?'

She opens the door a little wider and I decide not to stand on ceremony, marching in and placing the tray on the lovely chest of drawers that once belonged to my grandfather. Or so Mother said. I never knew if her stories were true or not.

Fiona's suitcase is open in the middle of floor, looking as though it has exploded, with half the contents scattered across the room. I close my eyes tightly for the briefest of moments. I find mess intolerable, but she's only just arrived, and she has a young baby.

There's a slight sour smell to the air. I turn and open the window just a crack.

'Fresh air is what this room needs. You didn't wake me,' I say kindly, turning back to Fiona. 'Now, what's this all about? He looks right as rain to me. Why are you upset?'

We both look down at Jake, who is sleeping soundly in the middle of the bed.

Fiona shakes her head, wipes the tears away with her fingers.

'I'm sorry,' she says. 'I just woke up this morning and thought . . . I can't *believe* what I've done. That we're here. I don't know what I was thinking.'

She looks terrified.

I take a seat on the bed. It'll need coaxing out of her, clearly, but she'll feel so much better once she's got it all off her chest.

'You poor girl. Why don't you tell me exactly what's happened? With the little lad's father. I promise you, I'm the soul of discretion.'

She looks at me, her eyes wide. The bruise on the right-hand side of her face is more visible today.

'Am I right in assuming that he was violent towards you?'

She bites her lip. Nods. But then she looks down, turning her hands over in front of her.

'It's such a mess,' she says eventually. 'But even so, I'm scared . . . We had to get away, but . . . now . . . I'm such an idiot, always acting on impulse. What if he finds us? He will. I'm sure of it. I've made such a stupid decision. And now . . .'

She bursts into fresh sobs. I've always found public displays of emotion quite distasteful, but I can't help but be moved by her obvious distress, and so I pull her towards me in an awkward hug.

'There, there,' I say, imagining she's a Girl Guide who's fallen over and grazed her knee. 'I'm sure it's exhausting, being a new mother, even without all this to deal with.'

'Thank you,' she stutters. 'You're so kind. I'm so sorry. To bring this to your door . . .'

'There's no need to thank me, Fiona,' I say, pulling away and staring at her hard.

111

She nods. I lean over and pull a tissue from the box beside the bed.

'I expect you are feeling just a little bit overwhelmed. I think, perhaps, bringing some order to the chaos . . .' I pause, glancing around at the once immaculate bedroom, 'might help proceedings. And we need to get Jake his own bed. I know there's all this newfangled attachment-parenting advice flying around these days, but the truth is it's just not safe for him to be in bed with you. You could easily fall asleep and roll on top of him and then . . .'

Perhaps that was a little strident. Her eyes are impossibly wide again, and filled with fresh tears.

'I'm sorry,' she says. 'There are so many things I need to buy for him. We left in such a hurry – we didn't bring anything. Not even a pram.'

'He needs his own bed, and a pram too,' I say briskly. 'I'm sure those slings are great while he's teeny, but once he grows, you'll end up with lumbago if you have to hoick him around in that thing all day. So, shopping trip in order, I think. There are plenty of baby stores in King's Lynn . . .'

I pause, swallowing. It's been a while since I went to town. It's not for me, all that noise, all those people. Kylie used to mock me for it. She took me Christmas shopping last year, and called me a whinging old fart when I complained about the crowds.

But she said it with a twinkle in her eye, and she treated me to a hot chocolate with marshmallows on top afterwards, so I didn't really mind.

'Anyway, they'll be sure to have all the things he needs.

Come on, cheer up. We'll get through it together. Now, how are you feeding him?' I swallow. 'Breast or bottle?'

She looks down again.

'Bottle,' she says, without offering any explanation.

I nod. She's a skinny thing, probably wasn't able to produce much milk. Looking at her now, it's hard to believe she's just had a baby.

'Right,' I say, 'well, we'll need a steriliser then too. Shall we make a list?'

She nods.

'Thank you,' she says, looking at me. 'For being so kind. Really.'

'Tsk, it's nothing,' I say, but inside I glow. 'As a mother myself, I understand how overwhelming it can be.'

This is what I was made for. Looking after these waifs and strays. They will be all right, living here with me.

FAYE

'Please,' I say to Rachel, putting a hand on her arm. 'Let me buy you a coffee or something? Or a slice of cake? To say thank you . . . for this . . .'

I wave a hand over the pile of shopping at my feet. I have spent nearly £500. It makes me feel sick to the stomach, but what choice did I have? Jake needs all of these things.

I had to put it all on my credit card. It would have looked too strange to have paid with cash. But now I'm worried that they'll be able to track me down through it. What will happen when it all comes crashing down around me?

In that split second when I took him, I really did think I was doing the right thing – for Jake, for me. How could I have left him with a father like that? But now I'm not sure. Louis has so much money. He could buy Jake anything he wanted. But me? My savings are dwindling by the day, and I don't have any easy way of earning more.

I can't teach the piano when I don't even have one. And what would I do with Jake, even if I did?

Rachel smiles at me. She really has been a lifesaver.

'I'll buy the cake,' she says. 'You've spent more than enough today. Anyway, it's been nice to get out and about for a change.

That's the problem with my age – so easy to get stuck in your ways.'

I pick up the shopping bags. My back is killing me. My body hasn't got used to carrying a baby around all day yet. It feels awkward, bent out of shape.

'Are you all right?' Rachel asks.

'What?' I say. 'Sorry, yes, just . . . I was miles away. These bags are so heavy.'

'Let me take Jake,' Rachel says, tutting lightly. 'You can't manage him and all the shopping.'

'Oh, right,' I say, and before I can say anything else, she has reached down inside the sling and plucked him out, holding him to her chest as we push through the streets in search of a cafe.

She's been very keen to hold him, offering constantly. It makes me nervous, seeing her with him. I feel anxious whenever he's not right next to me. Worried that someone could take him away from me at any time.

He's been a bit difficult today: crying more, leaking through his nappy onto his babygrow, and only sleeping for short periods of time. I'm sure it's normal but I wonder if the bright lights of the shops are too much for him. He's still tiny – not even four weeks old yet.

'How was the birth?' Rachel says, tucking into a huge piece of chocolate fudge cake. 'I must say, you're awfully skinny. Now I know that's rude, but it's true. You need feeding up. More of these!'

She forks a mouthful of cake through her lips.

'Oh,' I say, feeling my heart rate rise. 'It was fine, really. Nothing to write home about. I've always been very slim.'

I want to add that I was barely fed as a child, and that a malnourished child often remains underweight throughout their whole life, no matter what they do, but I don't want her to start asking questions about my parents.

'One of the lucky ones,' she says, nodding. 'And such a lovely little boy too. What was his birth weight?'

'Oh, I can't . . .' I begin, but then I pause. Why can't I remember this kind of thing? 'Seven pounds something.'

'A good healthy weight. Although he does seem a little bit out of sorts today, doesn't he? Perhaps he's overstimulated. Unfortunately, babies can pick up on stress.'

I look down at Jake, who is squeaking like an irritated kitten while she holds him in the crook of her arm.

'I'll take him, if you like?' I say, reaching out across the table to him.

'Oh, no need,' Rachel says. 'He'll settle in a minute.'

I bite my lip. She's been so kind to me, I can't demand she give me my baby back. But there's something niggling – the creeping sense that this kindness will need to be repaid someday. Somehow.

No.

I'm being paranoid. It's all because of Louis. He's destroyed my ability to trust. To see the good in people.

'I bought some dummies,' I say. 'Once we get home and sterilise them, perhaps they'll help him when he's a bit upset.'

'Dummies,' Rachel says, frowning. 'Well, he's your baby,

of course. But they can become a crutch if you're not careful. Babies should learn to settle themselves. And he will.'

All of Hannah's children had dummies. I wonder why Rachel has such strong opinions about babies. There aren't any photos of grandchildren in the house – or not that I've seen.

'Do you have children? You mentioned something before . . .' I say nervously, taking a sip of strong tea.

She nods.

'One,' she says. 'He's all grown up now, though. Brian. He lives in Australia.'

'Oh, I'm sorry,' I say. 'That must be very hard. To not see him regularly.'

'Well,' she says, 'we have the computer, Skype, you know. We talk regularly. In fact, that's something I wanted to ask you about . . . we speak on Sunday evenings at 8pm. But obviously, like I said, we have to do it in the living room, through my computer. So I'll require some privacy at that time. Of course, the house is yours to use as you please, but for that hour, if you could . . . well, I would say go out, but obviously that's difficult with the little one. So if you could just stay in your room on Sundays at 8pm, barring any emergencies, I would appreciate it.'

'Oh right, yes, of course,' I say. I would have stayed away anyway, instinctively. But it feels as though I'm being banned.

'It's just, I've never liked an eavesdropper,' she says, narrowing her eyes. 'And it's the only time I get to talk to my son.'

'Of course,' I say, making a mental note to never get under her feet. 'Of course, it's your house . . .'

'No,' she says, her voice stern. 'It's our house, but even so.

It's just that hour a week . . . it's very special to me. It's very hard, living so far away from your child, as I'm sure you can understand.'

'Yes,' I say, looking over at Jake, wishing that I was holding him. Rachel's whole body has tensed, and she's gripping him more tightly with her hand. 'Of course.'

She nods again, finishing up her cake.

'Do you have any grandchildren?' I say, staring down at Jake. He's yawning now. Hopefully the fidgeting has worn him out, and he'll fall asleep soon.

Rachel gives a brief shake of her head, but doesn't elaborate. Perhaps it's a sore spot for her.

'But you know so much about babies,' I say.

'Well, you never forget, do you? When you're a mother. It's an exclusive club; one we're lucky to be in. I worked in a school for years too,' she says, brightening slightly. 'Then I worked in a nursery for a while after I . . . retired. I also spent far too many years as a Girl Guide leader.'

I frown.

'The Girl Guides? I take it you weren't one. Anyway, I've worked with children my whole life. I've loved children for as long as I can remember. They're so . . . innocent.'

'I'm very lucky to have found you,' I say.

She nods again. I can't tell if I've upset her or not.

'The thing is . . . I . . .' I sniff, feeling tears threaten. 'I feel completely out of my depth. I wanted to have a baby my whole life, but . . . I imagined it differently. You know. A more trad-itional set-up – like my sister Hannah has. She's married, with four boys. That's all I ever wanted – a family of my own – but somehow . . . things haven't – my life hasn't – always gone how I'd wanted.'

'Well, you've had a traumatic time of it,' Rachel says. 'With his father.'

'It's not fair though, is it?' I look over at Jake. 'Why do I always pick the wrong men?'

'Oh, my dear child, life isn't fair,' she says. Jake has fallen fast asleep now, and her grip on him has relaxed slightly. 'Do you think he'll come looking for you? Is he that sort of man? Or will he just let it go?'

I wish I could tell her all of it. But it's too risky. I don't know her well enough yet. Maybe one day.

'I don't think he would let it go,' I say, shuddering. 'He's not that kind of man. In fact . . . I'm surprised he hasn't already come looking for us. Or gone to the police.'

'Well, it's not kidnap if it's your own child,' she says. She pauses, her gaze lingering on my black eye. 'Perhaps there's nothing they can do.'

I look down at my lap.

'Perhaps.'

'You're safe now,' she says, the tone of her voice telling me that she thinks I need to pull myself together. 'Both of you. That's all that matters.'

I hope she's right.

RACHEL

It's Sunday. We've spent a productive day building baby Jake's new cot. I'm very pleased that he won't be sleeping in Fiona's bed at night any more. I could hardly sleep myself for worrying about him suffocating.

In my day, babies slept in different rooms from their mothers from the moment they were born, but things are apparently more complicated now.

I hadn't thought what we would do about Brian's Sunday call before.

With all my other tenants, I had it written into their contracts. They had to go out on Sunday evenings, between 8–9pm, so that I could take the call in private. Some of them used the time to exercise, but most of them ended up going to the pub.

It became a running joke in the Royal Oak. Janice used to poke fun whenever she saw me, saying she should start paying me commission because, without fail, my tenants would come into her pub on a Sunday night, and stay long enough to buy at least two drinks.

'What do you get up to on Sundays, Rachel?'

'She scares them off mixing up her potions,' her husband, Paul, replied, winking at me.

The Witch.

That's been my nickname in the village for a long time.

I ignored it. It was none of Janice's business – or anyone else's, for that matter – what I chose to do in my own home on a Sunday evening.

But now it's difficult. I haven't even asked Fiona to sign a contract. It's not like me, but I'm worried it might upset her. She seems very concerned with not leaving a paper trail, in case the baby's father might find out where they've gone.

But what if Jake's having a bad day, or the weather is inclement? I can't ask her to go out and take a screaming baby with her. Instead, she's agreed to stay in her room, and hopefully she'll be too distracted to listen to our conversations.

When we got home from King's Lynn, I helped her unpack all her purchases, telling her that I was fine with her leaving out the steriliser on the side in the kitchen, so long as she kept it clean. I watched as she added the new bottles and the dummies to the water, and switched it on.

I restrained myself from commenting again on the dummies.

She stared out of the back door as we waited for the machine to tell us it had finished. I should have drawn the curtain. The weeds right behind the door are waist-high now.

'I think something's trying to grow through the gap at the bottom of the door,' Fiona said, pointing at it.

I squinted. My eyesight is not what it was.

'Excuse me?'

'There,' she said, taking a step closer. I followed, looking at the spot she was pointing at. She was right. A thin green

121

tentacle had curled itself under the doorframe and was poking into the room.

'Goodness,' I said, momentarily thrown off guard. It felt like a sign. As though someone was creeping closer towards the truth. 'I'll have to get the gardener in.'

'Are you not a fan of gardening?' she said, turning to look at me.

I could tell what she was thinking. She was thinking that most women my age love it.

'I'm far too busy to keep up with it, unfortunately,' I said, hoping that would be the end of the conversation.

'I could help you if you like?' she said. 'After all, you've been so kind to me.'

'No!' I said. 'Thank you. That won't be necessary. You have your hands full.'

I hoped my tone would encourage her to leave it, but she pressed on.

'But it must be a shame not to be able to use the garden when the weather's warmer,' she pressed on. 'How big is it?'

'It's not very safe,' I said. 'The ground is uneven and boggy. It's never been particularly nice out there. And we have the green just out the front.'

'Oh,' she said, and thankfully she left it there, retreating upstairs.

The lodgers often comment on the garden. Kylie didn't though. I liked that about her. She was completely oblivious. She only saw what was right in front of her.

I sigh. Out of all of them, I'm still the most upset about Kylie.

I tidy away the lunch plates and eye the tiny green shoot that's pushed itself underneath the doorframe. Nature always wins. One day, it will reveal its secrets. But hopefully by then, I'll be long gone.

As I put the plates back in the cupboard, I hear Jake start to cry. First just a few plaintive squeaks, but then they escalate into screams. Blood-curdling wails so loud they carry even through the solid floor of the cottage.

I don't remember Brian crying like that, but then it was so long ago.

Daisy has gone to hide somewhere, likely in disgust. She's always like that after a new lodger moves in. The way she looks at me! The disdain in her eyes, as though furious with me for allowing someone new into our sacred space.

But she doesn't understand how lonely I get. How much I appreciate having a human being to talk to.

I don't need the money, of course. I inherited a decent sum from Mother, along with this cottage. I have lived here all my life. Some people find that strange, but why would I move? In any case, I could never leave. I was born here, and I will die here, and I suppose you could find a comfort in that.

I turn to the small dining table and look down at my jigsaw, but Jake's wails continue, growing louder by the minute. I take a deep breath. It's not my business to interfere, but the sound is like a jackhammer to the senses, violent and repetitive. What is Fiona doing? Why isn't she taking care of him?

I saw the way she was today – uneasy, nervous. It would make sense that she's having trouble bonding with him, after what she's experienced. She hasn't told me many of the details, but I know that those first few days with your newborn are critical for establishing a bond between mother and child, and I can imagine they were very strained with the father still in the picture.

Those first few days are what I was denied, and it explains the distance between Brian and me. We're close, but not as close as we might have been. Not as close as we should have been.

I only have my parents to blame for that.

I tut. I mustn't get maudlin. It's a bad habit of mine. And things are good. If only Jake would stop that awful noise.

I can't concentrate.

I stand up, pushing my chair back crossly, and go to the cupboard, taking out Daisy's box of Go-Cat and shaking it vigorously.

'Dais! Daisy Doo!' I call, but she doesn't come. She's sulking. Not even her favourite treat is enough to lure her out, with that racket going on.

I give up after a minute or so. Jake's cries are even louder now, and when I turn around I see Fiona standing at the bottom of the stairs, holding baby Jake, tears streaming down her face.

Baby blues.

'He won't stop,' she says, desperately. 'It's as though he's in pain or something. Could he have hurt himself? I don't know what to do. I don't know what I'm doing!'

I look at the child. His lips are blue, his face red with the effort of screaming. I take him from her, and hold him over my shoulder.

'Oh Fiona,' I say, shaking my head. 'He has wind. Have you burped him? Feel how tight his tummy is. It's just wind. They should have shown you how to do this at the hospital.'

'Of course I've burped him!' she almost shouts at me. 'I've been trying for hours. Nothing works. He won't burp . . .'

'Well, he can probably sense your stress,' I say, as he quietens slightly over my shoulder. 'Babies are very good at picking up on it. You need to calm down. Go upstairs and wash your face. I know it's hard, but you're a mother now. You can do this.'

She stares at me. But then she turns on her heel and rushes back up the stairs. A few seconds later I hear her lock the bathroom door behind her.

Poor Jake. I sit with him on the sofa, trying to support his back and neck, keeping them as straight as possible while I tap him lightly on the back. Eventually, the loudest, most unlikely burp emerges from his tiny mouth, and he yawns sleepily and his eyes start to close.

'Poppet,' I say, looking down at him. 'That was a nasty tummy ache, wasn't it? All better now.'

I gaze at him for a little longer before I notice something. My trouser leg is damp underneath his tiny body. I hold Jake up against me again and pat his bottom lightly.

As suspected, he has wet through his nappy.

Thank God for the plastic sofa cover.

I take him upstairs, trying to ignore the cold, damp sensation through my trousers, trying to squash the knowledge that I must have urine on me too. *It will be fine, for God's sake, Rachel,* I tell myself. It's just baby urine. It's just milk.

Even so, it's a struggle not to dump him on the bed in Fiona's room and race into the bathroom for a shower.

I knock lightly on the bathroom door.

'Fiona?' I say through the thick pine. 'Jake's wet himself. Would you like me to change him for you?'

The door opens, and she peers out at me. She's stopped crying now, at least.

'It's OK. I can do it,' she says quietly.

Perhaps I spoke too harshly to her before.

'Apologies for my . . . frustration earlier,' I say.

She shakes her head. In one hand she's clutching a well-used tissue.

'I'm sorry. I was just overwhelmed,' she says. 'It's . . . much more difficult than I imagined. I looked after my nephews – I told you I've got four of them – so many times, and they were never like this. The minute I pick him up, he starts screaming.'

She stares at him darkly.

'It's like he hates me.'

'Of course he doesn't.'

'It's like I'm the wrong mother for him.'

'You're just tired,' I say. 'Did you look after your nephews when they were newborns?'

She shakes her head.

'Well, then,' I say. It feels as though the damp patch on my leg is burning my skin now. I have to get these trousers off, soon. I can't bear it. 'It's a completely different situation. Newborns are slippy little things. And his head control isn't great, is it? He's very floppy. Low muscle tone. It's very common.'

Her forehead crumples.

'Do you think there's something wrong with him?' she moans.

'No!' I say hastily. 'No, that's not what I meant. I just mean it's harder to burp them when they're so underdeveloped.'

I pause, taking a deep breath.

'It will all get easier with time,' I say, trying to sound re-assuring. I hope she starts to pull herself together a bit, or she doesn't stand a chance. 'Now, it's probably best you change him before that nappy leaks any more.'

FAYE

Rachel is cleaning again. She took a shower after she handed Jake back to me, and then she put a load of washing on and now she's downstairs, wiping down the plastic cover on the sofa.

But Jake's babygrow was only slightly damp. I can't imagine that it soaked through to the sofa. Still, I don't want to ask. I hold him to me, rocking him slightly, trying to sing to him, but I can't think of any lullabies. My mind has gone completely blank.

I search my memory, and then something comes back to me, and I start to hum . . .

Rock-a-bye, baby, on the treetop
When the wind blows, the cradle will rock,
When the bough breaks, the cradle will fall,
Down will come baby, cradle and all . . .

He screws up his face at me.

Why are lullabies so horrible?

'I'm sorry,' I say. 'I'm better at piano than I am at singing. And yes, it's not a nice song anyway, is it?'

Singing.

It makes me think of Hannah. When we were kids, she

wanted to be a professional soprano. She was good, but not good enough. My talent was perhaps the only thing she was ever envious of me for.

I wonder if Hannah is wondering where I've gone. If she has any idea that I'm even missing yet. Probably not. But by the end of the week she'll wonder, and then what? She doesn't know the whole story with Louis – I was too ashamed to tell her. But she knows we stopped seeing each other a while ago.

'Auntie Hannah will probably call the police,' I say.

Then it hits me like a train. What if I never see Hannah again? Or the boys?

What have I done?

I shake my head, then lay Jake down in his new cot. He's contented now, nearly asleep.

I wanted a new life, a change from my monotonous existence, but I didn't want this. I wanted the perfect family: me and Jake *and* Louis. I thought that's what I was going to get. But it's all gone wrong.

I take a look at the clock. It's nearly 8pm and I've been instructed to stay up here in my bedroom until 9pm at the earliest. I'm not in the least interested in Rachel's Skype chats with her son, but she was adamant that I'm not to come down while she speaks to him. I'm happy enough to stay in here. It's a good opportunity to tidy up a bit. The place has become a pigsty, and I've not even been here for a week yet.

It's amazing how much mess newborns make, especially given that they can't even hold things with their hands yet.

I start to tidy, making a pile of washing in one corner. Jake will need more babygrows soon, he's already growing out of the first lot I bought him. Then I take the nappy bin and empty it, tying a knot in the end of the plastic bag so the foul smell doesn't escape.

After that, I take the tray Rachel brought up for me yesterday and fill it with all his dirty bottles, and the dummy that I secretly let him have in the middle of last night, when he wouldn't settle and I was terrified that he would wake her up. I'll have to sterilise it without her noticing.

Once that's all done, I get to work on my own things.

This morning, I had to apply the make-up to my eye area in a rush, as Rachel was up and about before we were, and I accidentally left the purple and green eyeshadow palette out on the side. I can only hope that it's not something she noticed earlier when I came in to change Jake.

I'm not sure how quickly bruises fade, but the make-up I carefully patted around my eye socket earlier to mimic a black eye has almost completely vanished now. I add a little bit more of the purple into the hollow above my cheek, and tap it with my finger to blend it.

I'll be relieved when I don't have to keep this pretence up any longer. But I knew it was needed – the likelihood of anyone turning away a woman with visible injuries, on the run with a newborn baby, was minuscule.

And it worked. I saw the way Rachel's face softened as she answered the door to me that first time and saw my face.

I didn't like deceiving her, but what choice did I have?

I stroke Jake's sleeping face and a sense of calm washes over me. Everything feels so much better when he's asleep.

When he's asleep, I feel as though I've done the right thing in leaving Louis, and trying to build a life with just the two of us. Not exactly what I'd hoped for, but at least I won't be alone any longer.

But then, when he's awake, I feel completely out of control.

I make my bed and tidy away the last few things left out on my bedside table. Then I sit down, looking at the pile of washing in the corner.

I need that stuff to be washed and dried before tomorrow, or he'll have no clothes left, the rate he gets through them.

Surely she wouldn't mind if I crept down and just snuck into the kitchen to put the washing on? Surely she wouldn't even notice, if I was quiet?

And she's obsessed with hygiene – that much is clear. She wouldn't want me to leave this pile of dirty laundry festering in my room.

I check Jake one more time and then I bundle up the pile of babygrows inside one of his big muslins. I open the door to my room slowly, mindful of its creaks. Everything in this cottage makes a noise, as though the fabric of the place is trying to speak.

I wonder how long she has lived here. It has the feel of a home that's been passed down through the generations with care, the wallpaper so old it's come back into fashion. The bathroom looks relatively new, but that parquet floor downstairs is surely original?

I take a step forward on the landing. I've already worked out where the floor squeaks, and I'm careful to avoid the trigger points.

At the top of the stairs I linger, trying to hear if Rachel is already on the call or not.

My eavesdropping is interrupted by the sound of a loud miaow. Daisy the cat is standing in the middle of the staircase, staring at me with a haughty look in her eyes.

I frown at her, then take a step down. And that's when I hear voices.

She's on the call already, then. Dammit. I should go back to my room, but something makes me stay, straining my ears to listen.

'Of course, bonfire's coming up again,' Rachel is saying. 'Doug wants it to be bigger than ever this year. They've even been flyering Dalswood and Mitching this year! As though we need the hooligans from those villages to come. It's just greed, pure and simple. No thought about safety whatsoever. Last year, four kids ended up in hospital, but do they care? No. It's all "bigger and better" this and "best year ever" that.'

'Well, I suppose everyone wants everything bigger and better these days,' the voice from her computer says. What was his name? Brian, that was it.

'Yes, but it's nonsense. It's not the same any more. It used to be strictly a village affair, you remember. Now you get all sorts of out-of-towners gatecrashing. Antisocial behaviour . . . youths drinking, urinating on people's flower beds, all sorts. The police had a hell of a time of it last year. I've a mind to tell them in the Royal Oak to stop serving alcohol that night. We could really do without it. It used to be a family affair . . .'

Brian laughs.

'Rachel,' he says. 'Let the young people have their fun! You don't have to be quite such a miserable old cow all your life, you know.'

I'm shocked. I look down at Daisy, who is licking her paw, her head turned away from me.

'Shut your face,' Rachel says, and then – inexplicably – she giggles. Like a teenager.

I'm confused. She told me that Brian was her son.

I tiptoe down one more step and peer over the banister until I can see the face on the screen. It's hard to make out much definition as the image is so pixellated, but the man she's talking to looks much older than I imagined.

And he called her Rachel. Not mum.

Who is he? And why did she lie about it?

RACHEL

I always feel better after speaking to Brian. Even though, of course, as we log off, waving our goodbyes, there's an ache in the pit of my stomach that it will be another week before I'll hear his voice again. Australia is such a long way away.

So very far.

I've never been over there. Brian has asked me to go and visit many times but I've never travelled by aeroplane, and starting the experience with a twenty-four-hour flight seems a bit unwise. I've barely ever left Norfolk.

When I was younger I went to Switzerland once, on a coach with my friend Dorothy, but I didn't think much of the food. So much heavy, sickly cheese, although the scenery was nice.

I sit, staring at my computer for a few minutes after Brian's face has disappeared from the screen. I wish he would find someone and settle down. He's such a lovely man. He would be a wonderful father.

But he's a little awkward, like me. Misunderstood. Runs in the family, I suppose.

There's a creak on the stairs and Daisy slowly plods down. She walks towards me with purpose, her mouth open in complaint.

'Sorry,' I say, bending down to stroke her. 'You'll be wanting your tea, of course.'

In the kitchen I spoon food into her bowl and listen for any sound of Jake crying upstairs. Good. He seems to have settled more easily tonight. Perhaps because we had a quieter day.

He's been through a lot already in his short life.

'Is it all right if I use the washing machine?' Fiona says, and I turn to find her standing behind me, a bundle of baby things in her arm.

'Oh. It's rather late.'

Her face falls.

'Well, if you must, then you must,' I say. 'Of course.'

I give her a smile.

'Thank you,' she says, meekly.

I forgot how much washing young babies produce. I probably should have thought to charge extra for that. Running a wash costs a fortune.

I tut at myself. For goodness' sake. That would be incredibly uncharitable of me.

Fiona switches on the machine then fills a glass with water from the tap. The water splashes around the sink area as she does it, but she doesn't wipe it down after. Doesn't notice, I suppose. I take the dishcloth and soak up the puddle she's created, hoping she'll see and take the hint.

The water here is very hard, and water stains are difficult to shift.

Daisy sits by the back door, pawing at the plant shoot. I swear it's grown bigger since this morning.

'Don't you let her outside?' Fiona asks, and suddenly I feel

135

tired, and irritated that she hasn't just taken her glass of water and disappeared upstairs to her room with it.

I forgot about this. They are all different. Some lodgers are desperate to chat. Some hardly speak at all, choosing – like bats and mice – to only come out when there's no one else around.

Usually I prefer the chatty ones. After all, that was the whole point of getting a lodger in the first place, when Brian moved out to Australia. To stop me feeling alone.

To stop me feeling scared.

'She's an indoor cat,' I say stiffly.

'But why?' Fiona says. 'If you have a garden? It's safe here, surely. There's hardly any traffic in the village. Here, I can let her out . . .'

With horror, I watch her try to open the back door, but thankfully it's locked.

'You must never, do you understand me, NEVER let Daisy outside!'

I rush towards her and grab her hand, twisting her wrist upwards and yanking it away from the door handle.

'Ow!' she cries, her eyes wide. 'You're hurting me!'

I close my eyes, try to calm myself. I let go of her wrist.

'I'm sorry. But Daisy is a pedigree Scottish Fold. She's incredibly valuable. If she were allowed out, she would likely be kidnapped. Or worse, all the toms in the neighbourhood would take their turn with her, and I'd end up with a house full of mongrel kittens. Now, I hope you appreciate, Fiona, that there are certain rules that I really must insist you follow.'

She blinks.

'Yes, of course,' she says eventually, frowning.

'Good,' I say, pulling the heavy curtain across the back door. I've likely made everything worse. She'll be more eager than ever to go into the garden now.

I look at her. I can't tell if it's a trick of the light, or my poor memory, but the bruise under her eye looks worse than it did yesterday. Although, bruises can do that, I remember. They often look worse before they look better.

She stares at me. There's the briefest of moments when I regret it all: staying here all these years, getting Daisy, letting out Mother's room. I feel it pulling me, the familiar whirlpool of self-pity, and I try to resist. It's all in the past.

Perhaps I was naive though. Perhaps having a baby at the cottage was a bad idea. My temper is understandably shorter when my sleep is disrupted.

'I'm sorry,' I say. 'I shouldn't have . . . snapped like that. I'm a little bit tired, and there's so much to do with the bonfire coming up . . .'

'It's a big deal round here, is it? I noticed the huge mound on the green.'

'It's the biggest night of the year for the village. The pubs make a fortune. It's what Helston is known for.'

'I had no idea.'

'Well, you'll enjoy the view from your bedroom window next week. I hope the fireworks don't disturb Jake – they do tend to go on for rather a while. There's £30,000 worth, believe it or not.'

'What a funny thing to spend all that money on,' she says, and I frown. But she's right, of course.

'Well, it's tradition.' My voice is stiff. I sound like Mother. As the years roll on, I feel more and more like her, and it depresses me immensely.

'I haven't been to a firework display for years and years. Not since I was with my husband.'

She pauses. This is the first time she's mentioned a husband.

'He died.'

I'm surprised by this.

'Oh. So your husband . . . he wasn't Jake's father?'

She shakes her head.

'No, Jake's father is . . . someone else. Someone I should never have trusted.'

I purse my lips.

'Well,' I say. 'We all make mistakes.'

'Jake's not a mistake,' she says almost instantly.

'No, of course not. I just mean . . .'

'I thought we were going to be just a normal, happy family,' she says, staring down at the worktop. She runs a hand along the edge, leaning onto it. I'll have to wipe it down again now. 'I loved him. Louis. The way he used to look at me when I played the piano for him, he made me feel like I was the only woman in the world . . . But I was such a fool. He didn't want me, not really.'

My head is humming. I'm so very tired. I usually go straight to bed after speaking to Brian.

'Have you ever been used by a man?' she says, her voice suddenly bitter. 'You seem like the type of woman who wouldn't take any nonsense. But still. We're all vulnerable, aren't we? Deep down. We all have our weak spots.'

I shake my head, unsure how to reply to this.

'I should never have believed him,' she says, and I notice her right fist is clenched. 'He treated me like a commodity. Something he could use and then throw away when he was done . . .'

She's not making much sense, but something tells me not to probe further.

'You're safe here,' I say again, but I'm unnerved. The power balance between us has shifted. A minute ago she seemed frightened of me. I look again at her eye, take a step closer towards her. Her right fist unclenches, and then I notice it, on the tips of her fingers: a deep green smudge of something.

Make-up.

Make-up the same colour as the bruise under her eye.

'You have something on your fingers,' I say, pointing to her hand.

'What?' she says, and then she looks down, opening her palm. 'Oh . . .'

She rushes to the sink and washes her hands.

'Sorry,' she says, but doesn't elaborate further. Her anger has vanished. She's back to the meek little mouse she was when she first came here.

Now she's closer, I can see her eye even more clearly.

The brown and green colour staining the skin, and something else. A slight shimmer.

I drop my head to one side and look at her more closely.

She doesn't look like the sort of person who would fake a black eye. But she must have done.

But why? To garner my sympathy?

If so, it worked.

I'm momentarily impressed. It takes quite something to pull the wool over my eyes, but she's managed it.

Well, well, well, Fiona.

Clearly, I have more on my hands here than I bargained for.

FAYE

I escape back to my room as soon as I can without it looking too suspicious.

I can't believe I didn't think to wipe my fingers after I re-applied the make-up. I'm just so tired. I can't remember the last time I slept for more than two hours without Jake waking me up.

And now Rachel's seen what I've done.

She didn't say anything, didn't ask me any questions, but even so I knew she'd noticed. She kept looking at my eye, her nose twitching slightly.

What will happen now? Will she throw us out?

I paid her the six months' rent up front. Will she even give it back?

Marshall was right. I am hopeless. Useless. Good for nothing.

I look over at Jake. He's asleep, his chest rising and falling peacefully. I search for the rush of love I felt when I first scooped him up out of Louis' car, but I can't find it. I feel nothing towards him but responsibility. Pressure.

Just then, I hear the washing machine beeping. I hurry down the stairs, switching the machine off before it has the chance to disturb Rachel, and fill my arms with the washing.

I take it through to the little room off the side of the kitchen. No more than a store cupboard, really, but there's a window here onto the garden.

It's cold and damp in here.

I look out as I hang the tiny clothes on the rack Rachel has left out for me. From here, the weeds are slightly shorter, and I can see further, almost to the end of the garden.

It's a jungle – worse than the communal garden at the back of my flat. It doesn't look as though anyone has been out there for months. I shake my head, trying to understand it. Why would she let this space become so overgrown, to the point where it will surely start to threaten the structure of the house itself? She's so immaculately tidy and clean inside the house, it just doesn't make any sense.

I feel something rub against my leg, and I jump in surprise. But it's just Daisy.

'What do you want?' I say to her and she chirrups at me. I watch as she goes to the back door and paws at it. She has sensed an ally in me, it seems.

'You're not allowed out there,' I say. 'I've been told.'

I pull the door curtain back and look out at the darkness. The weed I noticed before has grown even longer. I lean down and yank at it, but it won't come loose.

Daisy watches, sniffing at the air that seeps underneath the doorframe. I'm seized by an irritation for Rachel and her rules.

'But you're right. It's ridiculous,' I say. 'You not being allowed out. You're a cat, for God's sake – and an ugly one at that, with your funny flat ears, so I'm not sure who she thinks might steal you.'

I turn the key in the lock. It's stiff at first but then it gives way with a satisfying click. The door opens outwards, and I can only push it a crack against the forest of plants that have grown up behind it.

Daisy puts one paw on the outside threshold and sniffs the air again. It's colder than I expected it to be, but I suppose we're further north up here, and the countryside is always chillier.

I crouch down and pull at the plant that had been growing under the door. After a fierce tug, it comes away in my hand. I look at it, the soil from the root crumbling away.

I shiver and fling it back outside. Daisy is still standing, one paw in, one paw out, sniffing the garden.

'It's cold,' I say. 'Are you in or out?'

She looks up at me and blinks.

'Oh, for God's sake,' I say, irritated now, and I pull her back into the house and lock the door again. 'Forget it, then.'

Once I've hung up all Jake's babygrows, I stand in the small storeroom and look around. I feel bone-tired. I'm overcome with an ache for my old life. The simple life, where I taught piano and slept until noon on Sundays and did what I wanted.

Despite what Hannah always says, I haven't been naive about this. I knew how hard it would be, having a baby. I've listened to her complain about it four times over. When she found out she was pregnant with Max, she poured herself a large glass of wine and sobbed into it at her kitchen island.

'I'm forty-one!' she wailed. 'What the fuck is God playing at? I can't do it again. Not all over again. Not after Arthur. I'm exhausted, Faye. Exhausted.'

143

At the time I tried to be sympathetic. Even though it cut like a knife. Hannah and her perfect family. She didn't know how lucky she was.

I turn to go back upstairs, and it's only then that I realise Jake is crying. I hadn't even noticed.

'Shit!' I say, hurrying up the stairs.

But it's too late. Someone else has beaten me to it. She's right in front of me, filling the space around me as she scoops him up.

Jake immediately quietens.

'Young man,' she is saying. 'That's not the sort of behaviour we expect from someone at this time on a Sunday night. Oh no, it isn't . . . Now, what's this I see in your cot? A dummy? Is that what you're so upset about? I see. Did Mummy give you a dummy and it fell out? Silly Mummy. Well, I did try to tell her she'd be making a rod for her own back by giving you one, but clearly she didn't listen to Auntie Rachel, did she? But let's not be too hard on her.'

She says all this in a soft, sing-song voice. Her eyes are fixed on my son, who's whimpering slightly now, the features on his little face softening as he calms down. She is stroking him ever so gently on the nose, her fingertips lightly brushing his eyelids.

Once he's quiet, she turns to me.

'Are you all right, Fiona?' she says, and I start at the use of my decoy name.

Fiona. I had forgotten that she doesn't know my real name. That's how useless I am at this.

What was I thinking? I should have known there was no way that I could pull a plan like this off.

'I'm fine,' I say, forcing a smile. 'I was just downstairs hanging the washing up . . . sorry. I didn't . . . I didn't hear him.'

I give a wry laugh but she doesn't return it. Instead she casts her eyes around my room. I'm glad I tidied up. She lays Jake down in his cot. She doesn't put the dummy back in his mouth, but she doesn't need to because he's fallen back asleep without it.

'You didn't hear him? Goodness me,' she says. 'I'm amazed that the whole village didn't hear him. He certainly has a strong set of lungs.'

'Yes,' I say. 'Sorry.'

She nods.

'Well, goodnight.'

'Goodnight, Rachel.'

Jake is still asleep in his cot, but the second that she leaves, he starts to shift around, moving his head and hips from side to side in a frustrated dance that I know will end with him bellowing his head off. Again.

I can't bear it. I knew how hard it would be, but I wasn't prepared for this. These feelings of irritation and frustration towards him.

I stand in front of his cot, looking down at him as he writhes from side to side. He starts to cry, softly at first, and then that familiar ack-ack-ack sound, a machine gun to the senses, as he gasps for breath.

I don't pick him up. I find myself biting down on my lip hard, feeling the blood rush to the surface. His eyes are open now and he looks up at me, judging me. The expression on his face is pure hatred. Anger.

Why aren't you meeting my needs? Call yourself a mother! You're getting everything wrong!

We're not bonding.

It's almost as though he can tell.

I am frozen to the spot, thinking of all I have done. Of how ridiculous it is to have got myself into this situation.

Another bad situation. I thought I could get away with it again. The madness of it. Act first, think later.

But it was completely different with Marshall. It was easy to get out of that situation. This time, I have bitten off more than I can chew.

I pick Jake up, and try to comfort him, but I'm a robot and he's a writhing pink pig of a thing in my arms, hating my touch, wanting nothing more to do with me.

I take the dummy and shove it into his mouth, harder than I should do. His eyes widen in shock but then he starts to suck, angrily.

He's probably hungry.

I should make him up a bottle.

I am a machine, going through the motions as I pour out some of the ready-made milk and screw on the lid with the teat. I take the dummy out of his mouth and he drinks, and I watch him, and we are locked in a co-dependent hatred.

Perhaps it's easier when it's your own child. Your own flesh and blood. Perhaps then you can tolerate more of this unending torture.

Perhaps it's easier when it's not a baby you've taken in a moment of lucid madness, stolen from the car he's been left alone in.

What kind of father leaves a baby alone in a car, even for a nanosecond?

And not just a car, but a car with the door wide open, the engine running, changing bag next to him on the seat, and the baby's only ID – his red child record book – poking out of the top.

What kind of father leaves a baby unattended?

Any stranger could have taken him.

And that's just what I did.

RACHEL

Two in the morning again.

The way she lets him cry! It's almost as though he's not her baby.

I keep track of how long it goes on for using the alarm clock by my bed. Nearly three minutes of him screaming before, finally, his cries lessen.

Three minutes is a long time.

I don't think she's coping. She needs help. An expert. And surely they should both be having check-ups with midwives or doctors? To make sure she's healing from the birth, and that he's putting on enough weight.

It's been years since I had anything to do with babies, but surely things haven't changed that much? And he'll need his vaccinations soon too.

Earlier today I noticed he has a red mark on his face that I hadn't seen before. Probably just a dry spot, the beginnings of baby acne. When she was in the bathroom, I looked around Fiona's room to see if I could find any cream for it, but instead I found something else poking out of her backpack.

A plastic-covered red book entitled *My Personal Child Health Record*. The names of baby Jake's parents were written inside.

Fiona Ivanov

Louis Horton-Jones

Louis Horton-Jones. What had he done to her?

Enough to make her run away.

Enough to make her pretend that he had punched her in the face. I should ask her about that, but now that I've had time to consider it, I can see that perhaps it was just an insurance policy, a way of making sure I didn't turn her away when she came to view the room. And it worked. I don't like dishonesty, but I can understand why she might have done it. She was desperate, after all.

And the sight of the red book reassured me a little. She had thought to bring that with her when she ran. She must be planning on taking Jake for a check-up soon.

I put the book back and left the room. Brian's right. I always get too involved with my lodgers. Look at what happened with Kylie. That was all my fault.

It's difficult to remain distant though, when you're sharing a home with someone. My home. My family's home. It's inevitable that you become close.

And deep down, I had so hoped for us to become like family.

When Jake arrived, it took me back all those years to Brian's birth. That special time that was ruined by my parents. My chance to become a biological mother was ripped away from me, and if I'm honest, I had hoped Jake and Fiona would be the next best thing.

And it was clear from the second I laid eyes on her – fake bruises or not – just how much help Fiona needed.

But there's something that doesn't feel right. The cold way

she spoke to me in the kitchen. The fact she didn't even hear him crying.

I understand trauma, and this isn't it. This is something else.

Jake's cries have stopped finally, and I creep out of bed in the darkness and open the door to my bedroom as quietly as possible, softly taking the two steps across the pink carpet towards her room. I put my ear to Fiona's door.

Even through the thick pine, I can hear Jake slurping away. At least she's feeding him now.

I smile with the memory of the first and only time I fed Brian. Mother was busy with something and said I could. His tiny little mouth clamped tight around the bottle while his eyes focused on the ceiling, a permanent frown furrowed across his forehead, as though he was trying to work out what on earth this world was all about.

Above the sound of Jake drinking, I can hear something else. Fiona muttering, or whispering.

I strain harder, but my hearing isn't what it once was, and I can't quite make out what she's saying to him. The words are lost, but the tone is not. She sounds mournful. Depressed.

It seems obvious then, what she's suffering from. It's always coming up in programmes on television: post-natal depression.

The next morning, her black eye has completely gone. Clearly, she has decided not to continue with the pretence any longer. Whatever that was about, we have both decided to let it be.

She's surprisingly cheerful when I come down into the kitchen.

'Morning,' she says, smiling broadly at me.

'Good morning,' I say, my nose wrinkling at the state of the kitchen counter. She's been sterilising Jake's bottles, and has laid them all out to dry on a tea towel, but there's water all over the counter, a pile of soap suds inexplicably bubbling away next to the sink.

Daisy wraps herself around my ankles and looks up at me, a quizzical look on her face.

'I've already fed her,' Fiona says. 'I hope that's OK? I just . . . well, she seemed hungry.'

I raise my eyebrows in surprise.

'Oh, right,' I say. 'What did you give her? She's got a very sensitive stomach.'

'Oh,' Fiona says, her mouth twisting. 'Just some of the dry food you keep in the tin. She practically showed me where to find it. She's a very clever cat.'

'Yes,' I say, reaching down to pick Daisy up. 'She is.'

Daisy sits in my arms for a few seconds and then begins to struggle, claws flaring. She's never been one for cuddles. Not like Patch, her predecessor.

I lower her back down to the ground, trying to keep my temper. Sometimes, it's very frustrating having a disappointing pet. But I know Daisy is similarly disappointed in me. She's been desperate to go outside ever since I got her.

'Rachel,' Fiona says. 'I just wanted . . . to say I'm very sorry about yesterday. I really was quite exhausted and I think the shock of everything that's happened to me and knowing that I can never go back to my place . . . it all just became too much. I was just . . . overwhelmed I suppose.'

'Apology accepted, although there's no need for it,' I say. 'I'm not surprised after everything . . . you've been through.'

'I know but . . .' she pauses, holding a piece of toast in mid-air. Where is the plate? Crumbs fall onto the tea towel with the bottles on. I stare at them. 'You've been so kind to me. It's just a difficult adjustment. I haven't lived with anyone else for a long, long time. And I'm just slowly coming to terms with . . . well, the enormity of what's happened to me.'

I nod.

'Would you like a cup of tea?' she says, gesturing towards the kettle. 'It's just boiled.'

'Thank you,' I say, although I'm very particular about my tea. Especially the first cup of the day. 'Is Jake . . .'

'He's asleep upstairs after his breakfast,' she says, smiling.

'Right. Good.'

I can't stand it any longer. I make my way over to the bottles and start drying them on the tea towel, screwing their tops back on.

'Oh . . .' she says. 'I was just about to do that.'

'It's no bother,' I say, stiffly.

'I know I'm a bit messy,' she says, looking down. I notice a bald patch at the back of her scalp. A perfect white circle, as though hair has never grown there. 'I was a piano teacher you know. Before. I lived on my own for a very long time. I guess I got a bit lazy.'

'Oh, I didn't know that.' I should probably have asked her

what she did, but what with Jake ... 'So we've both worked with children then.'

She nods, pouring water on the teabag. I notice with alarm that she's already sloshed milk into my mug. Doesn't the silly girl know how to make a cup of tea? You can't expect a teabag to infuse into milk!

'Yes,' she says, stirring the tea quickly and squeezing the bag, before spooning it out and letting it drip all the way to the bin.

I take a deep breath.

'You'd think, given how much experience I had with children that I'd find being a mother easy but obviously, babies are a whole different kettle of fish ...'

'It's very different when it's your own.'

She cocks her head to one side.

'Do you just have Brian?' she says. 'No other children?'

She's doing that thing again. The thing that makes my throat close up. It's what they all do. They push and push, going too far, until it's too late.

'Just Brian,' I say, shortly, hoping my tone will tell her to leave the subject there. But she's different today, as though someone has injected her with happy drugs, and she presses on.

'And Brian's father?' she says, her voice a little shaky at the end. 'He's not ...'

I glance at the back door. Sometimes I can't believe he won't just walk back through it at any moment.

'He died a long time ago,' I say, hoping that she has the sensitivity not to ask for any more details.

153

'Oh, I'm sorry,' she says. 'My husband died too.'

I frown at her.

'Yes, I remember,' I say. 'You told me before.'

She laughs, shakes her head at herself.

'Did I? My memory . . . it's the lack of sleep.'

She hands me the tea; a hideous pale beige.

'Thank you,' I say. I hate waste but I can't possibly drink that. As soon as she goes upstairs I will tip it down the sink and make myself a proper cup.

'I wonder if there are any children in the village who might like piano lessons?' she says, her eyes wide. 'I know you don't have a piano here but . . .'

'I have a keyboard,' I say, remembering. 'In the shed. It was Brian's. I think it still works.'

'Oh,' she says, wrinkling her nose. 'Right. Thank you. That's brilliant. I mean . . .very generous of you.'

'You're welcome to get it out and play it yourself. But I think it'll be a while before you can start teaching again, surely. You have Jake to look after.'

She blinks at me. And I see it there, the flash in her eyes: regret. The realisation that, like me, she can't do this alone.

Well, she doesn't have to. She only has to ask.

'Yes,' she says, looking down. 'Yes you're right, of course. I was just thinking ahead. Or should I say getting ahead of myself. Well then, I'll leave you to have your breakfast in peace.'

After she leaves the room, I stand in the kitchen looking around at the state she's left it in. I sigh. That's a couple of hours of my morning gone. At least I can have *The Archers* on while I clean.

And then my eyes fall on the back door. The curtain has been pulled back and the little green shoot is no longer there. No longer pushing its way into the kitchen, trying to invade my space. I frown and crouch down, arthritic knees grumbling at the manoeuvre, but there's no sign of it having been cut off from inside.

I look through the pane of glass at the bottom of the door.

No, Fiona must have opened the back door, and pulled the entire plant out, leaving a patch of black earth in its place. But did she actually go outside? It seems unlikely – the rest of the foliage is undisturbed.

I stare at the soil. A minuscule reminder of that day in November. The way the garden looked after we'd finished digging.

I close my eyes.

I'm going to have to watch this one. I really am.

ONE YEAR EARLIER

FAYE

I'm getting ready for my fourth date – well, *meeting* – with Louis, and I am carefully applying make-up following a tutorial I found on the internet, when my phone pings.

I snatch it up, whispering under my breath. No, please don't cancel. I'd been so looking forward to this evening. It feels like things are about to take a step forward . . .

Louis' job is incredibly busy and pressured. The company has fifty-two leisure centres across the UK, and he's constantly having to travel all over the place at short notice.

But it's just from Jonas.

Hey stranger, long time no see, pub tonight?

I reply that I'm sorry but I can't because I'm on a date with my new boyfriend and he sends back a string of exclamation marks. I know he's pleased for me, but even so, it feels a bit patronising.

As though he can't believe that I might actually have found myself a boyfriend.

Well, I have. Haven't I?

I swallow. Last night, I scoured the internet to find examples of people who'd started out co-parenting and ended up living together like a normal family. There were loads of them! That's what I really want. For the three of us to be a proper family.

And Louis is taking it slow – getting to know me first – rather than treating it as a straightforward, cold transaction. Which must mean he feels the same way too.

My phone pings again.

See you there at 7. Louis

My heart lifts. My eye make-up is a little uneven – and nothing like the woman's on the video – but even so, I smile at my reflection and head out of the door.

We're meeting at the private members' club Louis belongs to. It's not one of the trendy arty ones that some of my more successful musician friends belong to, but a more traditional affair that the internet informed me 'stinks of old money'.

It's a good job I left with plenty of time, as it takes me more than twenty minutes to find the entrance.

I feel like I'm in a film as I give my name to the lady waiting at the reception inside.

'Mr Horton-Jones is in the Blue Bar,' she says, her voice smooth as silk but with the trace of an accent. 'If you'll follow me, Miss Miller.'

This is a life I could grow accustomed to. I gaze into the side rooms as we pass, all filled with distinguished people having distinguished conversations. I'm drunk with glee at it, and saunter down the dark hallway, my eyes noticing all the details: the ornate cornicing above, the oil paintings that line the walls, the shiny conker floor beneath my feet.

I deserve this, after everything I've been through.

What would my father say, if he was still alive, and here

now? If he saw where I have ended up? The dark chip of anger in my heart pulses at the thought of it.

Louis is sitting in an armchair in the corner of the Blue Bar, on his phone, as the receptionist waves me towards him. I stiffen slightly, suddenly shy, my previous bravado vanished. I don't want to interrupt his call. But he looks up and spots me, and gestures for me to come over, so I do.

'Just sort it, Sebastian,' he is saying into the phone. 'If that's not too much trouble. Right. Yes. Goodbye.'

He puts the phone on the table in front of him and pauses for a moment, taking a deep breath and then looking up at me.

'I don't know what I did to deserve having such a moron as a stepbrother,' he says. His voice is sour. I've never heard him sound like this before.

It makes me nervous.

'Sorry. What would you like to drink?'

'Oh,' I say.

'Perhaps not alcohol,' he says lightly. 'We need to be careful, don't we. You are taking the vitamins I had my assistant send you?'

'Yes, yes, of course.'

'Excellent. Perhaps a ginger ale, then. That will be nice. Refreshing.'

He clicks his fingers at the waiter, who scurries over and takes my – his – order.

'I'm sorry for my mood,' he says. 'I'm having one of those days.'

'Sorry to hear that,' I say, my heart thundering. Out of the corner of my eye I notice that someone has spotted us, and is pointing and talking. I sit up a little straighter.

Yes, I want to shout. *Yes, I am dating Louis Horton-Jones.*

'Family, eh . . . never mind . . . How are you?'

He seems very cross.

'Very well, thank you,' I say, smiling as the waiter sets down the ginger ale in front of me. I don't like ginger – I never have – but I suppose Louis is right. It's not sensible to drink alcohol, even though I'm not pregnant yet.

'Glad to hear it,' he says, and then he reaches down and pulls out a large wad of paperwork from his briefcase. 'Now, sorry to bore you with this stuff, but, you know . . . you can never be too careful, can you? I've spoken to a solicitor who . . .'

I stare down at the pile of papers in front of me.

There are just two words printed on the cover.

Co-parenting Agreement.

I swallow.

'Oh,' I say. 'Right, yes.'

'Well, I guess you'll want to take this away and have it checked over by your own solicitor. Unless you feel you can trust me. Which, of course, you can. I have to say, Faye, I feel I can trust you.'

He pauses, staring at me for a few seconds. I feel a spark of connection between us that makes my body tingle.

'Oh, I . . . yes, of course.'

'Well, no rush. It's important you're satisfied that everything is above board. I just wanted to get it to you as soon as possible. I suppose . . . well, I'm as keen as you are to get things moving.'

He's so much more confident than me. So much freer. I wish I could be like him.

'It's all incredibly boring legalese,' he says, as I tentatively lift the cover of the agreement. 'But, you know, with my job and . . . my *status* . . . the lawyers get nervous. I've been burnt before by people in my real life who were only after one thing, you see.'

I feel my cheeks flush. What was it that attracted me to him when we met? His money? No, surely not. It wasn't that. It was his charm. The confidence with which he views the world.

I've never thought much about money. I forget how important it is to most people.

'I understand,' I say, my heart still pounding. 'That makes perfect sense. And I don't want you to think that I'm after anything . . . financially. I mean.'

'Oh, I know. It's the lawyers, they take the fun out of everything. What a job. There's really no need to read the whole thing unless you particularly want to. There's nothing in there that's not completely standard. And what I *love* so much about us is that we know where we stand with each other. Don't we? We're completely in sync. It's wonderful.'

I nod, take a sip of my ginger ale and swallow it swiftly in order not to really taste it. Still, it burns the back of my throat and I struggle not to cough.

Louis sits back in his chair, looking at me. I smile, embarrassed.

'Have you done something different with your make-up?' he says.

'Oh,' I stutter. 'Yes, just . . . well, I haven't been here before . . .'

163

'Faye, you don't need it, honestly. I still can't quite believe you're the age you told me you are.'

'That's so kind,' I say, but somehow it doesn't feel kind. I feel stupid, as though he's seen through my attempts to impress him.

'So, I in no way want to pressure you, but . . . I feel – and please, stop me if you disagree – that we're ready to take things to the next stage. How about you? Now, be honest with me. I have the tendency to be quite bullish when I want something, and I don't want you to feel railroaded into anything, but, well, time is marching on and neither of us are getting any younger, are we?'

'Of course,' I say. 'Of course I'm ready. I've been . . . I can't really believe it. It feels like fate has brought us together.'

'I quite agree,' he says, nodding, his face suddenly serious as he leans in closer.

'So . . .' I look over at him, taking in his blond hair, his slim Roman nose, and the way even his eyebrows look groomed to perfection, and I imagine him taking me in his arms and kissing me, long and hard.

My cheeks flush at the thought of it. I haven't felt this way since Marshall.

Louis is not my type. And he's so different from Marshall, who was all long hair and broken fingernails. Intense, always about the music. But his life was chaos. There were the drugs, the drinking, the chain-smoking, the fact that he never came to bed before 2am, and then slept until midday. He was slippery like a fish, impossible to pin down, impossible to get a straight answer from. He never looked me in the eye.

Not like Louis.

Louis is upfront and honest. A true morally upstanding citizen, with a reputation to protect.

'Oh, hello there,' a voice says from above, interrupting my daydreams. I look up to see a stocky man with a neat beard leaning down over our table. 'Thought it was you!'

He's staring straight at Louis.

'Jeremy,' Louis says, his mouth twisting into a smile. He stands and shakes the man's hand.

'Jonesy!' Jeremy says. 'Long time . . . sorry you didn't make it to Verbier this year.'

'Well, yes, work . . .' His jaw tenses. 'You know what's it like.'

I stare at them both. It's the first time I've seen Louis look flustered.

'And who's this pretty little thing?' Jeremy says, leaning down further towards me. 'You do know you're not safe with this one, don't you? His reputation precedes him.'

'Oh,' I say.

'Fuck off, Jez,' Louis says, and Jeremy gives a great belting laugh.

'Don't say I didn't warn you,' Jeremy says, winking at me. 'Anyway, I have to run. Here with the madre. But call me, and let's go for a drink and a catch-up sometime.'

'Give her my love,' Louis says, and he sits back down.

He didn't introduce me. I try not to read anything into it. But deep down, I'm thinking about what Jeremy said. His warning to me. What reputation? I should have asked Jeremy what he meant; Hannah would have done.

'I hate this place,' Louis says, once Jeremy is out of earshot. 'Would you like to get out of here?'

It's his thing, I realise. His way of bringing fresh energy to our meetings, switching up the location without warning. He's so enigmatic. If he could bottle his charisma and sell it, he wouldn't need to work for his dad's fitness business.

'Yes, why not?'

FAYE

The next thing I know, I'm in a black cab, Louis by my side, and we are travelling through the West End, towards Chelsea.

'Let's go back to mine,' he said when we left the club. 'We'll have some real privacy there.'

I can't believe I'm going to his apartment.

It's drizzling, and from the cab window I watch all the drab people wandering around in the rain. I can't remember the last time I took a taxi, but it feels right, somehow, that I should be in here and they should be out there. Finally, I am being appreciated as the special person that I am.

A prodigious talent. That's what someone wrote in a newspaper article about me once. And yet . . .

I've not had an easy life. My childhood was traumatic. My career didn't go the way I'd hoped. My short marriage ended with me as a widow. But perhaps it was all leading to this.

We cross Belgravia and soon we are driving down one of those roads you only see in films: white wedding-cake terraces, tall as the sky, each one marked out by two pillars flanking their shiny black front doors. These are the sort of houses that the parents of even my most wealthy of pupils could only dream of living in. These are the sort of houses that are owned by diplomats, politicians, royalty.

And, it seems, Louis.

'Here, please,' he says to the taxi driver, who pulls up outside number 42 Palace Terrace Court.

'That'll be £28,' the cabby says, and Louis rummages in his pocket, pulls out a wallet and hands the driver two twenties.

'Keep the change,' he says, and I follow him out of the taxi, noticing the way the cabby nods his gratitude, the expression not quite reaching his eyes.

I stare up at the house. Despite the fact that it's hemmed in on both sides by two other identical properties, it looks enormous. Leading up to the black front door is a wide flight of steps.

'Do you own the whole thing?' I say, stunned.

Louis lets out a brittle laugh.

'God, no,' he says. 'What do you think I am, a Russian oligarch? You are hilarious.'

He lightly climbs the stairs, gesturing for me to follow.

'I have the ground-floor flat,' he says, opening the door. 'If I sold up, I could buy something much bigger outside of Kensington, but if I'm honest, I just love the area. I'm settled here, you know what it's like . . .'

I *don't* know. Am I settled in my grotty basement? I suppose so, I've been there long enough. Not happily though.

'It's lovely,' I say, marvelling at the hallway, so unlike any of the other communal hallways I've ever set foot in before. The floor is orange marble, the wallpaper a delicately patterned floral. It smells of expensive candles, rather than damp.

'And here's me,' he says, opening the door nearest the staircase. 'Welcome to my humble abode.'

He pushes open the door and allows me to go in before him.

Inside, it is immaculate, the walls pristine white, the ceilings high, and the bay window at the front an unusual curved shape. In front of the window is a baby grand piano, the first thing that catches my eye. But not just any grand piano. I stare at it, then look away.

The flat is beautiful. You can see that someone – perhaps Louis, perhaps a professional – has spent time and money on the interior design. Everything is perfect. The whole place is so tasteful it feels like a dream.

'It's the only three-bed on the street,' he says. 'Flat, I mean. Most of the original villas have been converted to flats. But the one on the end – number 57 – that's still an original house and it sold for twenty-five million earlier this year. Insanity. I'm lucky that I bought this place when I did.'

He takes off his jacket and throws it over the chocolate-coloured leather sofa. I wander over to the piano, unthinking.

It's a Steinway. The case is made from the most unusual veneer I have ever seen – a kind of zebra pattern of dark and light wood.

Louis sees me looking.

'It's Macassar ebony,' he says, softly. 'One of the rarest woods in the world. Incredible, isn't it?'

'I've . . .' I'm speechless. 'I've never seen anything like it.'

I lift the lid, stroke the keys. I don't much care what a piano looks like. For me, it's all about the sound they make.

There's no music anywhere to be seen.

'And you don't play?' I ask.

He shakes his head.

'My mother did. Maybe one day you can teach me,' he says. 'Now, what would you like to drink?'

'A cup of tea would be lovely,' I say, feeling more out of my depth than ever. I take my own coat off, but wrap it over my arm.

He throws his head back and laughs.

'See, that's what I love about you. You're down to earth. A cup of tea, well, well, well. Of course. Come through.'

That's what I love about you. It's the second time he's used the word 'love' when talking about our relationship.

I blush.

I'm not entirely sure what's so funny, but I drag myself away from the piano and follow him through to the back of the room, where there's a perfectly painted cream door, surrounded by ornate cornicing.

On the other side is the kitchen. It's all marble and soft, muted grey wooden cabinetry. But there's something else in the room that surprises me into silence.

A woman, no older than twenty, carefully stacking a dishwasher. She stands up at the sight of us, dipping her head slightly, as though bowing in respect.

I stare at her. She is beautiful and slender, a pale face surrounded by thick dark hair. She has washing-up gloves on.

'Oh,' he says. 'You're still here.'

'I go now . . .' she says, looking directly at Louis. She pulls off the gloves and folds them neatly before putting them underneath the sink, then she goes back through another door at the side of the kitchen. She seems a little afraid of him, which is strange. After all, I've only ever seen him be utterly charming to everyone he meets.

I try not to be surprised that he has a housekeeper, even though he lives alone and doesn't have any dependents, not even a dog. Of course someone like Louis would have someone to do his cleaning. He's far too busy to do that kind of thing himself.

'So,' he says, clapping his hands together and opening cupboards. 'Faye would like tea. Now where would one keep the teabags, I wonder . . .'

He eventually unearths a box of PG Tips – 'I don't suppose tea goes off, does it?' – and pours hot water directly from a tap that's plumbed into the counter.

'Now you'll have to forgive me with the milk,' he says. 'My father's wife, Tamara, only drinks Earl Grey, and she takes that with lemon.'

He hands me a milk jug and I splash the tiniest amount into the mug. I have never felt more uncivilised.

He helps himself to a glass of sparkling water from a bottle in the fridge.

'Let's go through, shall we?' he says. 'To the drawing room.'

'Oh,' I say. 'I would love to see more of your home, if you fancied giving me a tour? It's so beautifully done.'

'My cousin Frances is in with the Chelsea Harbour lot,' he says, rolling his eyes. 'I confess I had nothing much to do with the decor. She oversaw the refurbishment last year. Before that it was a proper bachelor's pad. But yes, of course. Come and see. There's a room, you'll be pleased to hear . . .' He tails off. 'Well, let's not get ahead of ourselves.'

He opens the same beautiful doors to three bedrooms – the smallest of which just houses a desk.

'I very rarely actually work in here. So, this is the room that the baby would have,' he says. It's the smallest room, but it's still bigger than my bedroom, with an enormous window overlooking the back of the house, light from a streetlamp streaming in and landing on the soft, thick carpet.

'It's lovely,' I say.

'It has a bathroom too,' he says, opening another door, which I had assumed was to a built-in cupboard, but is in fact a stunning marble en suite.

'Oh!' I say, my eyes taking in all the details. 'It's absolutely wonderful.'

'Yes, well, it's criminally underused.'

I zone out, thinking of our future child. Growing up here, among such opulence. My hand rests lightly on my stomach, and I try to imagine the baby growing there. A baby destined for this life. How lucky it would be. How lucky I am, to have met Louis.

'So,' he says, 'that's the grand tour, really. Shall we go back to the drawing room and sit down?'

I notice that there's one door in the hall he hasn't opened, and I wonder why. Perhaps it's just a guest toilet or something.

'Yes,' I say. 'That would be lovely.'

'So, tell me about your week?' he says, as he takes a seat opposite me on the sofa. The piano looms large in the corner of my eye. I want to like it, but the truth is, it's ugly. It's a showpiece, not an instrument. I think of my battered Broadwood at home, the love it has brought me and my pupils over the years. 'Lots of piano lessons?'

'The same as usual,' I say. 'It's quite regular, my schedule.'

'I must say, I think you're an absolute saint, dealing with all those children,' he says. 'I'm sure some of them must be . . . challenging.' He pauses, his eyes flicking to the left. 'I was a right shit when I was a child.'

'Well, most of them are actually pretty good,' I say. 'It's the parents that are hard work. Jonas says . . .'

'Jonas?' he interrupts.

'Oh, Jonas is my oldest friend. We met at music college. He's a teacher too, but he works in a school.'

Louis pulls a strange face.

'I see.'

'He's not my boyfriend or anything,' I say, although I'm not sure why I feel the need to justify Jonas' existence in my life. 'We've known each other forever. We're just good friends.'

'But you did have a husband once?' Louis says, leaning forward and putting his crystal glass down on the coffee table in front of us. I notice that the coasters are inlaid with mother-of-pearl.

I bite my lip. I don't want to talk about Marshall. It feels disloyal, somehow.

'Yes, but sadly . . . he died. In an accident.'

'I'm very sorry to hear that,' Louis says, his eyes narrowing slightly. I feel as though he's examining me under a microscope, trying to get to the heart of who I am. It makes me uncomfortable, but at the same time, I know he's only showing an interest.

'Thank you,' I say. As always, I picture Hannah's face when I told her what had happened. The way she looked at me. 'It

173

was nearly twenty years ago now, though, so . . . well, I was just a child.'

Louis nods. I know he wants to ask for more information. Everyone does. Everyone wants to know the gory details.

But only I know those, and I have blocked them from my memory as much as possible.

He locks eyes with me, and then, when he realises that no more information is forthcoming, he smiles again and sits back on the sofa.

'And now you live alone?' he asks.

I nod.

'But you must have close friends nearby? People round for dinner parties and suchlike?'

I frown, wondering why he's asking this. Is he worried that I'm lonely?

'Not really. I see my sister quite often though.'

'Right. She has a family, does she?'

'Yes, four sons.'

He pauses, looking thoughtful.

'So Faye, there's something that perhaps it'd be good for us to talk about . . .'

My heart flutters. I want to pinch myself.

'Of course,' I say, a rush of energy seizing hold of me. 'There's so much to talk about . . .'

He shifts in his seat, adjusts his collar.

'I hope that you'll understand this. But my father and step-mother, they're very . . . old-fashioned. And I think if they ever found out how we met, well, they might find it quite difficult to . . . well, wrap their antiquated heads around.' He gives a harsh laugh. 'So, we'll need to be discreet about the app . . . and we'll need them to believe that we met in a more . . . organic way.'

'Of course,' I say. Of course he doesn't want to admit that we met over the internet, not least on a dating app that's just for people who want to have children. 'That's not a problem at all. I feel the same way.'

'I knew you would understand. It's very important, Faye. I can't emphasise that enough.'

I swallow. He looks stern, and I'm suddenly – briefly – frightened of him.

We sit in silence for a few moments, until I can't cope with it any longer. The piano feels like a literal elephant in the room. And so I do what I always do when I run out of conversation.

I glance back at the hideous Steinway.

'Would you like me to play something for you, Louis?' I say, staring into his eyes.

His face lights up and he leans in close.

'That would be wonderful.' He pauses, licking his lips. 'Do you know "Winter Wind"?'

FAYE

I suspect rule number one of co-parenting with a man you've just met online is *Do Not Fall in Love With Them*, but at the same time, the more I've researched it, the more people I've discovered who've been on this journey and done just that.

So it's not just me being naive.

I'm walking back from the Tube, my footsteps light with something that I assume might actually be joy. I can't be sure though, it's been so long since I've felt it.

It was the perfect evening with Louis. I played four of the Chopin Études for him – the ones I could remember – and he sat enraptured throughout. I was a little bit rusty, especially without the music, but it was the first time in a long while that I can remember having such a rapt audience.

Halfway through my final piece, he stood up and laid his hands gently on my shoulders. I could feel his fingers quivering against my collarbone, connecting us, as though he wanted to feel the vibration of the music through me.

As I played the final chord, he stroked my neck, ever so softly, then knelt down beside the piano stool and held my hand. His eyes were damp with emotion, and he thanked me.

'Not since my mother died have I heard music played as

beautifully,' he said. 'You are very talented. My mother would be so happy that I met you.'

I felt completely overwhelmed by his reaction. It made me want to cry.

I feel sure that next time we meet, we will take things a step further. And then . . .

I think he's as stunned as I am that we have connected in the way we have.

I feel so lucky, lucky, lucky.

'Just call me Kylie!' I trill to a pigeon that's attacking a takeaway box in the gutter at the end of my road.

Somehow, the splendour of Louis' neighbourhood has brought the grime of mine into sharp relief. How depressing my little corner of London is, with its discarded mattresses and ripped-open bin bags spilling their contents onto the pavements. How could I have ever thought otherwise?

I didn't realise when I moved here that it was just round the corner from Marshall's family. I once saw his mother at the Tube station, and turned away, keeping my head low so she wouldn't see me. I couldn't face seeing her again after all that time.

His family were the first people the hospital called. I remember his mother's face when I turned up, the way she stared at me without speaking. She grabbed my hands and we just stood there together, staring at each other, mouths open and heads shaking in shock.

I close my eyes at the memory. Marshall, lying on the floor, the blood trickling out of his ear and staining the concrete.

The way the nurse looked at me, her head cocked on one

side in sympathy. The inevitable black widow jokes that I knew people would be making behind my back.

How terrible, for a groom to die in such a tragic accident on his wedding day!

I look up at my building, turning the key in the lock and pushing my way inside. I don't want to think about that day. It was so long ago. Why does that memory haunt me, even in my happiest moments? As though it doesn't want me to move on.

I deserve to be happy. I've suffered enough in my life.

I take my bag off my shoulder and dump it on the sofa. It's a relief – a literal weight off. The contract Louis gave me was heavy, and it's poking out of the top, almost as though it's looking at me.

His lawyer has even had it bound.

I take it out and put it on my battered coffee table, remembering Louis' advice to get my solicitor to look it over. I don't have a solicitor. Do people just 'have' such things? There was someone we dealt with after Marshall died, but Hannah took care of most of it. I was in no fit state.

Other than that, I don't think I've ever spoken to a solicitor before.

In the kitchen, I run the cold tap until it's clear and fill a glass with water. I look round at my tiny, poky kitchen, comparing it to the luxury of Louis'. One thing is for sure – he can never come here. I couldn't bear the shame. The hob is thick with grease, and when the sunlight falls on the shelves and the floor, and even my beloved piano, the dust is thick, a coating of grey over everything.

I take the glass back into the living room and pull the curtains across. I sit down at the piano and rummage in the messy pile of music for my book of Études. Although Louis was impressed with my playing earlier, I was nervous and I made plenty of mistakes. I know I can do better.

I will practise and practise until I'm perfect, and then I will perform them all for him. Despite the rather vulgar design of his piano, the sound was magnificent – as you'd expect for a Steinway. So much power and depth.

When I finally look up from the piano, it is hours later. I glance at my watch. It's nearly 10pm, and I haven't eaten any-thing. But that's not that unusual. I used to skip meals all the time. I've never had a huge appetite. I got used to managing on one meal a day as a child.

I feel exhausted and my hands are aching. I stand up, a little light-headed, and walk to the sofa. The contract is sitting in front of me on the coffee table. I would sign anything Louis asked of me right now, without even reading it. But I pull it onto my lap anyway, feeling slightly like I'm betraying him.

He said he trusted me completely, but Hannah would say I was being stupid and naive not to even look through the contract before I signed it.

Louis was right, there's an awful lot of legalese, but once I get used to the jargon and the writing style, I find myself absorbing exactly what it says. None of it seems particularly remarkable – the same kind of things that the Acorns blog advised us to include – but then there's a section that brings me up short.

179

We have already talked about the future in vague terms. But there's something in this contract that we haven't discussed.

The biological mother agrees that the child's primary residence will be my client's primary residence. The child will reside there permanently. The biological mother will be allowed access to the child at agreed times, but limited to a maximum of two weekends per month, two weeknights per week.

My client will provide a full-time live-in nanny from birth to take care of the child until they reach the age of eleven.

The biological mother agrees that anyone outside of the co-parenting agreement will be told that the biological mother and my client were in a romantic relationship which unfortunately broke down. This is to save the child any future embarrassment . . .

I read on. There's more detail – a whole story, no less – of how Louis and I met, and how our relationship progressed and eventually ended.

I suppose they've had to put this detail in, because they weren't expecting Louis and I to actually feel romantic about one another. We could have saved them the job of inventing the story.

How funny.

There's also a whole section on education, saying I'll agree that my child will attend a primary school I've never heard of, somewhere in West London, and that they will be sent away to boarding school in Scotland when they turn eleven. There are two schools listed, the choice dependent on the sex of the baby.

I have vaguely heard of these schools. They are some of the most expensive and exclusive ones in the country. I once had a pupil and her parents were hoping desperately she would get a music scholarship to the girls' one, and blamed me when she didn't, even though she wasn't actually that good.

There's also a section saying that Louis will not be liable to pay me any child maintenance, above the legal requirement.

I take a big glug of my water, trying to remember the way Louis spoke of this contract when he handed it over. Some of it makes me feel a little bit uncomfortable. It's not quite as 'standard' as he made out.

But then again, I suppose boarding schools *are* standard for people like Louis, and wonderful for children – think of the opportunities. And anyway, Louis was dismissive of the contract. It wasn't his work. It was his lawyers. Everyone knows what lawyers are like. Bloodsuckers. Trying to justify their fees.

It's all fine.

I put the contract back down on the coffee table. It's just paperwork. It's not what's in our hearts. I know Louis feels the same way I do. I saw the way he reacted when I played for him. The way he looked at me.

He even said it: *that's what I love about you.*

I blush, remembering how I felt after I finished playing for him. We were staring at each other, both breathless from the intensity of the music. It was a connection like no other I'd ever felt. I knew in that moment that I had found someone good, and pure, and serious.

I snatch up a pen from the pot I keep by the piano and, without thinking, scrawl my signature on the contract. None of it matters. Not what school the child ends up going to, not where their primary residence is, nor how much money their father is legally obliged to give their mother.

Because their parents are in love, and that's all that any child can wish for.

FAYE

'When are we going to meet him then?' Hannah says, over Sunday lunch. 'This Louis?'

I look down at my plate. Marcus is heaping vegetables onto it, unsolicited. He always gives me far too much food. I know he means well, but it's infuriating being treated like a baby.

'Oh,' I say, 'well, he's very busy with his work but I'm sure . . .'

'Is he in a show?' Marcus asks.

'Oh no, darling,' Hannah says, placing a hand on his arm. 'He's not a musician. That's right, isn't it, Faye?'

I bite my lips, feeling the blood rush to them.

'Yes. He's not a musician. He's a businessman.'

'What sort of businessman?' he says, unfurling his napkin.

'His father owns a chain of gyms.'

I look around at my nephews. Albie has his phone on his lap, completely oblivious to the conversation around the table. Arthur is eating with just his fork, staring up at us all. And Max the baby is . . . being a baby.

'What sort of gyms?' Marcus says. I know what the

expression on his face means. I have seen it so many times before. He's pitying me. He thinks I'm pathetic.

'It's a chain called Fire Leisure,' I say, poking at a roast potato.

I sit back, wait for the penny to drop. Marcus is big in the business world. I don't understand what he does, only that it's something in sales and sounds incredibly dull and means he's always away and Hannah is always stressed.

'Not the . . .' Marcus says, struggling to catch up. 'Not the Horton-Jones boy . . . What's his name . . .'

'He's not a boy,' I say. 'His name is Louis.'

'Do you know them?' Hannah asks Marcus.

'Not exactly. Just by reputation.'

He puts down his fork, stares at me.

'Well, Faye,' he says. 'I'm impressed. They're one of the wealthiest families in the country.'

'That's got nothing to do with it,' I say.

'Oh, I know,' he says. 'That's the funny thing about you two sisters, your complete lack of interest in money. But even so. You should be proud of yourself. Life will be a lot easier with his deep pockets.'

I think of the contract, the way it specifically stated that I didn't have the right to any financial support. But it's gone beyond the contract now.

'We're in love,' I say, although technically he's yet to say it to me.

Arthur giggles. Hannah and Marcus exchange a look. Underneath the table, my fingernails dig into my own palm.

184

'Forget it,' I say. 'I should have known you wouldn't be happy for me.'

'Faye,' Hannah says, frowning. 'Don't say that. Of course we're happy for you, honestly. He sounds great. It's just . . . do you, you know, have anything in common? What do you talk about? I can't imagine he's interested in discussing the best fingering for the Czerny exercises.'

'He's a great fan of classical music, actually,' I say, rising to the bait. 'His mother played the piano. And he has a Steinway.'

'Oh,' says Hannah, her eyes widening. 'Wow. And have you met his mother yet?'

I shake my head.

'No, she's dead.'

It comes out blunter than intended.

'Didn't she take her own life?' Marcus says. 'I'm sure it was in the papers. Some massive scandal. His dad left her for another woman, and she killed herself.'

'I haven't asked him about it,' I say stubbornly. Poor Louis. If that's true, it's awful. 'I didn't want to pry.'

'Fair enough,' Hannah says. 'And how old is he?'

'He's forty-three. It's his birthday next week, actually.'

She nods. I notice the way she glances over at Marcus, her eyes widening. She can't believe someone like Louis would be interested in me, and it hurts that my own sister would think I was so worthless.

'What does he do at his father's firm again?' Marcus says eventually, pouring himself some more red wine.

'He's the MD,' I say. 'It's very hectic. Full-on. You know. It's

185

the curse though, of being born into an institution like that. Having to live up to family expectations.'

'Well, I'd like to meet him,' Hannah says. 'See if he's good enough for you.'

She thinks she's being nice, but in reality it's just because she doesn't trust me to make good decisions.

'He's lovely,' I say. 'And of course you can meet him. Eventually. It's just he's a busy man.'

'Let's change the subject, shall we? I think we've cross-examined you enough for one day, Faye,' Marcus says, spearing some cabbage. 'It's great that you've found someone who makes you happy. Did Hannah tell you that I'm training for the marathon next year?'

I try not to roll my eyes. I think what Hannah actually told me: *for fuck's sake, Faye, how clichéd can he get? The marathon. I ask you!*

'She did mention something,' I say, and I look over at Hannah. She grins, and for a second we are united again. Sisters.

'It's quite involved,' he says. 'You wouldn't believe the training plan my marathon coach has got me on.'

'Is red wine a core component?' I say, and Hannah snorts. I have got better at jokes over the years. It's taken me a long time to catch up with everyone else, but now, sometimes, I pull them off quite well.

Marcus frowns at me, missing the joke when it's directed at him.

'Well, it's not banned. No, it's quite interesting. I was very good at cross-country at school, of course, but . . .'

He drones on about practice runs and carb loading and I wish that everyone would hurry up eating so that I can say my niceties about what a delicious lunch it was and maybe spend half an hour building something out of Lego with Arthur and then leave.

Tonight I'm having drinks with Jonas, but I feel really tired and drained.

It's been difficult, juggling my lessons with seeing Louis. He's not particularly flexible – understandably with his high-powered job – and always texts me at short notice: *are you free this afternoon at 6? How is the Ravel piece coming along? I hope it will be ready for me to hear soon.*

We've met up six times in total so far. He said he had to be really sure that I was the right person before we went any further.

It feels like I'm being auditioned for a job, and it's a job I want more than anything in the world.

He hasn't spelt it out, but I get the impression he's tried this before and things haven't worked out.

'As I said,' he told me, 'with my financial status, it's hard to know who you can trust.'

I hope I've shown he can trust me.

I've been practising his favourite pieces for hours every day. They were all ones his mother loved, apparently, and most of them are difficult.

I'm not used to being out and about this much. I'm like a hermit that's finally come out of its shell. And it's all thanks to Jonas. If he hadn't given me that push I needed, the push to finally try to make my life what I wanted it to be, rather than accepting what it had become, then I wouldn't be in this situation today.

So I can't cancel on him. Even though all I want to do when I get back later is crawl into bed and pull the duvet over my head.

FAYE

Jonas is sitting outside the pub, smoking, as I approach.

'Long time no see, you absolute dirtbag,' he says, standing up and drawing me towards him. He smells unpleasant, a mix of fags and beer – but there's something comforting about it, and I find myself leaning on his shoulder, breathing him in.

'Hi Jonas,' I say. 'I'm sorry, I've been . . .'

'Yeah, yeah, I know. With your new man.'

I smile.

'Drink?' I say, even though he's got nearly half a pint left.

'What do I always tell you, Faye? You're an angel sent from heaven,' he says, grinning at me.

I am, I think, as I queue inside the pub. Because Jonas always gets me to buy him a drink, even though he has pints and I only ever have bottles. If I added up the difference over the years . . . But then he's even more chaotic with money than me, so I know it's not deliberate.

I bring our drinks outside and set his down in front of him.

'Cheers,' I say, and we clink glasses. 'It's absolutely freezing out here!'

'Sorry,' he says, waving his roll-up in my face. 'I'm nearly done and we can go back in. So, how are you doing? Not drinking?'

He gestures towards my lime soda.

'Oh, er, no. Just having a little break from it.'

'All well with love's young dream? What's the guy's name again?'

He blows me a perfect smoke ring.

'Louis. And yes, thanks.'

He nods, sipping his pint.

'And have you discussed the baby thing yet? Is he the sort you think might be keen?'

I swallow, staring straight at him. My oldest, dearest friend. He won't judge me. He knows everything – nearly everything – about me, and he has never judged me.

'Well, the thing is, we sort of met through this app . . .'

'I knew it!' he says, slapping his thigh. 'Told you that you needed to get online. Didn't I? Didn't I tell you?'

'Yes, but . . . well, the app I found, it wasn't just for dating. It was actually for . . . well, for exactly this. For people who want to have children, but haven't met the right person yet.'

He frowns at me.

'I've lost you. Sounds like a dating app to me.'

'Well, yes, sort of, but the point is that everyone on there . . . everyone wants to have a baby. So you sort of skip that stuff. You don't have to have those awkward conversations. Because everyone's on the same page. We all know we're there because we want to have kids.'

He wrinkles his nose, but doesn't say anything. It's not like Jonas to be quiet.

'But you're dating first?' he says. 'You're not just . . . meeting up and having a baby together?'

I hesitate, looking over at him.

'Well . . . it depends.'

He pulls another face. I think of all the research I've done.

'Some people choose to literally just have a baby together. Others . . . well, they do end up romantically involved, yes.'

Jonas is silent for longer than I ever remember him being silent for.

'What is it?' I say, suddenly worried.

'Nothing,' he says, draining his pint. 'Shall we go in?'

'No, it's not nothing,' I say, tugging at his sleeve. 'Tell me.'

'It doesn't matter,' he says, and he crushes the rest of his roll-up under his toe. 'Let's go inside.'

I follow him into the pub and we take our usual seat in the window.

'You're judging me,' I say eventually, when the silence has become unbearable. Jonas has never judged me. That's not how our relationship works.

'No,' he says, gazing past me and off into the middle distance. 'Believe it or not, Faye, I want you to be happy.'

'Well, what then?' I say, frustrated. 'It was your idea for me to try using the internet!'

'I know,' he says. 'It's just . . . this app. I don't know. I'm wondering . . . well, who's thinking about the children in this scenario?'

I'm so stunned by Jonas' reaction that my mouth falls open.

'What?'

He shrugs.

191

'Just seems a bit . . . well, like they're treating children like a commodity or something. An accessory. I dunno. Never wanted them myself, so I guess I just don't get it.'

I would never have expected Jonas to be so . . . old-fashioned.

'What are you saying, that all children need to be raised in a nuclear family? Mum, Dad, 2.4 kids, is that it? Do you think the mum should stay at home and bake cakes too?'

'Fuck no,' he says, and I can tell he's genuinely pissed off with me. 'For God's sake, my dad left my mum when I was seven. I hardly saw him when I was growing up, but my mum did her best. That's not what I think at all. I just think . . . this is different. Two strangers, just choosing to have a baby, and then share it? Like . . . I dunno, a carpool or something. It just feels a bit off.'

'That's not how it is at all,' I say, but I start to panic. Is this what other people really think? Have I been naive?

That word again, haunting me my whole life.

Faye's incredibly talented, but she's very trusting. Faye could go far, but her naivety means she's at risk of being taken advantage of . . .

'Just think how wanted the child will be,' I splutter, floundering a little. 'Unlike the teenagers who get pregnant by mistake and spend the rest of their lives regretting it . . . These children will be some of the most loved children on the planet! Their parents literally went the extra mile to get them. Don't you think that counts for something?'

He shrugs again.

'Yes, I guess,' he says. 'Sorry. I know how much you want a baby. I just . . . I wonder what kind of men feel the same way.'

'Plenty of men!' I say, my temper rising. 'Just because you're

192

too selfish to have your own kids, that doesn't mean there aren't men out there, all over the world, wishing that they could become dads!'

He holds my fierce stare.

'I think the reason I don't want kids is actually because I'm not selfish,' he says. 'Because I can't think of anything worse than putting a kid through the kind of childhood I had, and that's my blueprint, so how would I know how to do better?'

'That's an excuse. You just would. If you really wanted it. You'd do better.'

He sighs.

'Listen,' he says eventually. 'I'm way out of my depth here. I just want you to be happy. You know that. I hope the guy you've met on there is a decent one, but you're . . .'

'Don't you dare. Don't you dare call me naive or trusting or sweet! Don't you dare tell me you're worried about me.'

He smiles.

'I wouldn't. You're soft on the outside but you've got a core of steel, Faye. I know it. You're tougher than you look. I'm sure you've picked a good one.'

I smile at him.

'Well, if you had given me a chance . . .' I say. 'I was about to tell you about him. And the fact that we . . . it looks as though we might be one of the couples that actually work as a couple, and not just co-parents.'

'Now I'm really confused,' he says. 'I thought the point was that you aren't together? Christ, how on earth do the babies get conceived? Wait, don't answer that. I'm not sure I want to know.'

193

I shake my head at him.

'That's what I'm trying to tell you. I've been reading some of the case stories on the app's blog. Lots of the couples find that actually they end up in relationships. After all, most of them have similar ideas about things – similar priorities – and most people would prefer to be in a relationship with the other parent of their child. So really the app just filters out a certain type of person that might get drowned out in a normal dating app.'

'And so, the man you've met . . .'

'Louis. Yes. He's honestly so wonderful, Jonas. He's clever and cultured and confident and funny and he loves classical music . . . I really think . . .'

It feels as though my heart is about to explode.

'I think he's the one.'

FAYE

The evening isn't the same afterwards, even though Jonas tells me he's happy for me, and asks a few more perfunctory questions about Louis.

He thinks I've just said that we're in love as a way of trying to convince him that what we are doing is OK. But even if we weren't, I don't understand why he thinks there might be a problem.

How is it any different from single women using a sperm donor? Or choosing to adopt? There were so many things I should have said in defence, but I didn't think of them quickly enough.

But something niggles at me. Why *is* Louis choosing to do it this way? Surely he's had no problems meeting eligible, fertile women in the past?

I check my phone as I walk back to my flat, but I haven't heard from him. Panic starts to set in. He doesn't text me that often. I suppose he doesn't have time for great long text message conversations.

I'm being stupid. Anyway, our next date is already arranged. He's taking me to the opera on Saturday, to meet his father and stepmother.

Of course, I've been a fair few times before, but only on comp tickets from friends performing in the orchestra. But Louis has got us a box, and we're going to see *Rigoletto*, Verdi's masterpiece. And even though I've heard 'La donna è mobile' performed more times than I care to remember, this production has a new director who's supposed to be, well, experimental in his approach.

I'm excited. It feels like the start of a new life, one where I won't have to teach the spoilt children of south-west London how to play piano, but one where I can teach my own child, and play for Louis, and maybe even start to perform professionally again. Who knows? If I have the time to practise, without the constant worry of my pupils on my mind, perhaps I'll get back to the standard I was at when I was twenty-one.

I could even put on a series of concerts – a celebration of Chopin's Études, seeing as those seem to be Louis' favourites.

He has booked a room in a hotel in Covent Garden for after the opera. The kind of five-star place that fancy celebrities go to. Surely that's a sign he's ready to take the next step?

'I don't want you to feel you have to schlep all the way across London so late at night,' he said, when he told me about it. 'I think a night at the opera deserves to end the way it began, with champagne and opulence, don't you? Although, just the one glass for you. A special treat.'

I was speechless. I thought of how all my other nights at the opera had ended: with a McDonald's on the night bus home.

'Well, that's really very kind of you,' I said. 'But honestly, there's no need . . .'

'Shush,' Louis replied. 'There's every need! It's a treat. And I'll arrange for a cab to pick you up from outside your flat, if you'll just give me your address . . .'

'Oh!' I replied, thinking I couldn't take the risk of him ever turning up unannounced and seeing the squalor I live in. 'Thank you, but I have a lesson in West London that afternoon anyway; it'll be easy for me to make my way straight from there. They won't mind me getting changed in the house.'

'Well, if you're sure,' he said, and it was all arranged.

Saturday arrives and I'm so nervous that when I wake up in the morning I'm actually physically sick. Afterwards, I wash my hair, before marching down the road to the dry cleaner's to collect my blue velvet dress.

I haven't worn it since I last performed, but it still fits. If anything, I've lost weight over the past few weeks. I've had to buy a whole new wardrobe since Louis and I started seeing each other, and I'm spending money like I never have before.

I walk home, the sun on my face, my dress draped over my arm. I can't remember a time I felt this happy, or hopeful.

Dreams can come true.

It's difficult to get through my lessons that day but I manage it, praising every pupil overenthusiastically when they get even the most minor of details right.

'You're in a good mood today, Miss Miller,' Henry, one of my favourite boys, says. He's thirteen, knee-deep in learning the *Pathétique*, and is probably one of the most naturally gifted of all the children I teach. He's from a working-class family, and his mum works an extra job to pay for all his music lessons.

'I'm always in a good mood when I see you,' I say, grinning at him.

'And you've done something different with your hair,' he says. 'It suits you.'

It took me hours to pin it up this morning – a practice run for this evening – and I almost want to reach over and hug him, but I manage to contain myself.

'Well, that's very kind of you to say, Henry, but let's get back to Beethoven, shall we . . .'

Before too long, it's 5pm and my last pupil has gone. I haven't managed to eat all day. My lack of appetite is even more pronounced when I'm nervous.

But it'll be fine. Once I get there . . . once I'm immersed in the music, I'll relax a little. I'm sure of it. And the champagne Louis promised will help. Just one glass though, he was very opinionated about that.

'Not a good idea for you to be drinking. We want you in tip-top shape,' he said a few weeks ago, when I asked for a gin and tonic.

I wish I could have a drink now, before I leave. Just to take the edge off.

But no. I only have some ancient vodka in the house anyway, that Jonas brought round on New Year's Eve, and that's disgusting.

My blue dress is still in its plastic bag, hanging up on the outside of my wardrobe. I reach up and take it down, pulling the cover over the top of the wire hanger.

There it is, my most expensive clothing purchase. I

remember how I felt when I wore it. Like a Disney princess. It was even more beautiful than my wedding dress.

My eyes land on our wedding photo, on the side table by my bed. It's only guilt that makes me keep it there. But it's time to move on.

I march over and lay it flat on its face, so that only the back of the frame is visible.

I won't let my past ruin this day. This is the beginning of my new life. A new life with Louis.

I change into the dress, struggling a little to zip it up at the back by myself. Then I redo my hair, spraying a ton of hairspray into it, hoping it will hold. Natalie used to do my hair for me before concerts. I wonder where she is now. The last I heard she got a job with a touring philharmonic orchestra, and was in deepest, darkest Russia.

I miss her. She was a friend, of sorts. I don't really know why we lost touch. I've just never been very good at maintaining friendships.

Never mind. She wouldn't believe it if she could see me now.

I take great care with my make-up. I'm still not a natural, but I'm getting better at it. I trace my lips with red lipstick, and then I stand back and admire my reflection.

I've never cared much for my appearance before, but now I'm meeting Louis' family, I need to look the part. And in this dress I look like someone who belongs at the opera.

I take a deep breath, pick up my small overnight bag and then leave my flat to catch a cab.

FAYE

Louis smiles as he sees me approach.

He's wearing a black tuxedo, a starched white shirt peeping out from under his waistcoat. His bright blond hair is brushed neatly to the side, a little wax applied to keep it in place.

'My goodness,' he says, taking me in his arms and kissing me on both cheeks. 'Don't you look wonderful.'

I'm embarrassed.

'You look lovely too.'

'Oh God,' he says, looking down at his trousers. 'I hate being all trussed-up like this, but one must make the effort, I suppose.'

'Where are your parents?' I ask, looking around nervously. I hope they haven't cancelled.

'Inside,' he says, taking my arm. 'I didn't want to hit you with them straight away. They're looking forward to meeting you though. Don't mind my father. He's a little old-fashioned. And deaf.'

I swallow and nod, offering him a nervous smile.

Inside, he steers me towards the bar, where a smartly dressed couple are waiting. They are much older than I expected.

'Father, Tamara, this is Faye,' he says. 'Faye, this is my father, Hugo, and his wife, Tamara.'

My heart is hammering. Tamara pulls her lips in as she stares at me. Maybe she didn't like being introduced as Hugo's wife, rather than as Louis' stepmother.

I remember what Marcus said about them at lunch – something about Louis' father leaving his mother for Tamara, and breaking her heart. I suspect there's no love lost between her and Louis.

'Pleased to meet you,' I say, shaking their hands in turn.

'And you,' his father says, narrowing his eyes. 'Are you a fan of the opera, Faye?'

I pause, not sure how to reply to this. Louis hands me a glass of champagne. I glance at him. He gives me an encouraging smile and squeezes my other hand with his.

'I am,' I say, grateful not to be out of my depth for once. 'I've heard this interpretation is quite radical.'

'Radical indeed,' Tamara says, raising an eyebrow. 'I read the review in the papers at the weekend. Sounds simply dreadful, but Louis insisted we should give it a chance. He's quite obsessed with classical music, you know.'

'I think it's good not to prejudge things,' Louis says tightly, 'before you've had a chance to experience them for yourself. Don't you agree, Father?'

'What?' Hugo replies. 'Yes, I suppose so. I've never much cared for opera, truth be told.'

'Well,' I say, smiling at them both, 'let's hope we're all pleasantly surprised.'

'Hmm,' his father replies. He's not interested in me at all.

His eyes are scanning the room behind me, as though looking for anyone else he might know. I take a gulp of my champagne. Louis is still holding my hand.

'That's a bold fabric,' Tamara says, looking down at my dress.

'Oh,' I say, and I feel my cheeks turn red. 'Yes, I suppose it is.'

'Suits you,' she says shortly, as though she's thinking out loud. 'You're slim enough to pull it off. It would look like curtains on the wrong figure. And how long have you and Louis been seeing one another? He's very cagey, you know. Doesn't tell us much about girlfriends. This is the first time he's brought one to meet us. So you must be special.'

My eyes widen. I look at Louis. He leans down and kisses me on the mouth. He puts his arm around me and jerks me close towards him, and I almost topple over.

'She is,' he says, giving me a full smile. 'She's the most special woman I have ever met.'

I'm so taken aback by the kiss that all I can do is stare at him. It only lasted a second, and now I want more.

'And as for how long we've been seeing each other . . . it's been, oh, I don't know, what would you say, darling? A couple of months now?' Louis continues. 'Time flies when you've found the one.'

The one!

Darling!

He's never spoken to me like this before.

'Christ,' Hugo says. 'There's the Burton-Wells lot. Ugh. Now I'm reminded why we don't come to the opera.'

'Hugo, don't be such a grump,' Tamara says, prodding him.

'And don't make a fuss. We'll be taking our seats in a minute anyway.'

'How's Simon getting on?' Louis says, momentarily dropping my hand.

Tamara smiles. A full smile, for the first time.

'Oh, he's wonderful,' she says. 'He's coming up for eight months now. Sitting up and clapping his hands already. He's an absolute delight, isn't he, Hugo?'

She prods her husband. His eyes are still roving the bar.

'What?' he says.

'Simon! Your grandson!'

'Oh, yes, charming child.'

Louis' neck is flushed red. Poor Louis. I take his hand in mine and squeeze it. No wonder he doesn't introduce people to his family very often. They're awful.

The bell rings. As we make our way towards our seats, Louis pulls me ahead slightly.

'Listen, Faye. As I told you, they're old-fashioned about things like . . . well, what we're planning to do. It's important that they believe just how special we are to one another. Don't let me down now, will you?'

I'm not sure what he's talking about.

'Who's Simon?'

'My stepbrother Sebastian's son,' he says shortly. 'Waiting in the wings to step neatly into my shoes if I fuck up in any way.'

'Oh,' I say, understanding even less. Is he talking about a baby?

'Don't worry,' he says, and for the first time I see a flash of something in his eyes that frightens me. It reminds me of my father. 'We won't let that happen. Our child is going to inherit what's rightfully theirs. No cuckoo is going to push me out of my own family.'

He kisses me again, but on the cheek this time. The champagne has gone straight to my head, and so I reach up and pull him towards me for a proper kiss. My entire body feels like it's on fire when he pulls away.

'Sorry,' I say, giggling. My hand flies to my forehead. 'I'm a little tipsy.'

I hear a laugh behind us.

'Oh, to be young and in love,' Tamara says, and I bite my lip and squeeze Louis' hand.

'It's like you've done this before,' Louis says, a puzzled look on his face. But he's not cross.

I have no idea what he means, but I don't care. I've never felt so happy.

Halfway through the first half, Hugo falls asleep, his head lolling back against his seat, his mouth hanging open. I glance at Louis, who rolls his eyes, and we share a smile. From my seat I have the most amazing view directly into the pit.

I spend most of my time looking at the musicians, remembering only occasionally that I'm supposed to be watching the performers onstage. But I can't help but feel wistful, looking down at them all, remembering my childhood dream to one day learn the harp.

Perhaps I can. Perhaps it's not too late. With Louis by my side, it feels as though anything is possible.

FAYE

It's late by the time we leave and I'm tired, feeling almost as drained as the people onstage. I forget sometimes that music takes it out of me. How my shoulders tense and rise as I strain to listen, to hear every individual note, judging its accuracy and beauty, while also taking in the overall blend, the way the music comes together to become more than the sum of its parts.

It possesses me, as it always has done. Feels like electricity flowing through my veins: a sensory overload that leaves me weak and spent once it dissipates.

'I can't believe you slept the whole way through it, Hugo,' Tamara pouts, as we leave the opera house. Louis is holding my hand again. 'It's embarrassing.'

Hugo doesn't respond. He's clearly used to being chastised by his wife.

'What did you think of it, Faye?' she asks.

'It was . . . different,' I say, finding it impossible to lie. Not about this, the only thing I really know anything about. 'It's still early days on the production, and clearly there are some teething issues that need to be sorted. But that's normal. They will get into the swing of it before too long. It was certainly memorable.'

'I quite agree,' Tamara says. 'Right, well . . . we've arranged to meet our driver on Floral Street. Where are you two off to now?'

'The Savoy,' Louis says. 'I've booked a suite.'

'Oh, lovely,' Tamara says, kissing him on both cheeks, and then me. 'Well, enjoy.'

'Thank you,' I say. 'I'm sure we will. It was wonderful to meet you both.'

Hugo, who appears to be a man of few words, gives me a nod and slaps Louis on the back.

'I'll call you next week about the Manchester situation,' he says, and Louis nods, his top lip twitching ever so slightly. 'I'm not having them make fools out of us.'

We stand outside the opera house. It's cold but I don't care. I think this might just be the best evening of my life.

'We did it!' Louis says, clapping his hands together as soon as his parents are out of earshot. 'You were magnificent.'

'Was I?' I say. 'Thank you.'

'I can't tell you what a weight off my mind it is to have them on board with it all. The second kiss was a stroke of genius, by the way. Well done.'

He is beaming at me, and I know I've done well. I've passed whatever test I was meant to pass.

'They were fine,' I say. 'Just a little stuck in their ways.'

'Hmm,' he says. 'Well, like I said, *you* were magnificent. It was important to me, you know. That they were convinced by us. They would never have approved of our baby otherwise.'

'Oh,' I say. 'Well, it wasn't difficult to convince them, was it?'

'No. My goodness, how lucky I was to find you,' he says, and my heart flutters. 'I didn't tell you this, but there was another woman, before you . . . a friend. We discussed doing the same thing together. But then it all . . . got complicated. It was such a shame. That's why I'm so grateful to have found you, Faye. Someone I can really trust.'

He hails a cab and we sit together as it drives no more than four streets away, pulling up outside the Savoy. Louis pays the driver and we climb out.

'So,' he says, handing me a keycard after checking in at reception. 'I hope you had a good evening and that you have a good night's rest. It's a wonderful room. One of my favourites.'

'Oh,' I say, confused, 'but aren't you . . . aren't you coming up?'

He frowns at me.

'Well, I suppose I could come up for a drink,' he says, checking his watch. 'For a quick one. Let's toast our success, shall we? Sebastian can well and truly forget about Simon getting his hands on my father's empire now!'

I'm still confused about the Sebastian and Simon thing, but I don't say anything.

The hotel room is much smaller than I had imagined – not a suite after all – but stunning all the same, all swag curtains and chandeliers. It looks like something out of a Disney film.

Louis busies himself drawing the curtains.

'Shall I order us some drinks?' I say, looking down at the telephone by the bed. That's what people do, isn't it, in hotel rooms? In truth I have no idea.

'Have you eaten much today?' Louis says, turning to me.

'Oh, I . . .'

He's frowning at me.

'You should eat something. You're skin and bones in that dress. It's not flattering from the back, you know? You're all shoulder blades. I'll order you up a club sandwich.'

I'm too sick with excitement to even think about eating, but I don't want to disappoint him, so I nod.

Skin and bones. I hate that he's noticed.

He opens the door of the wardrobe. Inside is a small black fridge.

'Is that a minibar? I thought they were extortionately expensive.'

'Christ, Faye, must you always be so green? It's the Savoy. Everything is extortionately expensive.'

I'm chastised, feeling stupid.

I wonder if I could ever get used to this life, I think, as he unscrews a ginger ale and hands it to me in a crystal-cut glass.

After all, I'm getting used to ginger ale. It's not so bad if I swallow it quickly, without breathing in at the same time so I don't inhale the horrible smell.

I sit on the bed and wait as he selects a whisky, pouring it into the other glass, then he uses the phone by the bed to order me a club sandwich and a side of fries.

'I should have ordered some ice,' he murmurs after he hangs up. 'Never mind.'

I gulp down my ginger ale, pretending it's alcohol, and wait for him to join me on the bed.

'Cheers,' I say, trying to act more confident than I feel.

He clinks glasses with me, frowning, then immediately

picks up another miniature whisky and refills his glass, swallowing it quickly.

'Are you all right?' I ask, surprised.

The good mood he was in earlier seems to have vanished, and I don't know why, or what I've done wrong. I fiddle with the skirt of my dress. I wish I had a shawl or something to cover up my bony shoulders.

He waves a hand and stands up, turning away from me. I watch as he picks up the whisky glass again and refills it, drinking it down in one swift motion.

Is he nervous?

My heart swells with affection for him. For all his confidence, when it comes to romance he's the same as me.

I stand beside him and reach out, taking his hand and turning him to face me. He looks at me as I lean forward and kiss him again. He tastes sharp, of whisky, and it reminds me of the way Marshall would kiss me when he was drunk: aggressive and domineering, making me feel like a piece of meat.

I squeeze my eyes closed. This isn't Marshall. This is Louis. Lovely, gentle Louis.

I begin to relax, to kiss him more hungrily, and soon I'm tugging at his clothes, my hands anywhere and everywhere. This is it, I can feel it. The moment we've been waiting for. The moment when the plan comes together.

But then, within seconds, he pulls back, turning away from me.

'What's the matter?' I say to his back. His head is bent low, and he picks up his whisky glass again, pouring another measure from the final miniature whisky bottle in the fridge.

209

'Did you read the contract?' he says, turning back to look at me. His eyes are cold.

It feels like a test, and I don't know what to say to pass. He told me not to read it, he told me I should trust him.

'I, well, yes . . . some of it,' I mumble, ashamed. I hope he won't be hurt.

'The bit about the conception itself,' he says, swallowing. 'Did you read that?'

'I . . .'

His mouth is set in a line.

'The conception must take place using artificial insemination,' he says. Then he stiffens, standing up straighter, looking at me directly. 'That's what it says in the contract. I will provide you with a . . . sample, and the things you need to inseminate yourself. It's a very straightforward procedure, I've been told. Not painful.'

'I know how it works,' I say, confused. 'I looked into it when I signed up to the app. But . . . surely if we don't have to use that . . . er, method, then it's better not to? We can try to do it . . .' My cheeks burn. 'Naturally, instead? I don't know about you, but I . . .'

I feel humiliated. Underneath my desperation and misery, fury bubbles. How can he make me feel like this? I thought men *always* wanted it. That's what Jonas always tells me.

Am I really so hideously unattractive?

'I don't understand,' I say, starting to cry. I feel like such a fool.

He shakes his head.

'It's unfortunate,' he says, looking straight at me, 'if

tonight has confused things, Faye. I thought I'd been clear. We must stick to the agreed arrangement. I don't want any . . . complications.'

I stare at him.

'But why?'

His eyes flash and he slams the whisky glass down on the bedside table.

'Oh, for God's sake!' he says. 'I'm tired. It's been a long day. I thought we were on the same page. Surely you understand the situation? Don't make me spell it out.'

I shrink back, speechless.

Because I'm too scared to admit that I don't understand, and I wish he would.

NOW

RACHEL

They've started early this year. The kids from the village. Just a note this time, though. Not like last year.

I shudder, remembering the dog poo smeared all over my front door. The spray paint I couldn't remove, not even with the strongest detergent I had. In the end, I had to pay some spotty teenager £150 to repaint the wall.

In comparison with that, this is nothing.

I pick up the note, stare at it, shaking my head at the spelling.

Watch out for Bonfire Night – it's time for the which to burn!

For goodness' sake. They can't even spell.

'What's that?'

Fiona is standing behind me, holding Jake. He's awake, gazing up at her. And mercifully, he's not screaming for once, just whimpering with dissatisfaction.

'A love letter,' I say, screwing it up in my fist.

She frowns at me. Too tired for sarcasm.

'Just a stupid practical joke. Some of the kids in the village don't have enough to do.'

'Oh, that's horrible,' Fiona says. 'What did it say?'

'Nothing,' I reply. 'I worked at their secondary school, and a few of them have never forgiven me.'

'Forgiven you for what?'

'Disciplining them.'

Her eyebrows rise.

'How's Jake?' I say, changing the subject. 'Do you have plans today?'

I look at her. She's wearing the same grey jogging bottoms she wears every day and a long-sleeved white T-shirt with a hole in the arm.

I've never been known for my sartorial sharpness but even I make more effort than this.

'No,' she says, in a faraway voice. 'Just the usual.'

'You haven't left the house for three days,' I say. 'Perhaps . . .' I pause. I don't often like to invite my lodgers on my constitutionals, but I want to get to know her a bit better. Especially after all that business with the fake black eye.

Besides, it would do her good to get some fresh air. And Jake.

'Perhaps you'd like to join me on my 11am walk today? It's three miles. Round the village, across the fields towards Maltlick, and then back. Do you have suitable footwear? I suppose your boots would do.'

She looks at me, as though she's not really heard me.

'Oh, I . . .'

'Afterwards I'll be collecting branches for the bonfire,' I say. 'Nigel from down the road came round last night when you were upstairs with Jake. Apparently this year people have been

216

lazy about leaving theirs out. It's the bad weather, I suppose. No one wants to collect sticks in the rain.'

She looks past my head and out through the bay window. Colin and the rest of the team were working hard on the bonfire yesterday and it's grown several feet overnight.

'It must be absolutely huge when it's finished,' she says.

'Oh yes, the biggest for miles. People come from all over the county to watch the celebrations. It's very traditional. Of course, I've always been very involved with it all, having grown up here, but over the past few years it's become a magnet for antisocial behaviour. Teenagers drinking too much, that kind of thing. And then, of course, a few years ago, there was that terrible incident . . .'

'What?'

I shake my head. I can hardly bear to think about it now.

'A toddler wandered off, got lost in the crowd.'

She stares at me. I expect more of a reaction, but her face remains still.

'Anyway, he was found eventually, but he'd fallen over, hit his head on some rocks, and by the time they'd found him, it was too late. He was gone.'

'How awful,' she says, but she doesn't sound like she means it. She's definitely not herself. It's as though she's been drained of all her energy. She's just a shell.

I'm quite concerned she might actually drop Jake if she doesn't wake up a bit.

Brian's words ring in my ear: *you get too involved with these people. They're just your tenants, remember, not your friends!*

217

'Let me take Jake,' I say, stepping forward and scooping him up. 'Oh!'

She blinks at me.

'What?' she says.

He's wet through again.

'Nothing,' I say. 'He needs a change. Why don't you leave that to me, and you go and have a nap? I think you . . . could do with one.'

She blinks again, nodding and turning away. She doesn't even acknowledge her son.

I follow her up to her room. The curtains are still drawn, but even so I can tell it's a disgrace in here. I take a deep breath, remind myself that she's paying for the room and that if it's messy, then that's her prerogative.

But honestly, in all these years, only Elizabeth ever kept the place respectable. Darling Elizabeth. How I miss her. My first lodger. I suppose I've been trying to find someone to live up to her ever since.

'Try and sleep for an hour or so,' I say, picking up a fresh nappy, a change of clothes and the baby wipes. 'Jake will be fine with me.'

She climbs into the bed without replying, rolling onto her side, and I close the door behind me. I have to get that nappy off the poor mite before his skin starts to chafe.

I lay him down in the living room, and peel off his babygrow. It's absolutely sodden, and then I realise with shock that he's not even wearing a nappy.

Worse still, his skin is red and angry.

He starts to cry as I wipe it, but it's hopeless. He needs a proper bath.

'I'm so sorry, little one,' I say to him, standing up and leaning over him. 'But it's time you had a wash. A real wash.'

I carry him carefully up to the bathroom, trying to ignore the churning in my stomach at the fact that his urine must have soaked through to my sleeves too. I'll change later. I have to take care of Jake first.

I run a tepid bath – anything too hot will be painful for his rash. I add a little of my own bath foam – I have eczema myself and can only use the mildest of products, so I'm sure it won't do him any harm. Then I lay him down, keeping my hand behind his head, and watch as he wriggles in the water in delight, his face splitting into something like a smile.

I can't be sure though. I can't remember at what age babies start smiling.

I trickle water through my fingertips and onto his tummy. He gurgles. I think he likes it, so I do it again.

We play like that for several minutes before I worry that I'll dry his skin out even more. I pick him up and wrap him in one of my towels, arranging it so that his face just peeks out from the top.

He yawns, giving a slow blink.

'Are you sleepy again?' I say. 'Did that bath wear you out?'

I lay him on the bathmat and dress him quickly. Obviously I don't have any cream for his nappy rash, but I'll stop off at the chemist on the way back from my walk and get some. Poor mite. The skin is starting to blister now.

He falls asleep on the bathmat, and I pick him up carefully

and take him downstairs to the living room and lay him in his pram, tucking him in with one of my kitchen towels.

Once I'm sure he's fast asleep, I disappear upstairs and change clothes. The door to Fiona's room is pulled to, but not completely closed. I try to peer through the gap but I can't see anything.

I can hear something though.

Kylie was right about me: I am a nosey old busybody.

I strain to make out the sounds coming from Fiona's room, closing my eyes to help my concentration.

Is she crying?

I can't quite tell. But she's making a sound not too dissimilar. A muffled whimpering. And then, I hear her speak.

At first I think she's talking to someone on the phone, but as I look through the crack, I realise she's still lying down on the bed, now staring up at the ceiling, her arms outstretched as though in surrender.

Tears are rolling down the sides of her face.

'Hannah was right. Hannah is always right. Why am I such a fool?'

The poor thing. She's not coping. I'm angry with her for leaving Jake without a nappy, but clearly she's in no fit state to be looking after a young baby.

I can scarcely believe it. Another Kylie. But this one is worse. This one has a child.

I shake my head from side to side, slowly, thinking of Brian and what he would say.

Oh Rachel, what have you got yourself into this time?

FAYE

I can hardly bear to look at Jake any more. When I stare down at him, I don't see the baby I once dreamed of. Instead I see Louis. His face.

The way he looked at me that last time we saw each other. The disgust in his eyes. The way his lip curled as though I was something dirty, unclean. Shit on his perfectly polished shoe.

I had wasted his time – the one thing he couldn't get more of. Everything else in his life was easily replaced.

I'd hoped I could love Jake as though he were my own. As though everything had worked out as I'd dreamed it would that night at the opera. As though I had created this perfect child.

But that's not why I took him. I know that now. I took him because I wanted to hurt Louis the way he hurt me. To show him that he couldn't make a fool of me after all. But all I've done is hurt myself.

Every day, Jake develops a little more, shifting away from the anonymous baby I thought I was taking and into something else.

Every day, he looks a little bit more like his father.

And a little bit more like his mother.

I can't stop dreaming about Louis. And her too.

Fiona.

How must she feel, knowing that Jake is missing? And why haven't they reported it in the news?

I know why. Louis wouldn't want the attention. He's a public figure, and the way he went about procuring his heir – someone to make sure his stepbrother's family didn't inherit his father's business – was hardly ethical.

But even so, surely he can't be happy to just let Jake go? Surely, he must be beside himself with worry? What kind of father would he be if not?

I thought Louis deserved to feel the same loss I have felt. I thought I would love Jake, but the truth is I don't.

And the feeling is mutual. He hates me. He cries all the time; he kicks me and squirms if I try to comfort him. And I'm so tired.

I can't take it any more. It's the same way I felt after Marshall died, but worse, because I can't see a way forward.

I just want to turn back the clock.

But I can't. I'm stuck in this situation. And it's all my own fault.

I try to sleep as Rachel suggested. Perhaps that will help. But by half ten I give up and clamber out of bed. The sheets are wet with my sweat. It's not a great surprise. I haven't taken my medication for days now. I'm not even sure where it is – lost somewhere in the mess of my suitcase.

I can smell myself: body odour and sour milk and something tart that catches the back of my throat. Perhaps a shower will make me feel better.

In the bathroom, I turn the shower up to the maximum heat and climb in, enjoying the painful experience as the water needles my skin. I take some of Rachel's shower gel, which smells thick and unpleasant, but is still better than the smell of my own filth.

I forgot to bring a razor, but I wash under my arms as thoroughly as I can, and then I dry myself and put on clean knickers and a fresh T-shirt. I don't have another pair of jogging bottoms, so I put my jeans on instead. They are loose against my skin and gape at the waist, which means I've lost even more weight.

The bedroom is such a mess. I've never been tidy, but this is bad even for me. I scrape my wet hair back into a ponytail and set about trying to sort through everything, ending up with, as usual, a huge heap of washing in one corner.

I never would have imagined that a young baby would create so much washing.

The thought brings me upright.

Where is Jake? Rachel said she'd take care of him for me, but that was ages ago. I should rush downstairs, thank her profusely, and take him from her, but instead I slow my pace, tidying more thoroughly. Every second that I can string out this chore is another second away from the baby.

I can't believe I feel this way.

Perhaps the simple truth is that not all women should be mothers. I wasn't meant to be one, clearly. Biology put paid to that.

Mother Nature always wins.

I thought I could defeat her by simply taking what I wanted, but she's punishing me for my arrogance. Look how I've ended up. It's only what I deserve.

'Fiona?'

My time is up.

'Yes?' I say, trying to remember how tired I was earlier, when Rachel took Jake away from me. She was looking at something when I came downstairs. That's right: a note. Scrawled in thick black crayon. I hadn't been able to read what it said, but it clearly wasn't particularly nice.

'You're up,' Rachel says, and she pushes open the door to my room. She doesn't have the baby.

'I am,' I say, plastering on a bright smile. Perhaps I'm a better actress than I think. 'Thank you so much for giving me that little break. It was just what I needed.'

'Yes,' she says, staring at me like some kind of wise old owl. 'Well, you look better for it.'

'Where's Jake now?' I ask. Can she see through me? Does she know what I've done?

'He's asleep in his pram. I wanted to talk to you about him, actually.'

My stomach turns over. This is it, then. She's decided she's had enough of us both. She's going to ask us to move on, and then what will happen?

Where on earth will we go?

'I'm sorry if he's kept you awake at night,' I say hopelessly. 'I know he's been unsettled lately. I'm not sure . . .'

'I'm not worried about him,' she says. She flicks her eyes around the room, brushes her fringe away from her forehead. 'But when I took him from you earlier, he wasn't wearing a nappy. He was soaked through, Fiona. And his skin had started to blister.'

I stare at her in horror.

'I . . . I don't understand.'

'You're tired,' she says. 'You must have changed him and forgotten to put a new nappy on. You just put him back in his babygrow. I suppose it's an easy mistake to make, but it shows that you need a break. A rest. Or some help.'

'Rachel,' I say, trying to keep my composure. 'It's not your job to help me. I'm sorry that we've been such a burden. I'm supposed to be your lodger.'

'All my lodgers become friends,' she says rather stiffly. 'It's a bit difficult not to get involved when you live in such close proximity to someone.'

She pauses, staring out of my bedroom window.

'Why do you think I have a lodger in the first place?' she asks.

I shake my head.

'It's not for the money,' she says. 'I have enough of that. But I don't like living alone. It's lonely.'

'Even so,' I say. 'You didn't sign up for this. I'm sorry. I'll pull myself together, I promise. I just need to get . . . I don't know. Some kind of grip. A plan. I'm very routine-led. I find it difficult when everything is in chaos.'

'Well, babies are known for bringing exactly that,' Rachel says.

'I know. I'm really sorry.'

'I'm not saying any of this to chastise you,' she says. 'I remember what it's like to have a young baby. How difficult it can be. I just wanted to talk to you about . . . well, getting some support. What about your own family? Surely you have friends and relatives that could help you with him?'

'I can't go back to London now,' I say. 'And my family . . . they have their own problems.'

She nods, as though she understands.

'And Jake's dad?' she says, gently. I can see her trying to probe, to get under my skin. 'There's no hope of a reconciliation there?'

I almost splutter with laughter.

'No,' I say, in a low voice. 'Definitely not.'

Rachel sighs.

'My father was a violent man,' she says, after a while. 'Quick with his fists. He put my mother in hospital on more than one occasion. But he was a coward, deep down. As all bullies are.'

'I'm sorry to hear that,' I say. 'But Louis . . . he's not like that.'

'What is he like, then?'

'He's . . . manipulative. Clever. Selfish.' Like a dam bursting its banks, the tears erupt.

I thought it was Jake I wanted, but it wasn't. It was Louis. Louis, the man I loved.

'But he wasn't violent?' she says, softly.

I look at her through my tears. I shake my head.

'No,' I say eventually. 'Not violent. I . . . I loved him, Rachel. He broke my heart. I thought we were going to be a proper family. But he didn't want me.'

'The black eye?' she says, her voice even softer. 'I know you had make-up on. That it wasn't real.'

'I just thought . . .'

'You thought I would feel sorry for you if I thought you'd been abused?' she says.

I nod.

'I understand,' she says. 'Even so, it's a shame you lied to me, Fiona. You're living in my house, under my roof. Trust is very important.'

'I know. I'm sorry.'

'Never mind,' Rachel says, putting an awkward hand on mine. 'We won't say any more about it. But you are going to have to be stronger than this. I'm sorry if it sounds cold, but that's just the way it is. You're a mother now, and mothers put themselves last.'

RACHEL

Another girl with relationship problems. Just like Kylie. Except this one is nearly twenty years older. She should know better. She's got herself into all sorts of hot water and clearly has no clue how to get out of it.

When Fiona takes Jake upstairs for a feed, I power up my computer. I remember the name in the record book.

Louis Horton-Jones.

I have an incredibly sharp memory. No early-onset dementia here, thank you very much. I do the *Times* crosswords every day. Both of them.

As the computer warms up, I make myself a proper cup of tea and do a thorough clean of the kitchen. Daisy has taken to jumping up on the surfaces, something she knows is strictly banned. I came down the other day to find Fiona happily feeding her tidbits of tuna from her salad while Daisy stood on the counter, one paw on Fiona's arm. I nearly had a fit.

I managed to contain myself though. Fiona is fragile. Even Kylie didn't like my nagging.

I sit at the computer and open Google. I'm not sure what I'll find, or how I'll know I've got the right Louis Horton-Jones, but there can't be too many of them around, can there? He sounds like the most frightful toff. It's a dreadful name. Not sure what kind of parent would saddle their child with that.

I carefully type his name into the search box. How would I find contact details for him? I add 'email address' afterwards and click the button.

Lots of websites come up, but none of them look legitimate. There is, however, a page with people complaining about the conditions of their gym membership, and someone has posted something intriguing:

Email the MD directly, Louis Horton-Jones. Tell him how pissed off you are that they took the renewal fee without telling you first. His address is louis.horton-jones@fireleisure.com.

There are several people thanking them afterwards.

Wow, thanks! Will do.

Amazing knowledge, thank you! I did and got a refund almost immediately. Pays to go straight to the top, it seems!

That's it, then. I pull out a notebook from the drawer under my desk, ignoring the pages filled with scribbles about activities for the Guides. It still stings, that they threw me out just like that. I didn't get so much as a cake. All because of that stupid Lissa Martin. It was blatantly her big brother who posted that note through my door earlier. He always was a reprobate. Thick as bricks, as Mother would say.

Anyway, that doesn't matter now. I'm half tempted to rip the pages from the notebook and use them as kindling, but instead I fold over the spine and carefully copy down Louis Horton-Jones' email address.

I'm not sure what I'll do with it yet. Or indeed, whether or not I'll get in touch with him at all. But I'm glad to have it.

A security blanket, in case things with Fiona get too much.

In the end, Fiona decides she will join me on my 11am constitutional.

'It's an excellent idea,' I say. 'You'll see that fresh air can do you the world of good.'

She nods, looking unconvinced. I hope she won't slow me down. I like to walk quickly – another thing the local youths have taken to teasing me for.

'Left, right, left, right. Quick march, Witchy!' they shout if they see me on my strolls. I've half a mind to take my grandfather's cane from the loft next time I go and belt them around the legs with it.

Jake is tucked into a sling against Fiona's chest. He seems content. Fiona is a little more relaxed now too. Hopefully, while we walk I'll get her to open up more about this Louis Horton-Jones.

'He's had another change,' she says. 'Don't worry, he's definitely wearing a nappy this time.'

I nod.

'Glad to hear it. Let's go then, shall we? The weather looks like it might close in again before lunch.'

We leave the house and walk around the side of the green. Nigel and the usuals are still working on the bonfire.

'Don't you want to say hello?' Fiona asks.

'No, I see quite enough of them as it is,' I reply. 'Village life can be rather claustrophobic. I prefer to keep myself to myself.'

I pause, waving over at Nigel as he looks up.

'That's Nigel. He's seventy-two. That bonfire will be the death of him, but he insists. He's been in charge of the celebrations for forty years.'

Fiona waves at him too.

The road is coated with leaves and we trudge through them crisply. As ever, I keep my eyes peeled for any large branches that might have broken off in the recent storms, but it looks as though Nigel and the boys have already taken them. We'll have to go further afield.

'There's a torchlight procession too,' I continue as we round the corner of the green into the lane that leads out of the village. 'The boys and girls from the village dress up and carry torches to the bonfire. There's a marching band that leads them through the village, and then the torchbearers circle the bonfire and set fire to it together. It's quite a spectacle to behold.'

'No Guy Fawkes?' she says.

I frown at her.

'Of course,' I say. 'It wouldn't be much of a bonfire celebration without Guy Fawkes on the top. Some of the local children are currently building this year's. He's always a work of art by the end. Seems quite a shame to burn him.'

'It always struck me as quite terrifying,' she says. 'The idea of burning a body alive. Even if it is just a dummy. It's the symbolism.'

I sigh.

'For goodness' sake. It's just a tradition,' I say. 'Even the children are perfectly aware that it's not an actual *body*.'

She's quiet. I feel momentarily guilty. I shouldn't have snapped at her like that. But honestly. She needs to toughen up. Not sure she's fit to raise a child, if she's going to be this weak-willed.

'Didn't you say your great-aunt lived here?' I ask, as we make our way out of the village. 'In the village, I mean?'

'Yes,' she says. 'She did. A long time ago.'

'I probably knew her. Which house did she live in?'

'I can't remember,' Fiona says. 'I've been racking my brains but I can't think. I was sure it was a house set back from the green. I remember it had a red front door.'

I wrinkle my nose. That doesn't help much.

'Her name was Margery Miller,' she adds. 'If that helps.'

I stop short on the path.

'Oh,' I say. 'Say that again.'

'Margery Miller,' she repeats.

I close my eyes. The chances aren't as slim as you'd think, I suppose, in a small village like this. But even so. I take a deep breath, compose myself.

'It doesn't ring a bell,' I lie.

'She didn't live here long,' Fiona says. 'At least, I don't think she did. We only visited once. For a few days. It was summer and I just remember how different it seemed from London. It felt like paradise. So tranquil and peaceful. She was my father's aunt, but they didn't really get on. There was some kind of drama or something. We hardly saw her. I lost touch with that side of the family years ago, after my father died.'

232

'What about the rest of your family?' I say. I have to put this out of my head. It's not Fiona's fault, after all. She wasn't to know. But still. What are the chances?

'I have a sister,' she says, looking sad for a minute. 'But she's busy with her own life. She has four boys. My mother died when I was three.'

'I'm sorry to hear that.'

'It's fine,' she says. 'If I'm honest, I hardly remember her.'

'Still,' I say. 'I know what it's like. To feel alone in the world.'

We pause at the intersection of the lane and the main road. I look over at her. The autumn sunlight streams across her. She looks as though she's glowing.

'I used to think I liked it,' she says. 'Being alone. After my husband died, I thought . . . it was the safest way to be. To not let anyone close. Not let anyone near me. But then . . . well, then I met Louis. It was a mistake.'

'Like you said to me before, not a mistake,' I say, stroking Jake's head through his little hat. I think briefly of the other hat, still secreted under my pillow. Fiona may not be coping, but I can't let him go. He's too precious. Almost like a grandchild to me now.

I think about my own 'mistake'. My lovely Brian.

'It's never a mistake,' I say, gazing at Jake. 'No child is ever a mistake.'

FAYE

Rachel is right. I feel better for the walk. We cover nearly three miles in the end. Rachel walks impressively fast for someone so . . . portly.

I've lost weight recently. It's worse than it was after Marshall died. I suppose it's to be expected. It's my default state, honed by years of scrapping around for food as a child. And I barely have time to eat these days.

As we walk, Rachel scours the ground for branches, and when she finds suitable ones, she arranges them in piles at the side of the road.

Rachel is incredibly enthusiastic about Bonfire Night. But I'm grateful for it. Things could have been so much worse when she discovered I'd faked my black eye. She could easily have thrown us out on the street. Now I have to keep her happy. I have to get this situation back under control.

And she's right, the fresh air is helping clear my head a little. I glance down at Jake, asleep against my chest, take a deep breath of the frosty air and feel the greatest sense of peace I've felt for weeks.

A little way into the walk, we pass some teenagers on bicycles. They do wheelies up and down the road in front of us, looping back and riding right up to us repeatedly. There's something menacing about them, despite the fact they are literally just overgrown children.

'Shall we turn back?' I say.

'Don't be ridiculous,' Rachel says. Then she stops and pulls me round to face her. 'Listen to me, Fiona. Never turn back. Don't let them see your weakness. It's the only way to stop them having power over you.'

I'm embarrassed by her telling-off, and nod in reply. Thankfully, the teenagers mostly ignore us as we pass them, although one spits on the ground as we pass. Rachel spins on her heel.

'Disgusting habit,' she snaps. 'Go home, Jerome. Your mother would be ashamed.'

I hold my breath for a second, hardly daring to look at the boy she has admonished.

'Ooh, er, everyone, careful – the Witch is cross! Keep your wig on, you stupid old cow,' he says, and then he titters, cycling off in the other direction, followed by the others.

My heart is pounding. I stop short for a few seconds.

'The Witch?' I ask. 'Is that what they call you? That's horrible.'

'You're not very fit, are you?' Rachel says, ignoring my question. 'Here, give me Jake. I'll carry him the rest of the way.'

'Oh, no, it's OK, I can manage.'

But she's already rummaging around inside the sling, pulling him out gently.

'Right, put the sling on me,' she says. 'And I'll slip him back in.'

235

I do what she says, feeling guiltily pleased to be relieved of him for a while.

On the way back through the village, we call in at the chemist.

'Afternoon, Valerie,' Rachel says, marching through the small shop and up to the counter. I glance around. The display of make-up looks as though it's been there since the 1990s.

The chemist smells medicinal but in a comforting way. It reminds me of waiting for my prescription in the chemist by the Tube station. I wish I could ask for my medication here. I know it would help me with the sweating, the inability to concentrate. And, most importantly of all, my mood.

'This is my new lodger, Fiona,' Rachel says, pulling me closer to her.

'Oh! What happened to Kylie?' Valerie says.

'Kylie had to leave,' Rachel replies.

We stand for a few seconds waiting for her to elaborate. Something about her tone is strange. Kylie *had* to leave. Did she do something wrong? Perhaps she forgot to wipe down the kitchen counter after making a cup of tea.

'Right,' Valerie says, breaking the silence. 'I saw the ambulance a while back and I did wonder ... Shame. She was a lovely wee thing.'

The ambulance?

'This is Fiona's little boy, Jake,' Rachel says, ignoring her. She peels away the blanket from Jake's face.

'Oh, he's a beauty,' Valerie says, peering over at him. 'How old?'

'Oh, um, nearly five weeks,' I say, hoping I've got it right.

236

It's hard to remember the exact date at the moment. The days have blurred into one.

I suddenly panic. Should I be showing my face? The more people who know I'm here, the more at risk I am of Louis finding us.

'Isn't he something?' Rachel says, smiling. 'Just perfect. But he's got dreadful nappy rash, poor mite. Do you have anything for that?'

'Metanium,' Valerie says, lifting up the counter flap and leaning past us. She plucks a yellow box from the shelf. 'It'll sort him out in no time.'

'Thank you so much,' I say. 'How much do I owe you?'

'It's £5.99,' she says.

I take a ten-pound note from my pocket and hand it to her. She screws her face up.

'Do you have a card? I've hardly got any change left.'

'Oh,' I say, shaking my head. 'No, sorry. I . . . didn't bring my cards.'

She huffs slightly, taking the note from me and handing me my change.

It's going to get suspicious eventually, me always paying in cash. I can tell Rachel's thinking the same thing.

'Have you lost your debit card?' she says, as we close the door of the chemist and head back across the green. The bonfire team are still hard at work. Three days to go. I hope the fireworks don't stop Jake from sleeping. What I wouldn't give for a proper night's sleep. The type I used to enjoy. Sometimes ten hours or more!

'No,' I say, swallowing.

237

'But you're too scared to use it,' she says.

'I'm scared if I do, then Louis will be able to track us down,' I say, sticking to my story. I'm a woman on the run, terrified of my former partner. But perhaps I should never have mentioned Louis to Rachel at all. Perhaps it was stupid. I should have made up something else: that I was a single parent, looking for a fresh start. Anything.

'I used it when we went to King's Lynn that day but only because I was spending so much I didn't see another way. And at least King's Lynn is quite a big town. If I use it here, it's far riskier.'

'But you haven't committed a crime,' Rachel says. I can almost hear the cogs in her brain turning. 'It's not a crime to leave with your baby.'

I *have* committed a crime. The worst crime imaginable.

'But . . . I can't refuse him access,' I say. I am too tired for this pretence. How much longer can I keep this up for? The optimism I felt as we left on this walk is ebbing away. 'Legally, I can't stop him from coming and finding us and demanding I let him see Jake.'

'Is he on the birth certificate?'

'Yes,' I say quickly. Even though there is no birth certificate. Not yet. His parents never got around to registering him before I took him. I know this for sure because I followed them every day after his birth, and they never went near the register office.

Oh God, that's something else I'll have to do. And how can I? I don't have any ID that shows me as Fiona. It was only luck that Jake's child record book was in the bag next to him when I grabbed him from the car.

Rachel nods, sucks air through her teeth. The house is in sight now. I quicken my pace. I want to get into the warm and out of this conversation.

'Why do you think Louis hasn't come looking for you?'

She won't leave it alone.

'I . . . I don't know that he hasn't been looking for me,' I say. 'How would I know, if he hasn't found me yet? Perhaps he'll turn up tomorrow. I have no idea. I'm terrified.'

'Do you think he doesn't care?' Rachel says. 'Didn't he want to be a father?'

It's a good excuse. A 'get out of jail free' card tossed in my direction.

I nod, as though it's something I've been considering myself.

'I think quite possibly he's pleased that we are out of his life for good,' I lie.

It's the opposite of what I really think: that he has probably hired a private investigator and that it's only a matter of time before he shows up and has me arrested. Or worse.

It was a mistake, I realise. Running away to this tiny village. I stick out like a sore thumb here. Perhaps I should have stayed in London. I would be invisible, lost in the sea of people. I could have, I should have . . . there are so many regrets. They press down on me like weights.

'I think Louis didn't really want . . . didn't really know what having a baby entailed,' I continue. This much is true, at least. 'He wasn't prepared for it. He's a selfish man, used to his selfish ways. A baby was nothing more than an accessory to him. A box to tick. He's from a very successful and powerful family and they expected him to have an heir. It was all

239

just another purchase to him . . . another thing to add to his collection . . . he's just a showman. His whole life is about appearances.'

I tail off, gasping for breath. I've said too much. Rachel is staring at me, her eyes wide.

'I don't really want to talk about Louis,' I say, hoping that this will stop her asking any more. 'I'm sorry. It's very upsetting.'

'He has responsibilities to you,' she says. 'To you both. You and that baby. You should make him pay. Especially if he has means. At the very least, he should be providing for his son.'

'No,' I say, cursing myself for telling her so much. I should never have mentioned Louis to her at all. I'm an idiot. 'I don't want his money. I don't want anything from him.'

'But Fiona, it's not just about you, is it?' she says. 'It's about Jake too. What he needs. What he deserves.'

RACHEL

Fiona is upstairs with Jake, who is, as usual, screaming his head off. It's the same every day, between 7 and 9pm. The witching hour. He screams and screams and screams, and from downstairs, I listen to her cycling between attempts to soothe him, frustration with herself, and eventually, anger.

'For God's sake, what do you want?! Just stop crying!' she hisses. 'Just stop it, stop it, stop it!'

She's on the verge of another teary outburst. It's very wearing. Colic. Brian had it too, all those years ago, but of course I wasn't able to do anything to help.

'Go to your room, Rachel,' my mother would say, as she pipetted gripe water into his tiny mouth. 'He doesn't want your ugly face staring down at him when he's upset.'

I thought if she would just let me hold him, just let me kiss him once, then perhaps I could make his tears stop. I thought he was trying to tell us all something: that he could see what was happening, that he had been separated from his biological mother, and that, if he only protested enough, he would get her back.

He wanted me, not my mother.

But she was the one with all the experience. I was the fool

who had got herself pregnant at fifteen. My opinion wasn't valid or required. I was a disgrace, as they told me repeatedly.

I hear Fiona thump something in frustration. I can only hope it's the chest of drawers, and nothing near Jake. His scream has reached a fever pitch now, repetitive and hacking, the sound like a siren. It's a wonder Wendy next door hasn't complained. She likes to complain. Most often about the state of the garden, when the weeds grow so high they start to spool over the fence into hers.

I forgot to ask Fiona about opening the back door. Well, it's too late now. I've hidden the key, so she won't be able to do it again.

I was about to turn the computer on, but instead I go to the kitchen and prepare Fiona a hot drink. Not her milky excuse for a cup of tea, but my mother's special recipe. The drink she made for me whenever I was upset.

'Wash your face and drink this,' she would say. It was her version of sympathetic support. The most she was capable of. I've often felt angry with my mother, but the truth was, she was a weak woman in a difficult situation, and she was terrified of my father. She did the best she could.

I take a deep breath and climb the stairs. Daisy is lying on the landing, staring at me with disdain.

I lean down and stroke her. She's not really meant to sleep here – she has a perfectly good radiator bed downstairs – but I make allowances for her in November. She's eleven years old now. She understands what the tall structure on the green means, the terrifying noise and lights that are about to come her way.

'All right, Dais,' I say. 'Let's see if we can give Fiona a hand, shall we?'

I knock gently on the bedroom door.

'Yes,' she calls, sounding stressed. I open it. Jake is lying in the middle of the bed, screaming and staring up at the ceiling, his face bright red and his legs jerking angrily. Fiona is sitting on the floor, knees drawn in to her chin, her hands supporting her forehead.

'I've made you a drink,' I say. 'My mother's recipe. Calms the spirits.'

She stares at me as I place it on the coaster by the bed.

'Let me take him,' I say. 'You need a break.'

'Please,' she says quietly. 'Take him anywhere. Anywhere away from me.'

I take a deep breath. Now is not the time to pull her up on her attitude. I lean over her and pick up Jake. He's surprised by the change and momentarily stops crying. Then he passes wind. I feel the vibrations through his babygrow.

'Dear me,' I say. 'That was a tight tummy.'

Fiona lifts her head. Her face is streaked with tears, her cheeks and nose almost as red as his.

'It's very hard, having a newborn,' I say, trying my best to sound sympathetic. 'But it gets easier. Each day. You get a little more used to each other.'

'He hates me,' she says, a fresh tear making its way down her cheek. 'He literally hates me.'

'Of course he doesn't,' I say. 'Don't be ridiculous. He doesn't know you well enough yet. He doesn't even know himself.'

I look down at Jake, who is staring transfixed at my necklace.

A crystal pendant, inside of which is a lock of hair. It catches the light and I hold it up in front of his face.

'Do you like this, Jake?' I say, showing him. 'Pretty, isn't it? It was my mother's.'

I hear Fiona give a tiny sob.

'Let's leave Mummy to it,' I say. 'Shall we? She's feeling rather overwhelmed.'

I take him downstairs without asking permission. I lay him in his pram while I make up a bottle in the kitchen, sterilising it before I do so. I don't entirely trust Fiona's sterilisation routine. It seems rather haphazard.

Then I lift him up and sit on the sofa in front of the bay window, looking out at the green while I feed him. He's hungry, poor thing, and drinks almost the entire bottle straight away. Fiona needs to get into a better routine with his feeds. There *is* no routine, it seems, just her remembering every now and then that he might be hungry, and offering him a bottle.

'My mother put Brian on a very strict routine,' I say to Jake quietly as he slurps away. I remember it all so well. 'It was very regimented. Up at seven for the day, no matter what, fed every four hours, naps just as strict. And no eye contact before bedtime, which was 6.15pm on the dot. That always seemed a bit cruel to me. But we can do something a little less draconian, can't we, sweetheart? I think that sounds like a very good idea.'

As he drinks, I wonder what would happen if I contacted Louis. Would he help? I don't want him turning up and making everything worse for Fiona.

But at the same time, she's clearly not coping. She's been

here for nearly a week now, and I worry more about her each day. It's as though she's not truly present most of the time. Her mind is elsewhere, her body barely going through the motions.

She needs help. I can see it. But is Louis the right person to help her? I don't know.

It's not like me not to know what to do. I've always been decisive.

But there's more to it than that. There's also the fact that Louis is the baby's father. He has responsibilities, but he also has rights.

The right to see his son. She shouldn't have taken him away like that. And if her injuries were faked, then how can I trust that what she says is true?

But then, if he was a loving father, surely he would have called the police? Surely he would know that Fiona had taken him, and would be trying to track them both down?

It doesn't make sense.

Although perhaps Fiona's right. Perhaps he doesn't care that they've gone, and that's why he's done nothing to try to find them. But if that's the case, then he's a worse specimen of humanity than Fiona has made him out to be.

A sob escapes me, a strange release of grief. They ambush me from time to time, when I'm feeling low. The pain of that time, the shame that wasn't really my shame to feel.

But this is not the same.

I look down at Jake, now asleep in my arms.

'You just want to be held, don't you, little one?' I whisper. 'That's all babies want. To be held and warm.'

My mother would hiss that you mustn't spoil babies by

rewarding their crying. She put Brian in the airing cupboard when he wailed, turning up the tiny television set so that we couldn't hear him growing ever more desolate.

But I still heard him. He was my baby, after all.

I was angry with her then, but with time I've been able to forgive her. She went through a lot. And she did the right thing in the end.

Margery Miller. I can't believe she's Fiona's great-aunt. I shouldn't tar her with the same brush, but it makes me trust her even less.

Perhaps I should send Louis an email. Anonymously. To try to get some sense of what kind of man he is.

Perhaps that would be the right thing to do.

But then again, look what happened with Kylie. I think of the bloodstained scissors, hidden away in my tin.

Look what happens when I interfere with my lodgers.

Somehow it always goes wrong. Somehow someone always ends up getting hurt.

FAYE

I am going out of my mind. I can't continue like this.

I need to be able to talk to someone. To get some proper advice.

I take a sip of the drink Rachel brought me, then take my phone out of my bag, where it's stuffed in between the rolls of cash. My bank cards are buried at the bottom of my suitcase. But they have my real name on. I had to be so careful in that department store in King's Lynn, making sure Rachel didn't get a proper look at them.

I stare down at the phone, and then I do it. A moment of madness. I don't care.

I know his number off by heart, of course. He's my oldest friend, he has never changed it, and for a long time I didn't even own a mobile phone, so I got used to dialling it from my landline.

I type it in, hold the phone to my ear. My heart is hammering. This is wrong. So wrong. I know that. But I have to – I need to – talk to someone and tell them what I've done.

It rings and rings. The longer the ringing tone lasts, the more I have to fight the urge to hang up. But I keep the phone pressed against the side of my face, my ear growing hot as I listen to the repetitive tone.

He doesn't answer.

'Hey! This is Jonas. You know what to do.'

There's a ping. My breath catches. I don't know what to say. I hadn't planned this far. I hadn't planned what I would do if he didn't pick up.

In the end, I say nothing. I simply blink into the phone and eventually, it cuts me off.

He will know it's me. Won't he? Even though it's a different number, a new phone. Or perhaps he will dismiss it as a wrong number.

But maybe, just maybe, he will call me back and tell me what to do. Because I'm running out of ideas.

I have no idea how to get out of this situation, or how to clear up this mess I've created.

I lay down on the bed, my head suddenly thick with tiredness. I want to cry but I can't even manage that. Perhaps if I can get some sleep. Perhaps things will seem better.

I wake to the sound of a baby whimpering. I have been in such a deep sleep – the deepest sleep that I've had in months – that it takes me a while to remember.

Jake.

Rachel.

My stolen baby.

I wrench my eyes open and peer around in the darkness. But he's not in his cot. The bedside clock tells me it's 4.27am. I frown, trying to remember what time I went to sleep. I have no clue. The last thing I remember is Rachel, bringing me a drink that tasted of sour lemons and something else, something I couldn't put my finger on, and then calling Jonas and him not answering, and then feeling like I could sleep for a hundred years.

That was at about 8pm. Have I really been asleep all this time? And where is Jake now?

I lie back down. I can't hear him any longer; the whimpering sound that woke me. Perhaps I imagined it.

Perhaps I imagined it all. Perhaps there is no Jake. Perhaps I never stole a baby in the first place.

I close my eyes but then I hear it again. A whimper that turns to something more; a short, staccato cry, almost hiccup-like.

I didn't imagine it.

But he's not in this room. So where is he?

I climb out of the bed reluctantly, opening the door. I feel groggy from the sleep. Across the hall I can hear something else.

Rachel.

'It's OK, little man,' she is saying softly, in the tone she reserves for Jake. 'I know you're awake, but really, this is not a sociable hour. No, it's not. I know, you want food. But no, we don't get any sleep if we keep having sips of drink all night, do we? Better to have one big drink before bed, and then one big drink in the morning. So hush now, little one. Granny will take care of you.'

Granny?

I should go in, interrupt them, offer to take him off her hands.

But she sounds so much better at this than me. She sounds like she knows what she's doing.

Is he actually calming down for her?

She starts to sing, so softly I can barely make out the words. A lullaby: the tune is familiar but I can't place it.

I stand frozen on the top of the landing. My eyes are drawn to the staircase. I could just get dressed now, pack up my things and go. Back to my flat. Back to my old life. And no one would ever know. Would they?

No one would ever know I had taken this baby and then abandoned it again.

I could restart my piano lessons, my simple life of teaching. Go back to how things were before this . . . insanity took hold of me.

And the baby? What would happen to Jake? Would Rachel just take him on? I can tell how much she wants to. How much she loves him.

Perhaps that would be for the best.

The changeling child.

I'm seized by excitement and I turn and go back into my room, hurriedly starting to pack. If I'm quick, I can do it, I can walk to the town nearby and catch the first bus into the city.

But then there's a gentle knock on the door. It pushes open. She doesn't wait for me to invite her in this time.

'What are you doing?' Rachel says. She doesn't have Jake. He must be asleep . . . where? In her bed?

'I . . .' I say, red-faced. 'I was just tidying up.'

'At 4am?'

'I couldn't get back to sleep. How's Jake? Where is he?'

My heart is hammering.

'I kept him in with me so you could get a proper rest,' she says. She's wearing a pink velvet dressing gown with blowsy flowers embroidered on the lapels. 'Did you sleep?'

'Yes,' I say nervously. 'Yes, thank you so much. I did. I really did.'

'Good,' she says. 'Don't worry, I took the bassinet off the pram and he's been sleeping in that on the floor, so he's perfectly safe.'

Don't worry. I hadn't been worrying. Real mothers worry, don't they?

'Right,' I say. I can hardly catch my breath. 'Thank you.'

'I was just letting you know he was safe,' she says. 'I heard you moving around and thought you must be worried that he wasn't in his cot.'

'Yes,' I say. 'I was. Thank you.'

But neither of us are convinced. She can see through me. She can tell I'm not a mother, that I don't have what it takes – neither mentally, nor physically, so it seems.

'Well,' she says, as though waiting for me to speak. What would a real mother say at this moment? I have no idea. I am so tired of pretending. 'I'll leave you to get some more rest. Jake's quite settled.'

'Thank you,' I say. 'You've been . . . so kind to me.'

She nods, pulling the door closed behind her.

I sink down to my knees, and finally, I manage to cry.

251

RACHEL

Clearly, I have no choice.

Fiona isn't coping. She's hardly even here this morning, as she washes Jake's bottles and stares out the window, a vacant look on her face. When she does eventually feed the baby, she doesn't even look at him, and his eyes are wide with frustration. He needs the connection. He wants someone to pull faces at him, to blow him raspberries and tickle his chin and tell him how beautiful he is.

Because he is – absolutely beautiful.

Even Brian was fussed over. My mother fell quite in love with him. He was the second child she had always longed for.

I consider phoning my friend Janet, asking for her advice. Because much as I think I know the answer, I want the answer to be different. The truth is, I don't want them to leave. I want Jake to live here and grow up and go to the village school and call me Granny and for them to become like family and for everyone to mistake him for my grandson when we go out and . . .

But none of that is right.

What would Janet say? She'd sigh and say 'oh dear, Rachel, not again' and make some comment about me being taken advantage of – because she's always very defensive of me – and then she'd tell me straight that I must get in touch with this poor baby's father and sort this situation out before it gets any more serious.

She's right. But perhaps I could give Fiona one more chance to sort it out herself.

'Are you feeling all right?' I say, coming over to the worktop and wiping it down with Dettol.

She arches an eyebrow at me – the most her face has moved all morning. She's wasting away, her skin grey and slicked with sweat. She looks ill.

'Yes,' she says. 'Thank you.'

'Would you like me to get that keyboard out of the shed?' I ask. 'You might feel a bit more like your old self if you play for a bit?'

Her eyes widen.

'It's very kind of you, it's just . . . well, I was a professional classical pianist. I find playing on keyboards pretty intolerable, if I'm honest.'

'Oh, I see. Right.'

The atmosphere darkens. I see a flash of regret pass over her eyes.

'I'm sorry,' she says, pulling at the neck of her jumper. 'I just . . . I feel quite restless today. It's hot in here, isn't it? Or is it just me? I'm hot.'

She pulls the jumper over her head. That familiar white T-shirt is hiding underneath, replete with creases. I wonder if Fiona has ever heard of an iron. But that's ridiculous. Such things shouldn't matter when she's struggling so much, I know.

'That's better,' she says, giving an exaggerated smile.

'Fiona,' I say sternly. 'I think . . . I think you should seriously consider getting back in touch with Jake's father. It's clear that this situation can't continue as it is. Isn't it? You're not coping – but more than anything, you're not happy.'

She laughs at me. A laugh of shock, of terror.

'I'm sorry; I've always spoken my mind. I believed you when you said you were on the run from him. I believed you when you implied he was violent. But now I know none of that is true. I wanted you to settle here, to have the fresh start you asked for, but I've seen how you've struggled with Jake, how hard you're finding it, and I think you need more—'

'How can you say that?!' she says, anger rising. 'He's been a really difficult baby; he cries a lot. I've never looked after a tiny baby before . . . I'm trying my best! Everyone says how hard it is, but this doesn't even come close!'

'I know,' I say, trying to keep my patience. 'But like I've said, it's not just about you, how you're coping, how you're finding things. It's more important how Jake's finding things . . .'

'Look at him!' she hisses, pointing to him, peacefully asleep in the pram bassinet beside her. 'He's fine! He's absolutely fine.'

I sigh.

It's all so familiar. I think of Kylie. The way she looked at me when she confronted me. The hurt in her eyes.

'How could you have done this to me, Rach? Now he thinks I'm even more pathetic than he did before!'

I was trying to do the best for her. I was so very fond of

254

her, even if it didn't come across in the right way. It's no good though. This girl, like Kylie, won't see sense. Can't, won't, refuses to. I don't know which.

I can feel my pulse throbbing in my neck.

'I'm disappointed, Fiona. I had hoped we could become close. I'm very fond of Jake. I wanted you to feel settled and happy here. But . . .' I pause, softening my tone. 'I'm worried about you. About you both.'

She looks at me for a few seconds. I don't understand her. I don't know what's going on in her head most of the time.

I hardly know anything about her. All our discussions have revolved around Jake. Understandably.

'I'm sorry,' she says. She slumps. 'I shouldn't have snapped like that. It's just . . . being a mother. It's nothing like I imagined. It's nothing like I hoped it would be . . .'

'Well, I don't think you're the first mother to feel that way,' I say. 'But I don't think it's healthy to think you can do it all yourself.'

'I thought . . .' she says quietly, her eyes suddenly round like a child's. 'I thought you could help me.'

A warm glow spreads through my body.

'I want nothing more than to help you,' I say. 'If you'll let me?'

Her face relaxes.

'I think I need it,' she says. 'I think we can both see that.'

'Let me help you then,' I say. I take a step towards her, but stop short at drawing her in for a hug. 'You've done an amazing job so far. Despite everything.'

'Thank you,' she says, and this time she looks as though she means it.

Later that day, she takes Jake out for a walk around the green. The bonfire frame is nearly finished now, towering a magnificent twenty-five feet into the air.

I watch them as she rounds the corner. She said she's going to see if she can find her great-aunt's cottage. I know where Margery Miller lived, but I certainly won't be telling Fiona. I only hope she doesn't start asking around the village. There are only a handful of people still living here from that time, but those people have long memories.

I slip upstairs to take a look in her bedroom. She's tidied it up since yesterday. She's even made the bed. The nappy bin has been emptied, and the window opened.

Even so, I stare with dismay at the layers of dust on the furniture, the gritty texture of the carpet, and instead turn to her suitcase. She mentioned a sister; perhaps I can find her address written down somewhere? Since Fiona got here, I haven't heard her speak to anyone on the phone, although I know she has one. She's taken it with her now, of course.

I take her things out of her bag carefully – washbag, hairbrush, underwear – until I come across a diary. I open it, hoping I've struck gold, but there's nothing of interest inside except for the swirly writing on the first page, spelling out:

Faye Horton-Jones

Faye? I frown, wondering if it's just her handwriting that's difficult to read, and if it actually spells Fiona. But when I look more closely, I see that it definitely says Faye.

Perhaps a nickname? Although people called Fiona are more usually shortened to Fi or Fifi, as far as I'm aware.

I rummage further, unzipping the inner lining of the suitcase and pushing my hand in, groping around. And then I pull out two things.

A bank card.

And a small white box of pills.

I stare at them both, innocuous items that they are. But as I look closer, things stop making sense.

The name on the bank card reads MISS FAYE MILLER.

The name on the box of pills is MISS FAYE MILLER.

And the box is for medication I recognise. I know what these pills are for. I had them myself, a few years ago.

It makes no sense that someone like Fiona would need them, though.

I return to the suitcase, rummaging around for the red baby record book I found when I first came into her room. I open the cover, look at the names written.

Fiona Ivanov

Louis Horton-Jones

That doesn't make sense either. Did she accidentally pick up the wrong red book? But she can't have done, because Fiona – or Faye – told me that Jake's father was called Louis.

So why is she lying about her name?

And if she's not, then who is Faye Miller, and why does Fiona have her medication?

She must be another relation – she has the same surname as Margery Miller, Fiona's great-aunt.

But then why would this 'Faye' be practising writing her name with Louis' surname?

It doesn't make sense.

I put everything back where I found it. There seems to be no doubt what I must do now. I can't put it off any longer.

Back downstairs, I turn on my computer and type an email to Louis Horton-Jones.

ONE YEAR EARLIER

FAYE

Louis has left me here alone, in this beautiful hotel room.

I feel as though my heart is breaking.

The look in his eyes was just like the look Marshall had the night he died.

You think I loved you? Fuck. You stupid cow!

I close my eyes to the memory.

I go through to the hotel bathroom and throw up into the toilet.

Before he left ten minutes ago, Louis sat next to me and made me eat half of the club sandwich, demanding I promise to finish it later, even though I told him I was full.

Then he scurried out the door like a rat, barely bothering to say goodbye.

Leaving me here in misery.

I flush the toilet and sit down on the closed lid. I feel a little better now my stomach is empty again.

It's the most incredible bathroom I have ever seen. The walls are lined with marble; the claw-footed bath has gold taps. It's the sort of bathroom you might have in a honeymoon hotel. But I never had a honeymoon, so I can only imagine.

I start to cry, fat tears splashing down my velvet dress. I

should take it off. Water ruins velvet. But I can't seem to stop crying, and who cares if the dress is ruined? If he doesn't want to sleep with me when I'm wearing this, then he never will. It's all hopeless.

Artificial insemination.

I know, I've been a fool. I know that was the point of the app – to match people up who want to become parents together, not to match people romantically. But even so. We have been getting on so well. He took me to the opera, to meet his parents! I thought we were going to be a family. A proper family, like Hannah and Marcus and the boys.

He listened to me play the piano and told me it was the most wonderful thing he had ever heard. He kissed me and I could tell there was something there between us, and that my affection was reciprocated. Or did I get it all wrong?

What's been going through his mind all this time?

I scrabble back through to the bedroom, giving another sob as I stare at the sumptuous bed, perfect tasselled cushions lined up neatly against the pillows. But then my phone lights up with a message.

Forgive me for upsetting you. I find relationships difficult but I would still very much like to go ahead. I think we would make wonderful co-parents. L x

My heart lifts.

Can it be something else? Perhaps he was nervous? Perhaps he . . . perhaps he's impotent? You read about such things, don't you? Men who have problems in that department.

That would make sense. It would explain everything. I need

to give him another chance, and I mustn't put any pressure on him.

Relief washes over me.

I've been too suspicious. Too quick to judge him by Marshall's standards. Not all men are wolves in sheep's clothing.

I just need to play the long game. It'll all work out in the end, I'm sure of it.

I text back, my hands shaking.

I would very much like to go ahead too x

A week later, we are in an exclusive IVF clinic in Chelsea. Louis squeezes my hand as we sit in the waiting room.

'Do you remember what you need to say?' he whispers to me.

I nod. We have a story – Louis explained that it would be easier that way, to say that we have been trying for eighteen months to get pregnant naturally, to no avail. He said it would be easier than trying to explain to an IVF doctor that we intended to co-parent.

'Fewer awkward questions,' he said. 'Trust me. And it's no one else's business but ours.'

He was right. I didn't want anyone judging us.

'And I think it would be better for us to do full IVF,' he said. 'Rather than just artificial insemination. I'd like the embryo to be genetically tested before it's implanted. To make sure that it's . . . well, as healthy as can be. I don't want to take any chances. I'd also like to ask if there's a way we could check what the sex of the embryo is too. I'd prefer a boy. The world is kinder to men.'

I had nodded at that too. I thought I'd read somewhere that it was illegal to choose the sex of your baby, but he told me that the clinic was happy to do special favours for their most important clients, and then he winked.

'Welcome to life as a VIP, Faye. I think you'll like it.'

So now here we are, in one of the most exclusive clinics in the world. Known for their absolute discretion, according to their website. And eye-wateringly expensive prices, although Louis is covering all the costs.

'Money doesn't mean anything to me,' he said, when I had raised a hand in protest. 'It's a drop in the ocean, rather than a whole bathtub for you. I won't hear another word about it.'

And so I had nodded again. He was right, after all. Even one round of IVF at this clinic would have wiped out my savings.

'Mr Horton-Jones?'

I look up at the sound of his name. We are the only couple in the waiting room. The doctor smiles at us. I like her instantly.

'I'm Dr Wright,' she says, as we follow her through to a private room. 'It's a pleasure to meet you. Please, take a seat.'

Her office is vast, like no other medical room I've ever been in. A huge oak desk sits in the middle, and behind her there are floor-to-ceiling windows overlooking Chelsea Harbour.

'Please,' she says, once we're sitting opposite her. 'Tell me why you're here.'

Louis has told me not to speak unless I'm spoken to, so I look over at him.

'You came very highly recommended,' he says, and Dr

Wright smiles. 'And my partner and I – this is Faye – have been trying to get pregnant unsuccessfully now for eighteen months. We decided it was time to seek help.'

She nods, opening a folder on the desk.

'Let me just take some details.'

The questions go on for nearly twenty minutes. All aspects of our medical history are covered. Thankfully, neither of us seem to actually have any medical history, and at the end of the questioning, she tells us that we should be good candidates for IVF.

'You're both still relatively young,' she says.

She looks at me, her head cocked to one side.

'You're very slender, Faye. And I suspect your BMI is under where we'd like it to be. We'll need to get full blood work done for you, to test your hormone levels and make sure everything is working as it should be. We'll also do an internal scan, to take a look at your ovaries and womb. So please, if you could tell me the date of your last period, I'll get your blood tests booked in, and we can take it from there.'

I swallow, blinking. It feels like I'm in an exam, and I'm about to fail. From out of the corner of my eye, I can see Louis frowning, the vein twitching in his jaw.

'Oh, I . . .' I begin. My heart begins to thump in my chest. 'I'm sorry. I . . . I can't remember, actually. I . . .'

I scrabble around in my handbag, as though I might find the answer in there.

'That's OK,' Dr Wright says. 'I'd have no idea either. If you could work it out and then get back to me by phone or email, then I'll get one of the nurses to set up the appointment for you. It's important we test your hormone levels on the right days of the month, you see.'

'Right,' I say. 'Of course.'

My throat is dry.

'That won't be a problem, will it?' Louis says, and I glance at him quickly. He has that same look on his face that he had in the hotel room.

'No,' I say. 'I'm just . . . sorry! Just nervous. I'm sorry.'

I'm messing it all up. I'm ruining everything.

'Of course,' Dr Wright says, her voice smooth as silk. 'It's normal to be nervous. It's all very overwhelming, I'm sure, but rest assured we will take good care of you.'

I smile.

'And we'll arrange, too, for a sperm test. We can do them both at the same appointment. The sperm test will tell us whether IVF or ICSI is more appropriate in your case.'

Louis nods.

He doesn't seem nervous. I reach over to squeeze his hand but he looks at me, his brow furrowing. I put my hand back on my own leg.

'Right then, so if there are no more questions, I'll wait to hear from you on your dates, Faye, and we can take it from there.'

FAYE

'I'm sorry,' I say to Louis as we walk away from the clinic. 'I'm really sorry I didn't remember. I was just nervous. It's not the sort of thing you write down, really . . .'

I tail off, look up at him. He's not holding my hand. He was when we walked to the clinic earlier.

'It's not a problem,' he says. 'So long as you can get that information to them ASAP. We want to get moving on this, don't we? Time and tide wait for no man.'

I feel like I've let him down.

'I have to get back to the office,' he says, as we reach the Tube station.

'Oh,' I say. It's nearly 12pm. I had hoped we would be able to have lunch together. This is the first time I've seen him in weeks. After the night of the opera, we've only met up once, a rushed coffee date squeezed in between his meetings. 'Of course.'

'Send me a photograph of your lunch later,' he says, leaning forward and giving me a peck on the cheek. 'I want to make sure you're keeping up your calorie intake.'

There's no warmth in his words. I smile awkwardly. And then he turns and disappears down a side street. Once he's gone, I stand on the pavement for a while, watching the people walking past.

I don't know what I'm going to do. What I'm going to say.

In my pocket I have Dr Wright's card. She had a pile of them on her desk and I took one when we left her office. Louis had gone ahead so he didn't see. I suppose I'll have to phone her and explain.

I should probably have been honest at the time, but I was so taken aback by her question. I've never really understood how IVF works.

I scratch the side of my head, trying to remember when I had my last period. But it's no good. It's been months now. Possibly even a year. They've been irregular my whole life. And I haven't exactly missed them. I never kept track of them, and when they showed up, they always surprised me. They started lengthening out even further in my early thirties, with longer and longer gaps in between.

But when your life is as repetitive as mine, the days merge into one, and now I can't remember the last time I had one. The months seem to whizz past, each one the same.

You're very slender, Faye.

I've had comments like this my whole life. They infuriate me. After all, people wouldn't dare tell someone they were overweight, would they? But somehow, people think it's OK to comment on how thin I am. I never know how to respond.

There was a social worker I used to see when I was a teen. She used to go on and on about how skinny I was, telling my teachers I probably had anorexia, even though nothing could be further from the truth. If she'd dug a little further, she might have realised that the real problem was my dad not feeding me properly. But he was a convincing liar, and the people who were supposed to be looking out for me were stupid. They fell for his stories.

I don't want to think about my father. Or the past. It feels like another life, one I've put far behind me. But the repercussions of that time are back again, as always, to haunt me.

How will I give Dr Wright an accurate date? And how will she be able to test me on the right day if I don't know what day that is?

And how will I explain it all to Louis?

That afternoon I have two lessons. Anya comes after school. Her wrist is no longer bruised, but she has dark shadows under her eyes.

'Are you OK?' I say, after she plays me her scales perfectly. She has been practising, clearly.

'I'm tired, Miss Miller,' she says, staring up at me. 'That's all.'

'Why are you tired?'

'Mummy and Daddy were . . .' She pauses, a hand flying to her mouth, her eyebrows high. She has been told not to say anything and now she's said too much.

'Mummy and Daddy were what?' I say gently. 'You can tell me, Anya. You can trust me.'

She shakes her head. There's a pause as she thinks of something to say.

'Watching a loud film,' she says, a smile breaking across her face in relief. 'It woke me up.'

Watching a loud film.

When the doorbell rings, I take a good look at Anya's mother. She's wearing a lot of make-up, as usual, but even so, I can see the shadow underneath her eye. A bruise.

'Is everything OK at home?' I say.

'What?' she says, staring at me. 'Of course. What makes you ask that?'

Safeguarding rules, I think.

'Anya's very tired,' I say. 'She mentioned she hadn't slept very well last night.'

Anya stares down at her feet. I hope I haven't got her into any more trouble. I want to put my arms around her and tell her that it will be all right. That she won't always have to live with these people. That in just a few years she'll be able to do whatever she wants with her life.

'She reads for too long at night,' her mother snaps. 'I'm always telling her to turn her light off.'

'No, Mama,' she says. 'It's—'

'Come along, Anya,' she says, tutting. 'We'll be late to collect your brother.'

And then they are gone. And there's nothing I can do about it. About their clearly dysfunctional family.

It is so unfair, practically evil, that people like Anya's mother, people like my father, have children so easily, only to put them at the bottom of their priority lists, or worse . . .

When our child is born, they will come top. Before everything.

I close the door behind them and sink onto the sofa. And then, even though it's the last thing I want to do, I phone Hannah.

'Hi sweetie,' she says, as soon as she picks up. 'Are you OK? I'm having a bit of a day of it.'

'I'm fine,' I say. 'What's the matter?'

Hannah is always having a bit of a day of it, but I know deep down she is grateful to live this life, this hectic life she always dreamed of.

'Nothing, just Max is sick and the online shop's just arrived, and I've got the window cleaners coming and I haven't had time to even brush my teeth today, let alone have a shower like a civilised human being.'

'Poor Max, what is it?'

'Just a vomiting bug. It's ripping through the nursery. They've all got it.'

'I hope you don't catch it.'

'Me too. But more importantly, Marcus better not – he's got so much on this week. Anyway, what's up?'

I take a deep breath.

'Do you still get periods?'

'What?' she says, and then she laughs. 'Er, yes. And the mood swings to go with them.'

I can tell she's squashed the phone up against her shoulder and her ear, and she's unpacking the shopping as she speaks.

'Don't put me on speaker!' I say, terrified that Marcus might hear.

'I won't. What makes you ask that?'

'I don't,' I say quietly. 'Get periods. I can't remember the last time I had one.'

'Well,' Hannah says, her voice dropping. 'You always had problems with that, didn't you? Because of . . . the weight thing.'

I take a deep breath.

'Yes, but . . . they came back. Once I left home. They were always a bit sporadic, but I had them. I definitely had them.'

'You need to eat more,' Hannah says.

'I eat loads,' I say, although it's not strictly true. 'Do you . . . do you think it's fixable?'

'Oh Faye, I don't know. I'm not a GP.'

'Hannah,' I say. 'I'm really worried.'

'If you're not having periods, then you should go and see a doctor. That's not normal for someone in their thirties. But I'm sure they can sort it out.'

'OK,' I say. 'I'll make an appointment.'

She pauses.

'Is this related to . . . the new man?' She sounds less out of breath now. She must have finished putting the shopping away.

'Yes,' I say. 'We're hoping to start . . . trying for a baby.'

'You can't be serious!' Hannah says, her voice wary. 'Faye, you've only just met him.'

'I'm not getting any younger,' I say, because it's the sort of thing that she would say to me. 'And I love him.'

She sighs.

'Faye. Please. Be careful. You know what happened last time you thought you were in love . . .'

'It's nothing like it was with Marshall! How can you even say that? I was a child back then.'

'I know, but . . .'

'I know, I'm stupid and naive and trusting and no one could possibly be interested in me because I'm so gullible . . .'

'That's not what I was going to say. Please, Faye. It's been so hard, you know. Dealing with the fallout . . . and it was so hard, seeing you so distraught.'

'Don't make me feel bad.'

'I'm not. It's just . . . I'd feel a lot happier if we could meet this man, before you start rushing into anything.'

'Well, you can,' I say, even though the idea of asking Louis terrifies me.

'Great. When?'

'I don't know, let me talk to him.'

'Bring him round for lunch on Sunday,' she says. 'I'll decide if he's good enough for my little sister. And in the meantime, make sure you have three proper meals every day. No excuses, Faye. Listen, that's the window cleaner. I have to go. We'll see you then. Twelve-ish.'

And then she hangs up.

I swallow, thinking of two things: how I'm going to tell Louis about the lunch, and how I'm going to tell him about my periods.

FAYE

In the end I don't tell Louis. Instead, I make an appointment with my GP.

'Can you come in today, 10am?' the receptionist says on the phone.

'Oh, right, yes,' I say, surprised to get an appointment so easily.

I feel like I'm going to throw up as I explain to the GP why I'm here.

'Don't worry, we'll run some tests,' she says. 'Do you have any idea what age your mother went through the menopause?'

'Oh,' I say. The menopause? 'No, I don't, sorry. She . . . died when I was three.'

The GP looks up at me.

'Have you had any other symptoms? Hot flashes? Night sweats? Low mood?'

I swallow.

'Well, I've always been quite a sweaty person,' I say, thinking of the way I often wake in the night, my sheets drenched.

She frowns.

'How's your sex drive?'

I swallow again.

'Oh, I don't know, really,' I say. 'I've been single for a long time.'

'Shoes off and pop yourself on the scale over there for me,' she says, pointing to a huge contraption in the corner of the room.

I stare at it. It's just like the one they used to use when I was a teenager.

'Um,' I say, standing up. I keep my coat on as I step up onto the platform, staring down at the mechanical slide in front of me. The memories come rushing back; the way I would pray every week that the big slider would balance on one hundred pounds. But then, the disappointment in the doctor's voice when she would have to change it to fifty, and use the smaller scale to adjust it.

Today the big slider is on one hundred, and the small one is on ten. I breathe out. I've passed.

'How tall are you?' she says, frowning.

'Five foot seven,' I say.

'You're underweight,' she says, looking me up and down, and I nod.

'It's genetic.'

'Right,' she says, typing something into her computer. 'Well, let's not assume anything. I'll send you for bloods and we'll see where we are from there. Please book an appointment with the nurse on the way out.'

'Thanks,' I say.

Perhaps I just need to eat more. Perhaps that's the issue. I've lost a little weight since I met Louis, but if I put it back on again, then surely my periods will come back?

But if it was that simple, then why did she ask me about the menopause?

I don't know much about it, but I thought it was something that happened to old women. Not me. I'm only thirty-nine.

At home, I search the internet for reasons why my period has stopped.

Now I'm really thinking about it, I know that it has. I can't deny it any longer. It became more and more sporadic a few years ago, even though my weight was quite stable, and then it stopped completely. I didn't miss it, and perhaps I was an idiot for not wondering before.

None of the answers that Google throws up are relevant.

Pregnancy – haha.

Stress – unlikely seeing as they stopped well after Marshall died.

Sudden weight loss – not sudden, but perhaps?

Being overweight – no.

Doing too much exercise – no.

Taking the contraceptive pill – no.

The menopause – ?

Polycystic ovary syndrome – ?

Periods can also sometimes stop as a result of a medical condition, such as heart disease, uncontrolled diabetes, an overactive thyroid or premature menopause.

I don't like the sound of any of those.

Uncontrolled diabetes? There was none of that in my family that I'm aware of. Heart disease is more frightening, given that my dad died of a heart attack with no warning.

I click on the link for premature menopause.

It's like reading a description of my life. I hadn't even real-ised that these things I've been dealing with were symptoms. I thought they were just, well, me.

I start to feel nauseous. What does it mean for Louis and me? Surely it can't be good.

I know enough about the menopause to know that once you've gone through it you can't have children any longer.

I click on the section about treatment. There seem to be a few options, which reassures me slightly. The main one is something called HRT. Pills or patches. It rings a bell.

Hopefully it's fixable. I have the blood test tomorrow. I'll just have to keep all this quiet until I know for sure. It might be nothing. Whatever it is, I'm healthy. I hardly ever get sick. So hopefully it won't be too difficult to fix.

My phone buzzes, a message from Hannah.

What does Louis eat? He's not a veggie, is he? We were thinking lamb? Let me know – I'll get the meat from the nice butchers. X

She's really pulling out all the stops, but I haven't even invited him yet.

I tap my phone to call him. I've only rung him a few times before and he rarely answers, but perhaps this time I'll be lucky.

'Faye!' he says, sounding out of breath. 'What a coincidence. I was just about to call you.'

'Oh,' I say, smiling. The butterflies take over my stomach again. I can't read his tone.

'Yes, I had an email from Dr Wright, she said you hadn't given her the details of your last . . . well, you know. She hasn't heard from you. Tick-tock. We want to get this show on the road, don't we?'

'Yes,' I say, swallowing. 'I'm sorry. It's been . . . I've been back-to-back with lessons. I'll email her right away.'

'Let me know when it's done, please,' he says. 'How are you anyway?'

'Fine, thank you,' I say. 'I was ringing because my sister wanted to invite you for lunch this Sunday. I'm sorry, I'm sure you have a million things to do, so absolutely no pressure at all, but I promised I'd ask . . . she's doing roast lamb, she's actually quite a good cook . . .'

'*This* Sunday?'

'Yes, I know it's short notice . . .'

He sighs.

'Just a bit.'

'I'm sorry,' I say, sounding pathetic. 'I understand if you can't . . . but it would mean a lot to me. It won't be more than a couple of hours . . .'

'Well, I suppose I owe you one after your performance with my father and Tamara. What time?'

I don't know what he's talking about, but I'm so pleased he's agreed to come that I don't ask.

'Oh, great,' I say. 'I guess around twelve. She lives in Clapham so it's not too far from you. I'll send over her address.'

'Fine,' he says. 'I'll see you there.'

'Her husband's a bit of a bore,' I say, scrabbling around, worried that I've talked it up too much, that he'll be expecting something grand: civilised conversation and linen napkins, rather than my nephews throwing potatoes at each other over the kitchen table. 'I have to apologise in advance for him.'

'I have had decades of experience dealing with that kind of man. Water off a duck's back.'

'Well, thank you,' I say. 'It means a lot to me. I know you're very busy.'

'Don't make a fuss, Faye. I just told you, it's fine. What kind of wine do they like? Haut-Médoc? Goes nicely with lamb, I always think.'

'Anything,' I say. I have no clue about wine. 'Sounds lovely. Thank you.'

'Great,' he says. 'I know just the bottle. I'll see you there – text me the address. Oh, and don't forget to contact Dr Wright with those details. I hope you're having a big lunch too – send me the before and after photos of your plate, please.'

'Of course,' I say, swallowing. 'Thank you.'

We hang up and I put the phone down on the sofa next to me. I'll email Dr Wright and make up a date. It'll be OK. I've got the real blood test with my GP tomorrow, and it'll buy me some more time.

I dig out her business card and open my email account, telling her that my last period was five weeks ago. Any more recent and it wouldn't have rung true that I'd forgotten.

Then, I text Hannah back and say that lamb would be lovely and we'll see her there at twelve. And then I text Louis her address and tell him that I can't wait to see him.

Three days to go. Eight piano lessons. I find myself measuring out the days like this now – counting them down in the number of lessons, or episodes of *Coronation Street* I have to sit through, until I see him again.

I'm antsy though. Something is niggling me. This obsession with monitoring what I eat, and me having to send Louis pictures to 'prove' I've finished my meals. I feel stupid every time I take one. Is it normal? I know he's trying to make sure I'm as healthy as possible for the baby, but there's something a bit controlling about it.

Or is he just being kind and looking out for me?

Since I met Louis, Marshall feels closer than ever.

What's wrong with me? Not everyone is out to get me.

It has felt like that at times. People have betrayed me throughout my life.

'You're so naive,' Hannah once said, when a girl I thought was a good friend suddenly announced she wanted to move her boyfriend into our flatshare, which meant I had to move out, as he needed my room for a home office. 'Faye, you need to wise up a bit. Stop being so trusting. I would have thought after everything you had to deal with with Dad, you'd be the first to see when someone is being out of order.'

She can be blunt with me at times, but she's still my sister. She looks out for me in a way no one else can.

I know this is why she's invited Louis to lunch. Not just because she's nosey – even though that's part of it – but because she cares. Because she wants to make sure I will be OK.

FAYE

Dr Wright replies to my email and I book in a date for my second blood test this month.

Maybe, just maybe, everything will be fine.

I know that's wishful thinking though. I have a voicemail from the receptionist at my GP's on my phone, left on Friday evening, telling me to call them to make an appointment.

'The doctor would like to discuss the results of your blood work with you,' the woman who left the message said.

I was glad it was Friday evening. I could put it off until Monday.

I'm wearing the red star jumper again, with the smart jeans and boots. I was hoping Louis would want me to go to his flat first, so that we could arrive at Hannah's together, but he said he'd meet me there. It feels a bit strange, not turning up as a couple.

Like we're not really together.

I've bought Hannah some flowers. I don't know if they're the right ones – she seems to have fixed opinions about these things – but at least she'll know I've made some effort. I told Louis I'd get to their house a bit early so that he didn't have to worry about showing up without me being there, and he just laughed at me.

I forget that he has so much more confidence than me.

I catch the Northern line straight up to Clapham North. The train sits between Balham and Clapham South for ages – some issue with the signalling – and I'm almost hyperventilating by the time I rush to their terraced house. I so wanted to get there well before Louis.

This area has improved so much since they first moved here. I remember when it was pretty scruffy, lots of houses divided into flats, but now it's all Farrow & Balled front doors and box hedging. I open the iron gate and ring the doorbell.

As I wait for them to answer, I glance up and then I freeze. There's a face in the window, looking down at me.

Reuben.

The sight of him stops me short. I haven't seen him for months. What is he doing here? Why would Hannah not have told me he was here?

I want to turn and run but I can't. Louis will be here any minute. I'm trapped.

The front door opens. Marcus.

'Hello, Faye, how are you?' he says, taking the bunch of flowers from me. 'Where's the boyfriend? Hope he hasn't rained off?'

'No,' I say. 'He's coming straight from home. We didn't see each other last night.'

'Oh,' he says. 'All still going well though?'

I hand him my coat.

'Yes, absolutely. He just had dinner with friends.'

'I see. Lovely flowers, thanks.'

I follow him through to the large kitchen at the back of the house. Hannah is uncorking wine.

'Hi sweetie,' she says, kissing me on the cheek. 'You look nice. New jumper?'

'Yes. Thanks.'

She's wearing an apron. The archetypal housewife, cooking her whole family a Sunday roast. It was all she wanted, and it makes me happy, seeing her like this. It used to make me jealous, but now I can see that the same life is just within my reach.

'You didn't tell me Reuben would be here,' I whisper, when Marcus has left the room.

'I didn't know I had to? Don't worry, you're not likely to see him. He's vegetarian at the moment anyway. Or vegan or something. He's just back for the weekend. One of his friends did a gig at the Roundhouse last night . . . he didn't get in until 3am, I'm amazed he's even awake.'

'Still,' I say, trying to calm myself. 'You could have warned me. Is this why you've invited Louis over? Is having Reuben here a way of reminding me of all the bad decisions I've made in the past?'

'What are you talking about? You sound like a crazy person. It's nothing like that. I had no idea Reuben was going to turn up yesterday. And as for Louis . . . yes, I do want to meet him, because you're my sister and I love you and I want to protect you. I have to say, you being this jittery isn't particularly reassuring.'

She turns her back on me, and I swallow. Reuben doesn't know the truth about Marshall's death – he was only a baby when it happened – but even so, being around him makes me feel guilty and nervous.

'I don't need protecting.'

'Everyone needs protecting,' Hannah says, looking me up and down. 'You're looking skinny again.'

'I've been eating loads! I brought you flowers,' I say, trying to change the subject.

'I saw,' she says, raising her eyebrows. 'Thank you, that was very thoughtful.'

The doorbell rings. Hannah shoves a glass of wine at me and unfastens her pinny. She smooths her hair down and asks me how she looks.

I frown at her.

'Fine,' I say. Why does it matter how she looks? 'Nice. Honestly, you didn't need to go to all this fuss.'

'Marcus is so excited to have him,' Hannah says, tutting at me. 'He's a real big shot apparently.'

'Is that why you're so suspicious of him being interested in me?'

'Oh, Faye, for God's sake. I'm not suspicious of anything.'

And then she spins on her heel. I follow her into the narrow hallway, and watch as she flings open the door, greeting Louis enthusiastically.

I wonder what he will make of us all. My heart is fluttering with excitement. And then I remember what he texted me earlier.

Just checking before we meet that we're sticking to the same story with your family as we did with mine? Not sure my acting skills are up to yours but I don't want to embarrass either of us x

I didn't really understand what he meant. Perhaps the 'story' was that we've been seeing each other for longer than we really have.

'So lovely to meet you,' he says, smiling his most charming smile. 'And what is that delightful smell?'

'Oh, it's lamb shoulder,' Hannah says. 'We're so lucky, our local butcher is just great.'

Marcus is there too, all of a sudden, fawning over Louis and taking his mac from him, folding his scarf over his arm. The other boys are in the front room, playing a computer game. Hannah sticks her head through the door and tells them not to be so rude, and to come and say hello to our guest.

'Wonderful to meet you,' Louis says and they both smile and wait to be excused so they can get back to the Switch.

'Come through,' Hannah says. 'We've already started the wine.'

Louis hands her the bottle he's been holding.

'Hope you like Haut-Médoc,' he says. 'It's a rather good one I've been saving.'

'Oh, how lovely, thank you,' she says.

Then it strikes me; Louis has yet to even look at me, let alone say hello. But that's just his nerves surely? And I should be the one making the effort to greet him. We're in my territory, after all.

I glug down some of the wine Hannah handed me and march straight up to him, kissing him on the cheek. I have to take control of this situation.

He almost stumbles backwards in surprise, and for a split second he frowns, before kissing me back.

285

'Hello, Faye,' he says, taking a step back. 'You never told me what a delightful family you have. And this is your littlest nephew, I presume?'

'Yes,' I say, 'this is Max.'

Max is sitting in a playpen at the window, gnawing on a toy I recognise from when Arthur had it. His top is soaked in drool, his mouth hanging open.

'He's teething,' Hannah says apologetically.

'Adorable,' Louis says, his voice completely monotone. Even I can tell that he's lying.

But is that so bad? He's trying to be kind.

My flowers are wilting on the table.

FAYE

Reuben doesn't come down for lunch. I feel sick with nerves that he might appear any time. No one mentions him – they're all too wrapped up in their own chatter – but I'm constantly on edge, aware that he's just upstairs.

He never knew his real father. I feel sorry for him. But that doesn't mean I'm not also terrified. He thinks I'm just his eccentric auntie Faye – but he's also one of the few people alive who might one day be interested in finding out if there's more to Marshall's death than people were told.

Hannah is the only one who knows the truth about what happened to him. And she would never tell.

The truth is, she was glad Marshall was out of our lives.

'Not hungry, Faye?' Louis says, looking over at me. 'Remember what Dr Wright said . . .'

He tails off, realising that Hannah and Marcus might wonder who Dr Wright is, and why he's making a fuss. I look down at the food, the meat congealing on my plate. I pick up my cutlery and cut another piece of the lamb, forcing it into my mouth.

'Faye's always been slim,' Hannah says defensively, even though she was the one earlier who was telling me I was looking skinny.

'Well, the food is delicious,' Louis says, beaming at her.

He's right, he's brilliant at this. He answers all of Marcus' needling questions with great charm and ease, winning over the whole table. It's as though he's had coaching: a PhD in how to behave at dinner parties.

With the children he's not as comfortable. At one point, Arthur gets down and starts performing a song from his school play, and while the rest of us sit and listen and clap loudly despite his slightly off-key rendition, Louis' face is pulled into a tight smile. At the end, he grabs his glass of wine and takes a big gulp.

But I suppose it's to be expected. The boys are energetic company – Max has a proper tantrum right in the middle of the meal – and even though I have looked after them many times, I find them tiring and overwhelming too.

Louis is used to the civilised life, the refined life. A life of peace. Not the chaos of three boys around a Sunday lunch table.

'Thank you for the company,' I say, as we walk arm in arm away from their house later that afternoon. 'I hope it wasn't really terrible.'

'The lamb was a bit dry, wasn't it?' Louis says, pulling away from me, and I feel an instinctive flame rise within me.

'Oh,' I say, suppressing the feeling. 'Yes, I suppose. A bit.'

'I don't know what they were thinking serving that wine either,' he says. 'Everyone knows Haut-Médoc goes better with lamb. I thought they'd open the bottle I brought.'

He seems miffed.

'You should have said something,' I say. 'Hannah wouldn't

have minded. I'm sorry it wasn't more fun. I expect you're used to far more illustrious company.'

'Well, the boys are certainly . . . boisterous. Little bit out of control, don't you think? Hannah's very soft with them.'

I stop on the pavement. I know the boys can be annoying, but they're my nephews.

'I'm going to go back to mine,' I say shortly. 'I've got lots of teaching on tomorrow – one of my ten-year-olds has an exam coming up.'

'Right.'

A question flashes in my mind: why isn't he disappointed?

I feel stupid. All the old feelings come flooding back again. Marshall's voice, taunting me.

You thought I loved you?! Hannah was right about you . . .

I shake my head. I don't want these memories. Why do they keep hounding me?

'I've got a long week ahead too. And we want to make sure you get plenty of rest. We need you in top shape when we move on to the next stage.'

'Shall we arrange something for this week?' I say, folding my arms. 'Maybe I could come over for dinner?'

'Let's make an appointment with Dr Wright once your tests are done, shall we? And we can get the ball rolling.'

'But . . . that might not be for a couple of weeks.'

He stares at me, opening his mouth slightly.

'Faye,' he says sternly. 'I did tell you how busy I am at the moment, with the new northern branch opening and everything. I'll be travelling a lot. My time is very limited. I've spent all Sunday with your family, precious time I really couldn't spare. I really don't need any more pressure from you right now.'

I have never had a functioning relationship. The only one I thought I had – my marriage – was a sham. But even so, I can tell that this isn't right. That this isn't the way it should be. We should be desperate to spend every moment together, planning the future for our child. But instead it feels as though I'm just another one of his clients that he has to try to fit into his schedule.

'What about what I need?'

'Jesus, Faye,' he snaps. 'What *more* could you possibly need?'

He sounds mocking. Sarcastic. I feel myself start to crumble.

'I need . . . I don't know what I need! It's a big decision. I want to be sure . . .'

He takes a deep breath, exhaling it dramatically.

'I thought you *were* sure. I'm sorry if I've disappointed you in some way,' Louis says, breathing hard. I can see that vein pulsing in his jaw again, the way he's carefully measuring every word.

'You have,' I say. 'You have disappointed me. I feel like we have so much to discuss, and yet ever since we went to see Dr Wright, it's like you've been avoiding me!'

'Everything was set out quite clearly in the contract. Which you signed.'

'You told me not to read it! And we never talked any of it through.'

He looks up at the sky.

'Right,' he says, after a pause. 'Fine. How about you come over to mine tonight? We can discuss whatever it is you're concerned about then.'

'Really?' I say.

'Of course,' he says, and then he reaches out and takes my hand. 'If there are things you're worried about, you only have to ask. After all, I can't read your mind, can I?'

I feel wrong-footed. I search his eyes, looking for authenticity. This is what I wanted, but can I trust him?

Why do I feel like I can't? It feels as though he's just appeasing me.

'OK,' I say, taking a deep breath. 'That would be great. I'll go home and get some things and then come back to yours. Perhaps we could get a takeaway or something for dinner? Make up for the dry lamb?'

'Fine,' Louis says, giving a tight smile. 'See, we work perfectly well when we communicate, don't we?'

I nod, trying to fight that voice that's still there, telling me something isn't right.

FAYE

When I arrive at his flat later on, his housekeeper answers the door for me. Her hair is down around her shoulders, her cheeks slightly flushed.

She's wearing slim-fitting black trousers and a white shirt, the top two buttons undone to reveal a silver pendant hanging around her neck.

She's very young.

'Please, come in,' she says. Her accent is thick, difficult to place. 'Mr Horton-Jones is just taking a shower.'

A shower? Perhaps he's washing off the smell of Hannah's kitchen.

'Thank you,' I say. I feel a little uncomfortable. I don't even know her name.

'May I get you a drink?' she says, as she takes my coat from me and hangs it up in the slim closet in the hallway. There's a scented candle burning on a side table. Something smoky and woody.

'Oh,' I say. 'Just some water, please.'

She nods and disappears, leaving me alone in his living room. I'm surprised that she works for him on Sundays. Perhaps she lives here. But no, surely he would have mentioned it?

She comes back a few minutes later and sets down a crystal glass on a silver coaster. She also leaves a miniature bowl full of nuts.

'Thank you.'

She turns to leave, but then she pauses, and turns back.

'Your . . . playing,' she says, nodding towards the piano. 'It's so beautiful.'

'Oh,' I say, surprised. 'Thank you.'

She nods again and disappears through the door into the kitchen. I should have asked her name, but now it's too late, it'd be too awkward.

I sit there for several seconds, looking around the living room. On a side table by the piano there is a small collection of silver photo frames. I walk towards them to get a better look.

They're mostly black and white. Louis as a child, I presume, sitting in a pedal car in a huge garden, smiling at the camera. A couple on their wedding day. An elderly couple dressed smartly standing outside a church.

'My family,' he says, and I turn in surprise.

He's wearing jeans – possibly the first time I have ever seen him in them – and a pale pink shirt, tucked in. His blond hair is damp, his face glowing.

He looks more handsome than ever.

'I assumed so,' I say. 'Your dad looks young in this picture.'

'That's my parents' wedding day,' he says. 'When they were happy. Before Tamara got her claws into my father and wrecked everyone's lives.'

His eyes narrow and I see that same flash of temper I saw before.

'I thought you were on good terms with her?'

'I don't have much choice,' he says. 'She's determined to push me out completely. Constantly dripping poison into my father's ear about me, what an irresponsible and useless man I am.'

I'm surprised by the venom of his words.

'I didn't get that impression at the opera,' I say softly. 'She seemed nice enough. That must be very upsetting.'

'If it was up to her, she would have had me drowned as a child.'

'Louis! I'm sure that's not true.'

'You're very naive, Faye,' he says. 'Not everyone is as good and trusting as you.'

I shake my head.

'They packed me off to boarding school when I was seven. Got me out of the way. She was determined to replace me with Sebastian, right from the start.'

'Seven is so young!' I say, thinking of the pupils I teach who are that age. They seem like babies to me. 'What happened to Sebastian's father?'

'He died of cancer when Sebastian was a baby. That's when Tamara set her sights on my father.'

'That must have been really hard. For all of you.'

'Hmm,' he says, turning away from the photo table.

'I'm sorry,' I say, thinking back to my own childhood. The chaos of my father's tempers, the way it shaped every day. I never knew what was going to happen. It was exhausting.

294

'Don't worry. Everything will change when our little one comes along. Now, you already have a drink, I see?'

'Just water,' I say.

He nods his approval and picks up a slim remote control and points at a box on the wall. It turns on some kind of fake electric fire, the flames flickering on a screen.

'Will you play for me?' he says, and we both look over at the piano. 'I'm feeling a little . . . tense. It would help calm me down.'

My chest tightens.

'Is your housekeeper still here?' I ask, remembering the way she looked at me. I couldn't decide if I liked her compliment or not.

'My housekeeper?'

'She got me the drink,' I say, even though it must be obvious. 'It's just a bit embarrassing if she can hear too.'

'Why on earth is it embarrassing? Don't worry about her! I'm sorry if she's upset you.'

'She hasn't,' I say, confused. Something about the idea of having staff leaves me feeling queasy. I can imagine that in another life, if I hadn't had any talent for the piano, I might well have ended up in her shoes.

'Some Debussy then, perhaps? "Clair de Lune"? That was another of my mother's favourites.'

'It's a classic,' I agree, but I don't add what I also think: that it's overplayed.

'Go on then,' Louis says. 'It would mean so much to me to hear it played on my own piano.'

I glance over at the stripy Steinway that stunned me the

295

first time I saw it, but that in this evening's light just looks incredibly vulgar. I don't really want to play at all. I want to get to know him better.

'If you insist,' I say. I'm just being stupid. It's a crime not to share your talent, that's what my old teacher used to say to me.

I sit down and lift the lid.

'Wait,' he says, raising a hand. 'Two seconds.'

I watch as he vanishes out of the door to the kitchen. I hear his voice, low at first, then slightly louder, as he says something to the housekeeper.

Seconds later, she rushes through the living room, her cheeks red, and out through the door to the hall.

I turn my head towards the window and watch as she hurries away down the street.

'You didn't have to tell her to leave,' I say, feeling bad now.

He dismisses my comment with a wave of his hand. 'Christ, will you stop worrying about her?' He sounds snappy again. 'Just play the fucking piano!'

I put my hands on the keyboard, painfully aware of him watching as my fingers glide across the keys. But I don't put in the emotion that I know the piece needs. I've never liked it much. It's too pleased with itself.

At the end, I glance over at Louis nervously.

'Mama used to play that for me,' he says. 'When I was little. It reminds me of her. I miss her so much.'

I nod, unsure what to say.

'It's beautiful,' he says. 'Like our child will be. I hope he has your talent. He'll be lucky, having you to teach him.'

I smile and close the lid of the piano.

'I'm tired,' I say, before he has the chance to ask me to play something else.

'Come and sit here with me,' he says, patting the space on the sofa beside him.

I do as I'm told, and he leans back, throwing his arms out expansively, one landing behind my shoulder. He seems more relaxed again now, and I'm pleased.

'So what was it you wanted to discuss? Names? I was thinking . . . *Jake*,' he says.

'Oh!'

'What do you think? I've always liked it.'

'Jake,' I say. It doesn't really leave much impression on me, but I'm desperate to please him. 'Yes.'

I bite my lip. He leans back and closes his eyes. I shift towards him, until our bodies are pressed tightly together, hoping he'll take the hint. We sit in silence for a few minutes and then I lay my head on his shoulder.

'Food!' he says, moving away. 'What takeaway would you like? There's a Thai just down the road that's fairly decent . . .'

'Oh,' I say. 'If I'm honest, I'm quite full after lunch.'

'A cheeseboard then,' he says. 'Calcium and vitamin D, that will be good for you. Some olives? I'll go and see what's in the kitchen.'

I nod.

He disappears into the kitchen, leaving me alone on the sofa.

There's no denying what just happened. He pulled away from me.

He's not shy.

He just doesn't fancy me.

I look down at my lap. After all, why would he? I'm nearly forty. I'm socially awkward. My life is small, boring. I have nothing to say, nothing to offer. Only my music.

My only hope now is that once I have the baby, he'll see how perfect we are together. I just have to be patient. Fatherhood will change him. He'll see me in a different light too.

There's every chance once the baby is born, he'll fall in love with me and want us to live like a proper family. That's what happened to several couples who shared their stories on the app.

I have to stick to my plan and focus on the long game. That's my only hope now.

FAYE

The GP is smiling at me sympathetically as she discusses my treatment options. She hands me some leaflets. Apparently, there are many people who are in the same situation as me, who can help. At the end of her potted speech, she turns to me and asks me if I have any questions about my diagnosis.

Premature ovarian insufficiency.

The words seem suitably heavy and serious.

'Yes,' I say. 'Can I have a baby?'

She takes a deep breath.

'It's possible, yes. But the likelihood is that you will need to use donor eggs and fertility treatment.'

'Donor eggs?' I say, swallowing.

'I'm not an expert,' she says. 'But if having children is something you want to do, I'd suggest getting further advice. I can refer you, but the waiting list is pretty long. There's also your age to take into account. I'm afraid once you turn forty, you'll only be offered one cycle of IVF on the NHS, so you may want to consider getting advice from a private clinic.'

'It's fine,' I say. 'My partner and I were ... already investigating.'

'Is that what brought you to see me?' she says.

I nod.

'I was worried about the fact my periods had stopped. But I didn't expect . . . this.'

'I'm sure you have an awful lot of questions,' she says. 'There's plenty of support and advice available. But in the meantime, we'll get you started on some oestrogen-replacement HRT. As you are relatively young, we need to make sure we get your levels up to protect your health – women who go through early menopause are at risk of osteoporosis, as well as other conditions.'

I zone out as she tells me what she's prescribing, explaining that I have to take it for three months and see if my symptoms improve.

'Can I ask something else?' I say, when she finishes.

'Of course.'

'Why? Do you know why . . . I have this . . .'

She takes a deep breath.

'I read on the internet,' I say, 'that it can be caused by malnutrition. When I was younger . . . my father . . .'

I don't know how to put it into words. *My father was a sadist who withheld food as a punishment. I can't remember many days when I didn't go to bed hungry.*

'I didn't get a lot to eat when I was a child. I was very underweight throughout my teenage years. They tried to . . . my father convinced people that it was my fault, that I had an eating disorder, but it was him. He just didn't feed me.'

It's so basic, a human right. The bare minimum a parent should do for their child: feed them.

I start to cry.

'I'm sorry,' I say, spluttering into a tissue she offers me in haste. 'I'm sorry. I just . . . it's very hard to talk about . . .'

'I think it would be helpful if you had some counselling for this,' she says eventually, when I'm a little quieter. 'It sounds . . . horrific, what you went through, and I'm sure you could do with some support.'

'It's too late for that!' I sob. 'The damage has been done. Now I can't have children or a family of my own, and that's all I ever wanted.'

I stand and leave, before she has the chance to say anything else. It's not fair. Hannah has four healthy kids. Her mother was sensible enough to get away from our dad – Hannah only came to stay with us at the weekends, and when she did, he'd put on a cruel show, buying her all sorts of treats that I wasn't allowed. She was never malnourished. It can't be a coincidence that out of the two of us, I'm the one who's gone through the menopause prematurely.

What the hell am I going to tell Louis?

I stand in the cold street. The temperature has taken a turn for the worse and the wind feels like someone slapping me around the face.

You stupid cow! Did you really think you were just going to get it all? After what you did to me?

That voice in my head sounds like Marshall.

But it's not fair. It's not like I *meant* to kill him. If he hadn't been so drunk, he wouldn't have lost his footing so easily.

Even so, the sound his head made as it bounced down the concrete staircase has haunted me ever since.

Thump, thump, thump. Crack.

I don't remember much after that. Only the police, treating me like a devastated widow. Hannah arriving at my flat; the way her eyes widened and she simply shook her head at me as she pulled me towards her for a hug.

And another voice in my head, telling me that I wasn't a bad person. It was an accident.

But I have always felt like a bad person. Like a weirdo. An anomaly. A freak of nature. It wasn't normal the way I could play the piano. There was something wrong with me.

I was possessed. That's what my father believed. He once said he would starve the demons out of me.

I know, deep down, that he was mentally ill. That none of it was my fault. But even so, it turned out he was right.

I *was* a bad person. There can be no denying that I did a bad thing. I pushed Marshall down those stairs in anger. White-hot rage at the way he treated me.

I killed my own husband.

Later that evening, I am sitting at home, watching television and staring guiltily at my piano out of the corner of my eye.

All I can think about is Louis. What I'm going to tell him about my diagnosis.

I started looking it all up on the computer earlier. I began with the website the GP recommended to me, but before long, I had veered off-piste and was knee-deep in forums reading about other women's experiences of the early menopause.

None of it was good. It seems there's no way I can get away with not telling Louis my news. It will come out, whether I like it or not, when Dr Wright starts analysing the results of my blood tests.

I'll just have to be honest. There's nothing else for it. Be honest and hope that he understands it might be more difficult than we first thought.

It's not as though it makes much difference to Louis anyway. And it might actually be less traumatic for me, as I won't have to go through the rigmarole of stimulating my own ovaries and injecting myself with hormones.

I found one woman online who had managed to get pregnant while using donor eggs, so it's definitely a possibility. Just slightly more complicated, and expensive. Although money is not an issue for Louis anyway.

He'll understand. Won't he?

I stand up and switch the television off. Then I walk to the piano, opening the lid. I run my fingers across the ivory keys, and pull out the footstool. I remember my teacher when I was in my teens, telling me how impressed she was at my memory. I wanted to feel proud, but it came so easily that it didn't feel like much of an achievement.

I can play a piece through once, and then it's more or less burnt into my brain. A version of it, at least. Sometimes when I play things back, I realise I'm substituting notes that work equally as well. But the overall impression is the same. People are always impressed when I play.

In front of me is the music for *Peer Gynt*. 'In the Hall of the Mountain King'.

I start softly, the notes almost a distant echo, careful and slow. But of course, everyone knows how this piece goes — like so many popular classical pieces, it has been overplayed and ruined. And so I build the volume and the tempo until the end is just a muddy puddle of notes, thrown around my living room, and my wrists are sore and my fingertips ache.

I sit back on the stool at the end, slightly breathless.

And then I hear my phone ringing.

It's Louis.

NOW

RACHEL

It's time for the bonfire committee meeting. Tomorrow is the big day, and I've been liaising with the local police about their plans for stop-and-search.

More than one hundred children had alcohol confiscated from them last year. They think they're so clever, lacing bottles of Coke with vodka and expecting to get away with it. It gets worse every year. I don't know what's wrong with the parents of these children. They must know what their kids are doing – clearly they have no problem with their offspring breaking the law.

'I've written an updated alcohol policy,' I say, handing it to Nigel. 'For the website. I know it's a bit last-minute, but if you could get it typed up and put on there, I think that would be for the best, given that it's the young people who read the site. And you know, you could push it on the social networks.'

I look over at Felicity, the twenty-two-year-old media graduate who looks after that side of things.

Nigel glances down at it, nods.

'Well,' he says, scanning it. 'Thanks, Rachel. It's . . . great. I just think we could maybe tone it down a touch. So it doesn't feel like we're completely attacking the youth of today.

Threatening them with a night in the cells if they drink and they're under eighteen is a bit harsh.'

'Well, fine,' I say, sniffing. 'I just think you can't be too vague with this stuff. We need to set it out clearly – so that they understand before they come – that we have zero tolerance.'

'It's meant to be a welcoming, inclusive event,' says Brenda, the forty-something divorcee. She's relatively new to the village and has really pushed her way in. 'We don't want to vilify all teenagers because of the behaviour of a few.'

'One girl ended up nearly dying last year, thanks to alcohol poisoning,' I snap back. 'But yes, let's try the softly-softly approach again and see where that gets us.'

Nigel puts his hands up as if to stop us launching into fisticuffs.

'Right,' he says. 'Thanks, Rachel. I'll have a careful read through and I'm sure we can use this in some capacity, on the website at the very least. Now, what's next on the agenda . . .'

We rattle through the rest of the business, ending with a heated discussion over which time to close the road into the village before the procession. Too early and some residents struggle to make it back in time. Too late and all hell breaks loose.

I still haven't heard back from Louis Horton-Jones. I wonder if I got his email address right. Perhaps it was out of date. Perhaps he thought I was insane. I didn't give him any details. I just said I needed to talk to him about something important.

What still doesn't make any sense to me is why there've been no reports of a missing baby in the news.

I've racked my brains, but I can't get to the bottom of it at all. Is Fiona's real name Faye? If not, then who is Faye, and why did Fiona have her menopause medication in her bag?

Perhaps she stole the bag, and didn't realise the bank cards and the medication were in there.

I really hope this Louis replies. I need to work out what's going on and I can't trust Fiona to give me a straight answer.

When the meeting ends, I leave the hall without saying goodbye and cross the green. The bonfire frame is finished now, rising tall and majestic across the village. Soon it will be ablaze, lighting the sky for miles around.

Despite myself, I'm excited. The evening holds a special significance for me, after all. It's always been a celebration, of sorts.

When I get home, I call out for Fiona but she doesn't answer. She's not in her room either.

I'm confused. The pram is gone. Perhaps she took Jake for a walk. Sometimes when he's unsettled, pushing him in his pram helps him to fall asleep. I call her phone but she doesn't answer.

I log back on to my computer and load up my emails. But still nothing. I start searching again, trying to find a phone number for Louis Horton-Jones online. But there's only the number for the head office.

It's late. Nearly 9pm. I call it and get a recorded message telling me that the office is closed until the morning.

I send another email, just in case, leaving my phone number and address this time, so that he can tell I'm legitimate.

Please contact me. I need to speak to you urgently about a private matter. I'm not a time-waster, but this is not something I want to go into via email.

Rachel Morris

Laleham Cottage

Helston

Norfolk

07000 345984

I don't entirely know what I will say to him, but I know that this situation can't continue. I have to think of Jake, what's best for him. Fiona has been wandering around the house in a state of undress, humming to herself. She forgets to eat. I have to make food for her, and sit with her and force her to eat it.

She rambles on and on about what a terrible mistake she's made. How Jake doesn't love her.

I want to shake her and tell her that she's lucky to have this chance. The opportunity to be a mother at all.

Because I didn't.

Brian was stolen from me when I was just fifteen, and he still doesn't know that he's mine. He still thinks I'm just his big sister.

She eventually comes home at nearly 10pm. It started to rain about half an hour ago, and she's drenched by the time she comes in. Drenched and shivering, her hair hanging in dark tendrils by her face.

'Thank God you're back,' I say, standing up as she pushes the pram into the front room. I don't even care that the wheels are caked with mud, leaving great marks on my parquet flooring. She's had the foresight to put the waterproof cover on the pram at least, so that Jake is dry.

'Where on earth have you been?' I can't hide my temper.

'I don't know,' she says, staring at me, dead behind the eyes. 'I was trying to get him to sleep. I pushed him and pushed him and pushed him. It was the only way to stop him crying. Then we got lost.'

I ignore her and wrench the cover from the pram. Jake is tucked up snugly, both hands thrown up beside his head, his eyes fixed shut. I touch his forehead lightly. He's warm, but not too warm.

'You must be frozen to death,' I say to Fiona. I sigh. 'For goodness' sake. I'll run you a bath.'

We leave Jake asleep in the pram. I pour a good glug of my bath foam into the bath and turn the water on hot.

'Here,' I say, handing her a fresh towel from the airing cupboard. 'Get in and warm up. I'll make you something to eat.'

She nods.

I leave her to it and go back downstairs to check on Jake. He's still asleep, and I unzip the cover of the pram and change his nappy as quickly as I can, trying not to wake him up. Thankfully, he seems fine.

I check my email again while I wait for the kettle to boil. But nothing. No reply from Louis, just a message from Nigel telling me that he's uploaded my alcohol policy to the bonfire website.

I don't reply to him. I'm too agitated.

Instead, I turn my computer off, wait to hear the sound of the bathwater draining, and take Fiona up her hot drink and some cheese on toast.

She's in her bedroom, pyjamas already on.

'Here,' I say, handing her the drink. 'Bovril. That will warm you up.'

'Thanks,' she says again, but the distant look in her eyes is more pronounced than ever. She stares down at the plate of toast in front of her.

'You need to eat that. Really, Fiona, you'll make yourself ill.'

She nods.

'Jake is still asleep downstairs,' I say. 'He's fine.'

Nothing.

'Well, it's getting late,' I say. 'I'll bring Jake up to you, shall I?'

'I really thought he would love me,' she says, after a long pause. 'I thought we were going to be a family.'

I take a step forward towards her.

'Who? Louis?'

She nods, sinking onto the bed.

'I really loved him,' she says. 'But he made a fool out of me. That's what everyone does. Makes a fool out of me.'

'You're not making sense. You need to get some sleep,' I say. 'It'll all seem better in the morning.'

I consider asking her who Faye Miller is. But if I ask, then she'll know that I've been in her room, and looked through her things. Personally, I think privacy is overrated, and that it's only fair for me to know who I'm sharing a home with, but other people can be funny about it.

'He was so charming to begin with,' she says, but I can tell she's not really talking to me. She's just thinking aloud. Getting it all out. 'He took me to the opera, to meet his family, but it was all a ruse. He was putting on a show for them, and using me as part of the act. I thought the reason we didn't see each other much was just because he was so busy with work. But really, he was never interested in me at all. He just used me . . . he just chewed me up – and when I didn't taste how he wanted, he spat me out . . .'

I try to make sense of her words. Is she telling me that he just didn't care about his child? Perhaps that's why he's ignoring my emails.

But we've been through this. If that was the case, then surely she wouldn't have needed to run away?

She stares up at me, as if remembering I'm in the room. Her hand swipes across one eye, removing the tear.

'I'm really tired,' she says eventually. Her voice, just seconds before so passionate and animated, now sounds robotic and detached. 'I think I should try to get some rest. Thank you for the food.'

I pause. She hasn't mentioned Jake. It's as though she forgets he's even here sometimes.

Never mind. He has me. We'll do just fine without her.

'Of course,' I say. 'Goodnight.'

FAYE

I can't stop dreaming about her.

Jake's mother.

Fiona.

It feels as though she's in the room with me, right now. She started out far away, in the distant corner, but then gradually she moved closer to me, until she climbed onto the bed itself and sat on my chest.

And that's where she is now.

She isn't speaking, she's just staring at me, her eyes becoming wider and wider until her head is all eyes. Eyes that are like black holes, sucking me in, destroying me.

I am frozen in the bed, the weight of her body on my chest, and then she stands up, one leg either side of my body, and I see that she is bleeding. Blood pours out of her, soaking me, the bed, and then the whole room, until we are both swimming in her blood.

We are going to drown in it.

But then I wake up, gasping for breath.

Jake isn't in the cot beside me. Where is he?

I am alone, and it's the middle of the night and the flowery curtains still hang at the windows and the air is still, and I realise it wasn't real. Just another dream. Another bad dream.

Even so. There's something not right about this house. About Rachel. There are ghosts here. I can feel them. The ghosts of the women who shared this room before me.

And Rachel. *The Witch*. People in the village, they don't trust her. There must be a reason for it. Something she's done.

She's been so kind to me, but it's all too good to be true. Why haven't I learnt my lesson by now? These people, who say they love and want to spend time with me, they're all the same. They're all tricking me. Using me for their own ends.

I tiptoe out of the room and listen in at Rachel's door. He is in there with her, I'm sure of it. She wants him for her own.

What was in the drink she gave me? It's the second time she's given me something that's knocked me out completely. She must be drugging me, it's the only explanation. I haven't felt right since I arrived here.

I remember how confident I was when I scooped Jake up out of that car, bundling him up inside my scarf. How right it felt, to be taking my baby back. The baby I should have had. The baby he was going to pass off as mine.

And I wanted to hurt him too. The way he had hurt me.

But that certainty – that split-second decision which felt so right at the time – began to dissipate as soon as I got on the train to Norfolk. As soon as I looked down at Jake's face and didn't see my own reflected back at me. And ever since I arrived here, with lovely, kind Rachel, who on the surface has been so good and caring, I've lost a little more confidence every day.

She's been making me feel worse about myself, not better. And now I see why. It's all part of her plan!

She wants Jake for herself.

The pram is still blocking the front door in the living room, but otherwise, the room is neat and tidy as always. She's obsessed with tidiness. And cleanliness. She's constantly cleaning up after me. Even though she thinks I don't notice, I do. I've seen the way she washes Jake's bottles up again, after I've done them.

She doesn't trust me. She thinks I'm hopeless. And I've started to believe it too, but I'm not.

I'm not hopeless.

It's all her. Undermining me.

I walk around the front room, staring at everything. The weird brass dogs that stand proudly at each end of the fireplace. The gold carriage clock that stands in the middle of the mantelpiece, in front of a painting of some lilies. The neat pile of wood on the hearth. She lights a fire every night, prodding it with a brass poker and muttering to herself.

The Chinese rug, with the tasselled edges, and the sofa still encased in plastic.

She doesn't leave anything out. She doesn't even have a pile of magazines or post or a pair of discarded spectacles on a side table, like most people.

I walk through the back to the tiny kitchen, staring out at the garden.

The crazy, overgrown garden. Why aren't we allowed to use it? She doesn't even let her beloved cat go out there. What is she hiding in all that wilderness? I want to see for myself.

I try the handle but the back door is locked and there's no sign of the key that was there last time I opened it. I stare out of the glass at the dark jungle of weeds behind.

I turn back to the kitchen. It's immaculate, as always. Nothing is ever left out on the counter. Just the kettle and a rack on the draining board, the dishcloth wrung out and folded neatly over the side of it.

I open cupboards, looking for the key. Mugs in one, glasses in another, crockery in another. Then the larder cupboard with tins lined up in order of size, their labels always front-facing like they are in the supermarkets.

Last Christmas Hannah gave me a fake baked beans tin that you could hide valuables in. Perhaps one of these is like that?

I start to take them all out, to get to the ones at the back, but they're all heavy. Just beans and soup. No key.

I put them back slowly, sighing.

The final cupboard is the one under the sink – just cleaning products, but as I reach further back, I find something tucked sideways behind the U-bend.

A metal box, with a pretty picture of a swan on the lid.

I frown. Why is this box in the cupboard with the limescale remover and Marigolds?

It's heavy. I sit on the floor in the kitchen, the lino cold through my pyjama bottoms. Then I lift the lid.

The first thing I notice are the scissors. Dressmaker scissors, but old. I pick them up, feeling their weight in my hand, slotting my fingers through the handles and opening them in front of my face.

There's a stain on one of the blades. Rust. I peer at it.

No. Not rust. Something else.

I put the scissors down, frowning.

The next thing I notice in the box is a plastic key ring. On one side is the logo for a theme park. I turn it over, finding it hard to believe that someone like Rachel goes to theme parks.

But on the other side there's a picture of a young couple, screaming their heads off on a rollercoaster.

I don't recognise them. There's a single key attached to the key ring. I try it, but it's the wrong shape for the back door.

I put it down next to the scissors, and turn back to the box. The next thing inside is a mauve leather glove. It's old and worn, soft under my fingers.

Under that, there's a small leather pouch. Inside is a miniature photo album, with space for three pictures. One of the pictures is black and white, a couple sitting in the garden. The other two are passport photographs – one of a middle-aged man, the other a middle-aged woman. I have no idea who these people are.

But then, there's something I recognise. A soft cotton hat. I pick it up, confused. It's the hat Jake was wearing the day I took him from the car, I'm sure of it. White, with a small embroidered sheep on the front. I thought we'd lost it somewhere on the journey up here.

But no. Somehow, it's ended up in this box, underneath Rachel's sink.

She's stolen it from me. Do all these things belong to other people too?

I look back in the box, and pick out a plain gold ring. It

looks like a wedding band or similar. I hold it up, squinting in the darkness to try to read the inscription on the inside.

Elizabeth and Ray

Who were Elizabeth and Ray? Why does Rachel have one of their rings?

I'm so confused. I slump into myself, looking at the strange collection of things around me. They are all personal items. Mementoes.

Apart from the scissors.

There's an envelope at the bottom of the box. Cream, heavyweight. I take it out and open it. Inside, there are some photographs, faded with age. A baby, sitting on a woman's knee. The baby is dressed in full knitwear, round in the face. The woman looks stern.

I turn the photograph over.

Brian and Mum, 1962

Brian, Rachel's son. Although he doesn't call her mum, and the woman in this picture is definitely not Rachel.

There's another photograph. The same baby, lying flat on his back in a maroon pram. On the back someone has written: *Brian, Summer 1962.*

I put the photographs down. I don't understand the connection with the other items in the box.

Inside the envelope there's a piece of paper. I pull it out, read what's written on it.

Elizabeth: September 1995 to August 1997

Heather: September 1997 to March 1998

Abigail: April 1998 to June 1999

The names and dates go on and on, filling the piece of paper and spilling onto the back.

I turn it over.

And then I see the last two names on the list: Kylie's, then Fiona's.

The name I borrowed.

I look back at the box, pick up the ring again, running my finger over the inscription. This is Elizabeth's, then, but what about all the other things? Which of these belongs to which woman?

How could she steal things from all these women? And why would she?

The scissors glisten at me in the moonlight.

Why would you keep a pair of dirty old scissors?

I pick them up again, run my finger along the stain, lifting it to my nose to sniff. And that's when I realise it's definitely not rust.

It's blood.

RACHEL

Daisy wakes me up, padding across the bed and putting a paw to my face. Jake is fast asleep in the bassinet beside me. I couldn't leave him with Fiona. Not when she's so unstable.

'For goodness' sake,' I mutter to Daisy. I love her, but she's infuriating. She doesn't seem to understand boundaries, despite me repeatedly trying to explain them to her.

It's my fault. I must have left my bedroom door ajar.

My head feels heavy as I lift it. I attempt to push her off, but she keeps springing back onto the bed and nudging me with her paw.

'I should have shut you in the cupboard under the stairs,' I hiss, but she hisses back. 'What is it? What on earth do you want at this ungodly hour?'

This ungodly hour is nearly 4am.

'For goodness' sake,' I say, but she simply sits down in front of me and starts licking a paw, as though waiting for me to do her bidding. 'Right, fine. It's food you want, I presume? But then I'm locking you in for the rest of the night. I can't have this at my age, Daisy. I really can't.'

It's exhausting enough dealing with Fiona and Jake.

I climb out of bed and pull on my dressing gown.

'Come on then,' I say, my voice cross, but I lean down to stroke her flat ears and she purrs, looking up at me. I melt. She has me wrapped round her paw.

It's a new thing, this nocturnal hunger. I spoke to the vet who said it might just be because she's getting older. But even so, it's far from ideal.

The vet suggested leaving out extra food when I go to bed, but he doesn't know Daisy. They say cats aren't scavengers, but she is. She'd eat that the second I set it down and then still come and wake me up for more.

On the landing, I look across to Fiona's room. The door is slightly open. I peer round the corner. She's not in her bed.

I look over at the bathroom. The door is wide open, the room dark and empty.

A cold fear takes hold of me. Has she run off? Done something to herself?

I think about Kylie. All that blood.

Brian is right. I shouldn't invite these women into my home. These damaged, difficult women. It's too much for me.

Daisy nudges at my leg. I had forgotten all about her.

'Right,' I whisper into the darkness.

I'm nervous about going downstairs, and of what I might find. I love this house, but I hate it too. Everywhere I look there are memories; some ancient, others more recent. The sight of Kylie, lying at the bottom of the stairs. The blood spilling out of her, staining my carpet.

The way the scissors felt in my hand.

I give myself a little shake and head down the stairs. I'm being ridiculous, but even so, I find myself tiptoeing. I know these stairs intimately. Know exactly which stairs creak. I used to lie in bed when I was a child, waiting for the sound of his footfall. He was a heavy man, and so were his footsteps.

Each step made a different sound, had a different timbre. I would count them down in my mind, knowing when he had reached the top. And then, I'd hear him creak across the landing, and I'd dive under my blankets in fright.

He's long gone. But there's someone else in my house now. Someone else I can't completely trust.

I peer over the banister as I inch my way down the staircase. Despite the dark, there's a full moon tonight and the light from the bay window illuminates the small space.

I search with my eyes until I find her.

There she is. Sitting on the floor in the kitchen, with her back to the stairs. She's still. Not moving. Hunched over something in her lap.

Not bleeding at least.

Not crying either.

What is she doing?

I take another step closer, then another, and another, until I am right behind her.

I look over her shoulder, and I see the box in her lap. The collection scattered around the kitchen floor. The photos of Brian as a baby, tossed to one side.

Worst of all, I see the list, in my own handwriting. The only record I've ever kept of my lodgers.

She is poring over it. She will be wondering: who are these women? What are these things? And why are they in this box?

And then I see the hat. Jake's little snow-white baby hat.

I only put it in there earlier today. Stupid.

I stand frozen. What can I do? What can I say?

But I don't have a chance to think, because Daisy grows impatient and miaows loudly and angrily at me.

And then Fiona turns. She sees me there and I watch as her whole body convulses in shock and surprise.

'What . . .' she begins. 'When did you . . . ?'

Briefly, I imagine the sight I must make in the darkness, as I loom over her. My hair pinned up in its net. My pink velvet dressing gown gaping open to reveal my floral nightie. I have never been a slender girl.

And now, I'm aware more than ever of my size in relation to Fiona. She's so slight, so insubstantial, so pathetic. Barely even here. Just a collection of frail body parts, sitting on the floor.

I don't want to play this role, but enough is enough. She has crossed a line, and there's no going back.

I brace myself, pulling my shoulders back so that I stand even taller. And then I speak, my voice low, the way his used to be.

There's never any need to shout, he would say. *Keep your voice quiet. That's what unsettles them. It's unsettling you, isn't it?*

Her eyes are wide in the moonlight. Deep and terrified as she stares at me.

'What exactly do you think you are doing?' I say.

FAYE

I'd never given much thought before to the way Rachel looks. But seeing her standing over me like this, the clear view I have straight up her flared nostrils, makes me wince.

She is horrifying.

'I . . .' I say, scrabbling away from her on the floor. 'I was just looking for something and . . .'

'What exactly were you looking for in the cleaning cupboard in the middle of the night?'

Her eyes are narrow; they bore into mine. She looks like a wolf. I imagine her reaching forward, her mouth open wide, and swallowing me whole.

I begin to shake. This house. It's all wrong. Everything in it is wrong. I should never have come here. She wants Jake. She wants Jake and she wants me gone.

'I spilt . . . something . . .' I say. 'In my room.'

She stares at me. I look away and start shoving all the things back into the metal box. But as my fingers hunt around on the floor beside me, they fall onto the little white hat. Jake's hat.

A wave of courage rushes over me.

'Why did you have this?' I say, holding it up to her face. 'It's Jake's. He was wearing it when . . .'

When I took him.

'When we got here.'

She wrinkles her nose, looks at the hat.

'I found it outside the house,' she says. 'Months ago, before you arrived.'

This floors me. Is she going to try to claim this is some sort of lost property box? I stare at her.

She takes a step towards me and leans down, picking up the box and closing the lid firmly.

'What is all that stuff?' I say. I don't know why I'm asking. Clearly, there's something not right about her, and I'm trapped here in her house. Vulnerable.

The blood on the scissors. Whose was that?

'It's none of your business,' she says. 'Just old family things. I'd appreciate it if you didn't go rummaging through my belongings. As my lodger, I need to be able to trust you.'

Her tone is strange. She's playing me. My head begins to ache. I'm hot again, even though I'm only in my pyjamas. I want to unbutton my top and throw it off. It feels sticky against my skin, under my armpits. Sticky and disgusting.

Does she know I saw the list? The list of names, ending in the one I borrowed?

'I'm sorry,' I say, biding for time. 'I was looking for carpet cleaner.'

'In the middle of night?' she says, sighing. 'I don't think you're well, Fiona. I think perhaps you need to see a doctor. The postnatal period can be incredibly overwhelming. There are all sorts of unfortunate conditions. And really, your behaviour. It's not normal.'

'My behaviour isn't normal?' A warning voice creeps into my head again. *Don't lose it. Stay in control. You can't afford to blow your life up again.* 'What about your behaviour? What about all these creepy things in this box? Who do they belong to?'

'I told you,' she says, shaking her head at me as though I'm a misbehaving child. 'They're things from my family.'

'But that's not true. I don't believe you. I saw Kylie's name on the list . . . she was the lodger before me, the woman in the chemist said! She ended up in an ambulance! And what's with the scissors? Why do they have blood on them? What happened to all these women?'

'Nothing happened to them,' she says. 'These are just things they left behind when they moved out.'

'So they weren't family things, then?' I say, my mind suddenly sharply in focus. 'That was a lie.'

'All of my lodgers have been like family to me,' she says softly. 'And those scissors were my mother's. She was a dressmaker.'

Daisy miaows impatiently in my face. She has never liked me. I thought cats were meant to be friendly.

I think of Rachel's nickname. *The Witch.*

Rachel takes a deep breath and then walks past me and towards the kitchen cupboards. She reaches up and pulls out the Go-Cat box, pouring a small amount into Daisy's bowl.

'That's enough for you,' she says sternly. 'No one likes a fat pussycat.'

The metal box is sitting on the kitchen counter next to the sink, the white hat soft in my hand.

'Why did you have a list in there? Why did you keep a record of everyone like that?'

She shakes her head.

'I'm disappointed in you, Fiona,' she says. 'I thought . . . I hoped . . . I've grown so fond of your little boy. I thought we could create a home together. All three of us. That we could build a strong relationship. Something that would last. But you haven't been honest with me, not from the start. Louis never abused you. You faked that black eye. So what's the real story? He just didn't want to know? Wasn't interested in becoming a father? He didn't want to be tied down, did he? Did you trick him? Trap him into having that baby?'

'No!' I shout. My hands are shaking. I stare at her in the moonlight. How dare she? 'That's not it at all. Louis wanted a baby more than . . . more than anything!'

'If that's the case, then what went wrong?'

'He . . .'

'What?' she says, coming closer. 'Tell me the truth, Fiona. I've done everything I can for you. I've taken you in, looked after you both. I deserve the truth.'

'*You* deserve the truth? What about me? You're lying about this box . . . these things. And where's Jake? What have you done with him?'

'Jake is asleep upstairs. The state you were in yesterday, how could I trust you with him? Look at you, you're pathetic. You can't even look after yourself.'

'How dare you! Ever since I got here, you've been undermining me, trying to take Jake away from me, convincing me that I wasn't fit to be his mother. And it's worked! There's something creepy in this house . . . and now this box – full of things you've *stolen* from people. Everyone was right about you! You're evil.'

'No!' she says, her voice low. 'Fiona. You're not well. You need help.'

'I don't need help from you! You're a creepy old woman who nobody loves! I should never have come here.'

She takes a step forward as if to grab my arms, and in a rush of anger I push her away from me as hard as I can.

It's just the same as with Marshall, except that time it was down those concrete steps and he was laughing at me as I pushed him, laughing right up until the second when he saw that I meant it, that I wasn't going to stop, that the force inside me was uncontainable.

It was only then that his face turned from laughter to something else, a wide-eyed look of surprise as he freewheeled backwards down the steps, arms flailing pointlessly to try to grab for something – but there was nothing to grab, no handles or banisters outside the pub, and nothing but cold hard stone to break his fall.

I open my eyes. I hadn't even known they were closed. Rachel is lying in front of me, in a heap on the floor.

What have I done?

Oh God. Not again. Not again.

FAYE

I stare down at her crumpled shape.

Daisy deftly picks her way around Rachel's body, then leaps up onto the work surface – a forbidden manoeuvre – and nudges over the Go-Cat box that Rachel hadn't yet put away. The contents spill out onto the work surface and the floor, and she miaows satisfaction at herself, burying her face in the brown biscuits.

It's the first time I've really lost my temper since that night with Marshall.

You think I married you because I loved you? You stupid cow. It's a marriage of convenience. For us both, if you're honest about it. After all, who'd want to marry you?

Even though on some level I suppose I had known. I had always known that Hannah was his first choice. After all, Marshall was Reuben's father. Everyone thought it was weird when we got together. Incestuous. But even so, I didn't expect that.

Not on the happiest day of my life. I had spent so long looking for that dress. I had loved him ever since Hannah first brought him home. He was so cool, so talented, so comfortable in his own skin. What did it matter that my sister didn't want to come to the wedding? She was just jealous that he had picked me over her. Or so I thought.

She tried to warn me that he was just using me to get to her after they broke up, but I didn't want to listen.

Listen, little sister, I married you because it was the only way to stay in their lives. Hannah wants to cut me out. Stop me from seeing my own son! Well, she can't. And I'm going to be in their lives forever now. Whether they like it or not.

It turned out Marshall was the one who was jealous. Not Hannah.

He was high as a kite the night of our wedding. He could often be nasty when he was on something. He liked to poke fun at me. I didn't mind. I was used to it, and some attention was better than none.

He was the only man who had ever paid me attention before.

But this time, I could see he really meant it. He was proud as a peacock, laughing at his success. He had trapped me. Trapped us both. He thought I was too weak, too pathetic, to leave him.

It broke me. I was sobbing in his face when he laughed at me.

Cheer up, Faye! It won't be so bad. We'll both get something out of this little arrangement, won't we? I've always liked the idea of being with sisters, you know . . .

And then, just like tonight, something switched. My devastation turned to anger. The visceral sense of unfairness overtook me. Hannah had always had everything I wanted.

And that was when I pushed him.

Not that hard. But hard enough.

And now, I've done the same to her. Except this time there are no stone steps. There's just a linoleum kitchen floor, and an old lady lying at my feet.

It's not her fault. But she kept pushing and poking me. There's only so much I can take.

What am I going to do?

RACHEL

When I wake up, it takes me a moment to work out where I am, and what has happened to me.

My eyes peel open slowly, and I look around the room. I'm in my bedroom. It's morning. It must be, because there's light creeping under the edges of my curtains.

I sit up. My head is throbbing and my throat is dry. I don't remember what happened. Fiona and I had a fight. And then what?

I don't remember coming to bed.

She pushed me over! But then . . . then there's nothing. Just a blank, unwritten page in my memory.

My head is full of different memories. And that's when I realise – I have been dreaming of the night my parents found out that I was pregnant.

'How could you do this to us?' Mother said, when I couldn't hide it any longer.

It hurt Mother more, I know, because she wasn't able to have any more children after I was born. Something went wrong – I was the wrong size or shape as a baby – and I broke her. She never got over that.

And then I got pregnant.

She had a triumphant look on her face when she told me they had made a plan.

'You should be grateful, Rachel,' she said. 'For getting you out of the mess you are in. You're lucky. Lucky you have us. That we've found a way to make it work.'

I glanced over at Father.

I didn't feel lucky. I didn't feel lucky at all.

'We'll take the baby on,' she said. 'Say that it's mine. We will go away and stay with your Auntie Vi while you get . . .' She paused, swallowing. 'Bigger. And you'll have the baby in the hospital down there. We'll explain to everyone in the village that my pregnancy has made me very sick, and so I'm having to spend the duration in hospital, being taken care of. Then, once it's born, we'll come back.'

'But won't people wonder where I've gone?' I asked, but deep down I didn't care. I worked out the dates in my head: six months of not seeing him. But what would happen when we got back? Perhaps things would be different.

'I'll tell them where you've gone, of course,' she said. 'I'll explain that while I'm in hospital, your father can't be expected to look after you as well as work, so your Auntie Vi will be.'

She had it all worked out. It made me feel sick.

'What do you say?' she said, into my silent face.

'Thank you,' I replied, because that was what she wanted to hear. And I was thankful, in a way. Auntie Violet was kind and funny. And perhaps if I was good, and behaved myself, then I wouldn't have to come back. Perhaps Auntie Vi would let me stay there forever.

'You're a lucky girl to have such understanding parents,' Mother said, and I realised my gratitude wasn't enough. 'Most girls would be thrown out in disgrace if they came home pregnant at your age. And it's a good job you won't tell us who the father is, because *your* father would beat him black and blue.'

I looked at Father then, quickly, but he had opened his newspaper, started to read.

I didn't think about the baby. What he or she would mean to me. I didn't expect to feel anything for it. I just wanted the whole thing over with and for it to all go away.

But then, at Auntie Violet's house, I started to get bigger. And bigger and bigger and bigger. And Mother would look at me, pulling a face, as I heaved myself up from the couch, or strained to do up the buttons on my cardigan.

She only made me two dresses, when I was too big to fit into any of my normal clothes, and I alternated wearing them. I was so sick of them both by the end that I wanted to burn them.

Mother and I had never been particularly close. She wasn't warm like Auntie Vi. She provided for me; she fed me and clothed me and helped me with my homework. I got a present at Christmas. But she never told me she loved me. She never kissed or hugged me. She was always distant, distracted, a life spent tiptoeing around Father.

I imagined when she looked at me she was always thinking of what I had cost her: the big family she so longed for.

And now, it felt like she hated me. She was so jealous of my pregnancy and the fact I could grow a life inside me, when she no longer could.

Brian's birth was traumatic. I don't remember much – only that he got stuck and then the place went mad with people and they put me to sleep and had to cut him out of me in the end. When I came round from the anaesthetic, Mother was sitting beside my bed, Brian in her arms. She was cooing at him, tickling him under the chin, kissing his soft head.

'It's a boy,' she said.

'Can I see him?' I said weakly, because I still felt woozy and strange.

Our eyes met and she beamed at me, and I felt it then – the feeling of love that I'd so longed for from her, all my young life. She leaned towards the bed and lowered Brian a little so that I could see him.

He looked angry, like a grumpy old man.

'A beautiful, healthy boy,' she said. 'Well done.'

'My stomach hurts,' I said. 'Can I have some water?'

She frowned at me, but only for a second.

'Of course,' she said, as if remembering that I was her child too. 'I'll fetch a nurse.'

She laid Brian down in the small cot next to me and left us alone. I looked over at him. He was tightly swaddled, bundled up like a glow-worm, with just that angry little face, eyes closed, visible.

I leaned over – with some difficulty, as my stomach felt as though it wasn't attached to the rest of my body any longer – and I stroked his tiny cheek. It was the softest thing I had ever felt. It was almost unreal.

'Hello, baby,' I said. 'I'm your . . .'

I was going to say big sister, because that's what I'd been

coached to say, by Auntie Vi and Mother, but I found the words sticking in my throat.

'I'm your mummy,' I whispered, as though I was committing some terrible transgression.

I had never called my mother Mummy. Lots of my friends did for their mothers, but when I said it to her once, my mother frowned and corrected me. *Mummies are for babies.*

Well, he was a baby.

I stroked his cheek with my finger, up and down, ever so softly, right until Mother came back into the room.

'Your father's decided,' she said, handing me a glass of water. 'His name will be Brian.'

Brian.

I didn't like it. It sounded like an old man's name to me. But I was too tired and too scared to say anything, so I just nodded.

'You need to get some rest,' she said. 'I just wanted to show you the baby. The midwife will take him into the nursery now.'

'My chest feels strange,' I said, as she turned to leave. 'It's achey and heavy.'

She wrinkled her nose at me, in that way she did.

'I suppose it's your milk,' she said, as though it was something distasteful. 'I'll speak to someone to see if there's something they can do. Now, get some sleep. You need to recover. I'm going to need lots of help now I have my little Brian.'

She leaned over and kissed him on the forehead, then smiled briskly and left the room.

No kiss for me. But Brian was still there, and I stroked his cheek again until I fell asleep.

I realised then that I loved him. I had felt nothing for him while he was growing in my tummy, apart from irritation when he kicked and woke me up, or when he gave me heartburn.

But when I saw him lying there in the cot beside me, his tiny face scrunched right up, I felt something I had never felt before. An absolute devotion to this perfect creature, and the determination that he would feel differently from me as he grew up.

The first time I heard him cry, it went straight to my heart. I remember trying to reach for him, but Mother got there first, scooping him up and turning away from me.

I remember the sound his crying made. It's the same sound I can hear now.

But it's Jake who's crying, not Brian.

Where is Fiona?

How did I get up here? I remember the fight, Fiona pushing me, and then . . .

I glance up at the clock on the wall. It's 3.28pm! The light I can see under the curtains is actually the sun beginning to set. It's Friday. Bonfire Night.

My stomach growls. How can I have been asleep for so long?

I remember now. She was looking through my box when we had that fight, asking me why I kept those things.

I shouldn't have lost my temper. I made everything worse. She didn't seem to understand that all my lodgers feel like family to me. I wanted to have something left of them when they moved out. Because they didn't all feel the same way. Some of them found me annoying, I know that. Some of them found me pernickety and fussy and boring. Some of them liked me, but only in small doses. I could see the way their eyes would glaze over when I tried to talk to them about something I was interested in. How they would make their excuses and take their cup of tea up to their room to drink it alone.

I have been so lonely. My whole life. Ever since my parents stole Brian from me.

And now, Jake is crying the way Brian used to. But no one is going to him. No one is helping him. So, even though it might not be my place to, I will.

I walk to my bedroom door and try to open it, but I can't. I rattle the handle, confused. But it won't budge.

And that's when I realise.

Fiona has locked me in.

FAYE

Dragging Rachel up the stairs was almost impossible. She weighed an absolute ton, and now my back is killing me as well as my head. But I had to get her out of the way so that I could buy some time to think.

Once she was in her bed, I put her in the recovery position so that hopefully when she came round, she would be OK. I checked that she was still breathing, and she was. Perhaps she would wake up and not remember what had happened.

Perhaps it would all be OK.

And then I remembered: I had forgotten to take off her dressing gown when I put her back in her bed.

She would know that was strange. I locked her room from the outside, just in case. Just to give me some time to work out a plan. Who knew what she was capable of?

I fed Jake, then set him down for a nap in our room, in his cot.

I went downstairs, and I cleared up the mess in the kitchen. I spent the rest of the day pacing round the living room, trying to think, as the sun rose and began to fall again.

Now I'm running out of time. I have to make a decision.

It's getting dark again, and from the living room window

I can see the village green is already alive with people, all crowded round that fucking bonfire, attending to it as though it were a wedding cake for a royal couple or something.

I think Rachel mentioned she had another meeting with the bonfire committee this morning. A final run-through before the festivities tonight. At one point the house telephone rings, but I don't pick up. It's probably them, wondering where she's got to.

I consider calling Hannah, but I don't think she'd come through for me again. And anyway, she's miles away now.

Right after Marshall fell down those stairs, I went to her flat. She hadn't been at our wedding. She had tried to talk me out of it beforehand, right up until the last minute, telling me that he didn't love me.

'Please, Faye!' she said, practically crying. 'I wouldn't lie to you! He's an arsehole. He's just using you to get to me and Reuben. Trying to make me jealous, trying to make my life difficult. You know what he's like. Please!'

But I didn't want to hear it.

'You're just saying this to hurt me!' I shouted. 'You never want me to have anything good!'

Hannah had always had it easier than me. It wasn't fair. I wanted to believe Marshall, not her. I was stupid, naive, blinded by my own love. My own gratitude.

He was standing outside the back of the pub when it happened. I'd gone out to find him. Our meagre collection of friends had drifted away from our post-wedding 'celebration' in the pub. Most had only come for the free bar. He'd hardly spoken to me all day, and I was so pleased when I found him there, smoking, at the top of the fire escape.

341

I can hardly bear to think about what happened next. The way he pawed at me, drunkenly laughing to himself at what a success it had all been. How he'd managed to fool us all.

And afterwards, when he lay in a twisted heap at the bottom of the steps, I had nowhere to turn. I didn't know what to do. So I ran to Hannah's and told her she was right, as always. My big sister. She would make it all better.

After Marshall fell, I had slipped down the stairs, stepping over his body and out through the beer garden at the back. There was no CCTV at the pub. No one even knew I'd been there.

They would assume he just fell because he was drunk. And that's what they did. I couldn't believe there wasn't a proper investigation, that they didn't come after me. But everyone believed it was just a tragic accident.

His own fault, for being so inebriated.

I got away with it then. But would I get away with it again?

'Think, think, think!' I hiss to myself.

I consider ringing Jonas, but he never even called me back after the last time.

Upstairs, Jake has started to cry.

I glance up at the ceiling. I can hear something else: movement. Is she awake?

What the hell am I going to do? How am I going to explain it all?

I think of Rachel's box – the bloodstained scissors – and the way she stood over me, the fury in her eyes. And then, the way the chemist sounded when she asked where Kylie had gone. Something about an ambulance.

What happened to all her previous lodgers? Did she do something to them? Why does she have a box full of mementos?

When serial killers keep things, they're called trophies.

I start to shake. There's no getting away from it: I have to leave the village. I have to go. Now.

If I leave during the bonfire, hopefully nobody will notice me. I can lose myself in the crowd.

I go to the kitchen, open the drawers and take out the vegetable knife. Just in case. It's not big, but it's better than nothing. I secrete the handle up the sleeve of my top. Then I grab my coat and throw some things into a bag.

Jake has really started to build up some steam now. He's properly wailing. I picture his pinched little face, bright red with the effort, his uvula vibrating with the force of it.

I hesitate for a moment, one foot on the bottom stair. She won't hurt Jake, I'm sure of it. She loves him.

And I don't have any choice. I have to leave him.

After all, he was never mine to take in the first place.

RACHEL

I can't get this door open. I can't get to Jake.

I rattle and rattle it.

Where is she? Why isn't she taking care of him? Has she just left us both here?

No, surely not.

If she'd done that, why would she have locked me in? It doesn't make any sense.

'Fiona!' I call, thumping on the door. 'Fiona, let me out! For goodness' sake!'

But nothing. There's no response and Jake's screaming is getting even more intense. That poor mite. He'll be sick if he doesn't stop soon.

I turn back, take a look around to see if there's anything I can use to break out of the room. But there's nothing in here. Just my bed, chest of drawers and wardrobe.

Wardrobe! That's it.

I fling the door open and grab the closest coat hanger from the rail, throwing my blouse on the bed.

'It's OK,' I call to Jake, although he won't be able to hear me over his distress. 'I'm coming, little one.'

I crouch down at the lock and try to bend the coat hanger

into a hook shape. Then I thread it through the lock, twisting it. I don't really know what I'm doing, but I've seen this work on television programmes, so surely it must be possible?

I keep twisting and twisting it but it won't budge.

'Oh, darling,' I say, tears streaming down my face now. What is she doing to him? This crazy woman that I let into my home. I'm so stupid. After Kylie, I should have learnt my lesson. I should have just got used to being alone. 'I'm coming, I'm coming!'

The coat hanger is too big. I'm desperate now and I stand back, wondering if it might be possible to bash the door down with something. But it's impossible. The pine is thick; I'd have more luck smashing down a wall.

I turn back to my chest of drawers, scrabbling around in my jewellery box. I definitely have some hairpins somewhere. I'm sure of it.

Eventually I find one, and I twist it into a smaller hook, threading it through the lock. But I'm panicked and stressed and my fingers are fumbling and useless. I keep dropping the hairpin on the floor.

Jake is still screaming. It feels as though he's been screaming ever since he arrived.

'I'm so sorry, my darling boy,' I say, my face streaked with tears of my own. 'I'm coming, I promise.'

It reminds me of Brian. My boy. The way he would howl and howl as I sat downstairs, eating my dinner. I so wanted to go and comfort him, but Mother insisted.

'He has to learn,' she said, putting a firm hand on my shoulder as though she knew I was about to leap up at any moment. 'He has to learn to settle himself.'

'But he sounds so sad,' I said, and she shook her head at me, laughing.

'Oh, so you're the expert now, are you?' she said. 'Have you ever raised a child? No. Didn't think so.'

I hated hearing Brian cry. It felt like he was sobbing for us both. For me, his real mother, for what had happened to me, and for himself, knowing that he now faced a childhood similar to mine, when it might have been so different.

But Mother was right. I had never raised a child. I was still at school. I didn't have any money, no time to take care of him. I had no choice but to give him up.

But listening to him cry – that's something I will never forget. I can't stand it. And now, for poor Jake, it's the same.

'Oh, for goodness' sake!' I shout, exasperated as the hairpin falls out of the lock again. I wipe my tears away and pick up it up again. I can't remember the last time I cried.

I have to focus. I have to get a grip.

I pause before putting it back into the lock. I tell myself that this time, it's going to work. And I take a deep breath and push it into the hole.

I'm calmer as I twist it this way and that, and eventually I hear a satisfying clunk as the lock turns.

'Thank God!'

I practically fall out into the hallway, rushing through to Fiona's room. Jake is lying in his cot, still crying, but more pathetically now, as though he's run out of energy. He's covered in sick.

'Oh, you poor darling,' I say, scooping him up. The vomit

is cold and I change him quickly, my hands still shaking. His nappy was wet through too.

'I'm so sorry.' I smooth down his rumpled hair as I dress him in fresh clothes. He looks up at me, his lips twisting into something like a smile. But surely not? Surely he's too young for that?

I feel my heart lift, and I pick him up and kiss his little cheek.

'I promise I'll make sure you're OK,' I say, looking into his bright blue eyes. 'I promise. I will look after you, Jake, as long as I'm alive.'

FAYE

The procession has almost reached the bonfire. I can see the lights at the edge of the green. Rachel was right. There's something quite mesmerising about it.

The crowd outside is rowdy. People start to cheer as they see the trail of torches approach. There's the sound of laughter, glasses clanking, people chatting and shouting.

Across the other side of the green, a man is pumping out soulless pop music through a sound system, punctuating it with occasional updates on how the procession is going and shout-outs for missing children.

The green is absolutely rammed with people now. This is the perfect time to escape.

I'll have to walk the three miles to the next village, but from there I should be able to catch the bus into King's Lynn.

I try to keep my head down as I push my way through the people. But then I hear a shout that makes me look up.

'Fiona! Hello!'

It's Valerie, the woman from the chemist.

Shit.

I turn away from her in a hurry, pretending not to hear. But as I rush to get away, I stumble and bump into someone.

'Sorry,' I say, looking up without thinking.

But the face I see in front of me makes no sense.

Louis.

Louis is here. On the village green. Standing in front of me, his eyes filled with fury.

Am I hallucinating? I can't be sure.

'Hello, Faye,' he hisses, his eyebrows rising. 'Fancy seeing you here.'

I'm not hallucinating. It's really him.

I turn to flee.

FAYE

Louis is quicker than I give him credit for. He grabs me in a chokehold, his arm around my neck, his chest pushed against my back.

'Well, well, well,' he snarls. 'Long time no see. What have you done with my son?'

'Get off me,' I stutter, but it's difficult to speak with the way he's compressing my throat.

'Not until you tell me what you've done with him.'

'I . . . don't know what you're talking about!' I say. I look up, desperately trying to catch someone's eye, but they're all oblivious to us, and it's too dark for them to see what he's doing, that the way he's holding me isn't just a bear hug from behind.

'Listen to me, you pathetic little bitch. Tell me where he is, and you won't get hurt.' His breath is warm against my ear. 'I'm not messing around. You've wasted more than enough of my time.'

'I haven't . . .' I say, gulping in shallow breaths. 'I haven't got your son. I don't know what you're talking about. How did you find me?'

'Dear me, Faye, liars never prosper. Be careful. I know he's here. I know you took him. Tell me where he is, you little psycho, and I might not actually kill you.'

My fingers clutch the knife. But it's no good. I can't move while he's holding me like this.

My mind races. I don't have any choice. If I take him back to the cottage, perhaps I can escape again while he's distracted with Jake.

'He's . . . back at the cottage,' I stutter.

'That's better. Now we're getting somewhere. Now, walk.'

He pushes me forward and I stumble across the green towards Rachel's house, one of his hands pinching my shoulder so tightly that the bone starts to ache.

The front door is ajar. I must have forgotten to close it when I left earlier. I push it open, stepping inside the living room. The lights are off and the room is silent.

'You'd better not be messing me around,' Louis spits, looking around the room. 'Where is he?'

As if answering his call, Jake gives a wail from upstairs. My heart pounds.

Is Rachel still locked in? How am I going to get out of this situation?

'Shit,' Louis says, and for a split second he loosens his grip around me.

For the time it takes for him to consider his course of action, I picture it all.

My hopes and dreams. The life I thought we would live together. The way he charmed me, promising me the world. Telling me he loved me, when in truth I was nothing to him. Just a piece of meat. A womb for hire.

351

You pathetic little bitch.

That's how he sees me. Just like Marshall.

Dispensable.

Easily replaced.

Easily replaced by his poor, naive housekeeper who needed the money.

Fiona.

Another woman manipulated by a man who felt nothing for anyone. A man who saw people as accessories, pawns in the performance of his life.

The arm Louis has wrapped around mine relaxes for just a millisecond.

But it's long enough.

I wrench myself free, turn and plunge the vegetable knife into his neck, as hard as I can.

His eyes pop with shock and he raises a hand to the knife, stumbling backwards.

It takes a second before he realises what I've done.

Before *I* realise what I've done.

More bloodstains on Rachel's floor. She'll be upset.

Another hopeless lodger bringing trouble to her door.

RACHEL

I stand in the window of Fiona's room, holding Jake and looking out across the green. I can hear voices downstairs. What is she doing down there? And who's down there with her?

The procession is coming closer. They'll be down Pack Lane, having set off from Dayle Farm. A snake-like trail of torchlight, making its way towards the bonfire, keeping time with the slow drumbeat.

It's almost mythical, the procession. People stop and stare, speechless, as they watch.

It's a clear, dry evening. That makes all the difference. When it rains, it's no fun at all. But usually, we're lucky. Usually, Bonfire Night is clear.

All our plans have come together, and yet . . . I hold Jake close to my chest.

I am paralysed at the top of the stairs. I know I need to go downstairs now and confront Fiona. Take charge. If she's even still here.

But I think back to when I found Kylie, and shudder at the memory of it.

I had known, of course, that Kylie was having a hard time of it. Her boyfriend – the useless weasel of a man – had broken her heart just a few months before. I don't know what she saw in him, but I have never understood romantic love. It's not something that's ever afflicted me, thankfully.

I tried to console her, to remind her she was young and, relatively speaking, attractive; that she would find someone else who was more worthy to love her. But she didn't listen. She became more and more depressed.

I thought if I contacted him, and asked him to consider giving their relationship another try, that would help cheer her up. But it backfired, and he sent her a string of abusive messages calling her a loser, among other juvenile insults.

Unfortunately, rather than this helping her to realise what a nasty piece of work he was, she was utterly devastated.

I think that night, with the scissors, was just a cry for help. We had argued, and I'd stormed upstairs to my room, leaving her downstairs in a state.

It was just a cry for help from a desperate young woman, but she went too far.

Catastrophic blood loss.

Bad things happen in this house. That's what my mother said, right before she died.

And bad things have happened again, tonight. Fiona isn't who she says she is. She's unhinged. She locked me in my room, and left her baby to scream until he was sick.

I snuggle Jake to me, kissing his soft head. Part of me wishes we could just disappear together, the two of us. Wishes we could escape somewhere, start a new life. Just me and him.

Could we?

But he's not Brian. I know that. Brian is grown up now, living in Australia, working as a software developer. He's happy. He's built a good life for himself, away from this house and its ghosts.

Brian still thinks I'm his big sister Rachel. Mother made me promise not to tell him, and I've kept that promise. But it's been so painful. Over the years, the pain has become more engrained, a scar that's so deep it will never fade.

I look at Jake. He yawns, his eyes closing sleepily.

It's no good. I have to go down there, and take back control of my own home. I have to be strong.

FAYE

I stare down at Louis' body.

It was no more than he deserved. I'm sick of being treated like this. Of people telling me I'm worthless.

The room is cold; freezing air is rushing in through the open front door. I gaze out of it and onto the green beyond. The crowds are thick now, obscuring the view of the bonfire. The torchlight procession is getting closer, and I can hear a distant slow drumbeat growing ever so slightly louder. As though they are coming for me.

What am I going to do?

I slump down by Louis' side, momentarily exhausted by it all. Upstairs, I hear Rachel moving about. Jake is no longer crying. It's only a matter of time.

Louis' eyes are wide open, fixed like two glass beads. His lips are slightly parted, as though he's about to speak. The knife is still sticking in the side of his neck, his hand wrapped around it, coated in treacly blood.

I don't even know if he's dead yet.

'You hurt me more than anyone has ever hurt me,' I say to his body. 'I thought you loved me. I was so sure . . . that we had something special. I thought we were going to be a family. But you made a fool out of me.'

His chest isn't moving any longer.

'You should never have left Jake alone in the car,' I say. 'What kind of father does something like that? It's almost as though . . . as though you were telling me I should take him.'

The last time Louis and I actually spoke was on the phone. He rang me, and as soon as I answered, I could tell something was wrong. His tone was different. He was short with me. Irritated.

'Dr Wright said the results of your blood test don't make any sense,' he said. 'That your levels are way lower than they should be or something.'

I remember thinking, even before I knew the cold truth, *oh, he isn't going to be sympathetic, then.*

Premature ovarian insufficiency.

Insufficiency. I was *insufficient* to his needs.

I told him what the GP had told me.

'What does that mean?' he said, and from the way he was speaking I could picture his face, his forehead wrinkling into a frown. I had learnt enough by then to know that Louis didn't like it when things didn't go his way. He had to be in control.

'It means I've gone into early menopause,' I replied.

'Menopause? But that's . . .'

'Yes,' I said. My heart was racing at the prospect of losing him. 'But it's possible that I can still conceive. We might just have to use donor eggs, that's all.'

'Donor eggs?'

I should have recognised that there were no words of

357

comfort for me, that he had gone straight past that and on to how it affected him and his plans. What he wanted.

'I know it's not what we wanted . . .'

'You could say that,' he said, his voice dry with sarcasm. 'Listen, I'll have to . . . I'm going to have to think about this.'

'Of course,' I said, like a pathetic sacrificial lamb. 'Of course. I'm sorry. It's a shock . . . it's been a shock to me too.'

'Yes, let's take some time to process, shall we? Catch up soon.'

And then he hung up. And I never heard from him again. The very last time he saw me, I was standing outside his house in the rain, crying, and he walked straight past me as though I wasn't even there.

I look down at his lifeless body. It's his fault that it's come to this.

It's amazing, really. That someone could be that cruel. To switch from being so charming and wonderful to being, well, evil. Just like Marshall.

And I had fallen for it twice. Stupid, idiotic me.

I tried to call Louis a few days later, but of course he didn't pick up. Then he blocked my number. I left messages with his assistant, until she started screening my calls too.

I turned up at his place of work. I stopped eating completely. I drank every night, the red wine we drank when we first met, remembering the night at the opera, the way he called me magnificent, the dreams I had had of us becoming a real family.

I turned up at his flat, banging on the door until his housekeeper came out and told me he was away.

Fiona.

She looked at me with pity.

'Mr Horton-Jones does not want see you,' she said, and I felt a surge of anger. I wanted to reach forward and claw at her face. She could see the state I was in – my face swollen from crying, my hair unwashed, my desperate expression.

'I am sorry. He said if you don't leave, he will call police,' she said softly, and that made me cry even more as she closed the door and I slumped down onto the steps outside his expensive London home.

I had been so stupid to believe what he had promised. That he could love me. When all the signs were so clear, if only I hadn't fooled myself into ignoring them.

He was callous and determined. He had picked me precisely because I was vulnerable and isolated, someone he could easily manipulate.

I went underground after that. Whenever I wasn't teaching, I was looking into where he was, what he was doing and who he was doing it with.

Stalking, I suppose you could call it.

I cut my hair short and hid round the corner from his flat so that I could follow him whenever he left.

One day I followed him all the way to the riverside, and watched as he disappeared inside a door underneath the railway arches. The sign above the door said PleasureBox. A massage parlour. But when I looked it up online, it turned out to be a brothel.

He had so many secrets.

It all came to a head about seven months after he ghosted

me. I sat at the bus stop over the road from his flat, my parka hood pulled down low over my head. And I waited.

I'd got used to the waiting. I quite liked it: watching the people of Palace Terrace Court coming and going. The lady with the two tiny dogs she pushed around in a buggy. The old man with the horn-rimmed spectacles and holey cardigans, who looked homeless, except he must have actually been incredibly wealthy, because he had the whole of one of the terraced houses on the street.

But that Sunday, something else happened. Louis came out of his front door, and my skin prickled in something like excitement. The truth was, it was exciting, stalking him. Every time I saw him and he didn't see me, I felt a rush of adrenalin, as though I was playing a real, live-action computer game, and I'd just scored another victory.

But trailing behind him today was his housekeeper.

I stood up, crossed the road, and crouched behind a parked car, pretending to do up my shoelace.

I only learnt her name that day.

'Come on, Fiona,' he said crossly. 'We'll be late.'

She nodded and turned to shut the door.

And that was when I saw it.

Her bump, bulging beneath a fitted white T-shirt. Her *pregnant* bump.

He put his arm around her as he guided her into his car. I strained to hear their conversation above the drone of the traffic.

'The doctor will be waiting,' he said. 'And I don't have long. I need to be in Manchester tonight.'

'Yes, Mr Horton-Jones,' she said.

A womb for rent.

That's all she was to him. He had replaced me – his failed attempt at securing himself an heir – with someone a little closer to home. A little less likely to cause him problems.

After that, I was obsessed. I came back to the flat as often as I could to watch her as she grew and grew and grew. And one day, after he left home and disappeared down the street, I pulled my hood over my head and rang the doorbell.

Before she had the chance to realise it was me, I kicked the door open with my foot and forced my way into the hall and through the front door of Louis' flat.

'Oh!' she said. Her hands immediately wrapped themselves around her stomach. 'It's you!'

'You're pregnant,' I said when she followed me into the front room. It looked the same. The showy Steinway sitting proud in the bay window. The room was just as immaculate as it was the last time I was there, apart from a vacuum cleaner that was sprawled in the middle of the expensive Chinese rug.

'He's making you clean!' I shouted, indignantly.

She looked down.

'How long until the baby is due?' I asked, and she stared at me, then shook her head. 'It is his baby, right?'

She nodded then. I could see how frightened she was. Did she think I was going to hurt her?

'Tell me,' I said, taking a step towards her and grabbing her wrist. 'What the situation is. Are you a couple now?'

She shook her head.

'For God's sake,' I said. 'You can speak!'

'I ... I'm ...' she began. I wondered just how good her English was. 'I'm ... like you? Su ... surrogate?'

'Oh,' I said.

'It a favour for Mr Horton-Jones. He so want to be a daddy.'

She looked so young. Barely twenty.

'He say it didn't work with you,' she said, smiling at me. 'I'm sorry.'

I felt tears threaten.

'He used me,' I said. 'He ... took advantage of me. Like he's taking advantage of you! You mustn't let him ...'

'Oh, but,' she said, smiling at me nervously, 'it's good money. Good money for baby.'

It shouldn't have surprised me, but it did.

'He's paying you! How much?'

She looked confused.

'I send it home to my mother. She's very sick. She needs it, for the hospital.'

'How much?'

'It was £50,000,' she said, hanging her head. 'I thought ... you the same. Surrogate.'

I shook my head.

'But the baby,' I asked, staring down at her bump. For a minute, I couldn't understand. Louis was *buying* a baby? 'Don't you want ... don't you want to keep it?'

Her eyes filled with tears then, mirroring mine. She didn't reply straight away.

'I'm still young,' she said. 'I'm going home after, with the money, and take care of my mother.'

She hung her head.

'I'm sorry,' she said. 'I have to do it.'

'What are you sorry for?'

She sniffed, wiped an eye with the back of her hand.

'What I don't like . . . after baby comes, Louis tell everyone the baby is yours. That you leave him heartbroken. He doesn't want foreign mummy for his baby. Not servant's baby. But I have no choice. I have to help my mother.'

'You mean he's lying to everyone about me? He's going to pretend that I'm the baby's mother, and that I abandoned it?'

She nodded. I could see she was terrified, not just of Louis, but of me too.

'Please. I'm sorry.'

'It's OK,' I said. 'It's not your fault.'

I turned and left. What more was there to say? It was game over. Louis had got what he wanted – found the woman he could use, found a way of using her that was far cleaner than the sticky situation he got into with me. Cold, hard cash. That was Louis' language. The only language he spoke.

But now.

I look down at his lifeless body.

Now he'll never speak again.

RACHEL

I take a deep breath, one hand on the banister, the other wrapped tightly around this innocent bundle of a baby who deserves all the love in the world, and, screwing my courage to the sticking place, I inch my way down the stairs.

I am four steps from the bottom of the stairs when I peer round the banister into the dim light of my living room. The light from the torches on the green floods through the open front door.

My heart starts to hammer with fear. Has someone tried to break in? Drunken teenagers. I was right all along. Little hooligans.

Where is Daisy? I hope she isn't hurt. I hope she hasn't made a run for it and got lost among all the people on the green.

My anger is superseded by fear this time. Where is Fiona?

I'm holding Jake. I'm vulnerable.

I consider calling out to her, but what would be the point? If she was interested in Jake – in me – she wouldn't have locked me in the room and left him screaming and covered in his own vomit.

I take another step down.

And then I crane my neck to look back into the bowels of my little cottage, towards the dining table that I sat at eating miserable meals with my parents, towards the run of units along the back wall that constitutes the kitchen.

And that's when I see it. A body, lying on the floor in the darkness.

I close my eyes, think of Kylie. I can't believe this is happening again.

Mother was right. This house is cursed.

Too many bodies have lain on this floor. Even though I have scrubbed and scrubbed the parquet, it has never seemed clean to me. Stained with blood that won't ever wash away.

'Fiona!' I call, because I'm too scared to go straight up to the body. I can't tell who it is, if it's even her. I can only see a pair of legs sticking out from behind the sofa.

'Are you there?'

But nothing. My voice is almost drowned out by the hubbub on the village green.

I have the same feeling of fear I had that Bonfire Night all those years ago. But the difference is then I had Mother there, telling me what to do. This time I'm all alone.

Apart from Jake. Jake needs me. I have to be strong.

I nearly lose my footing as I take the final step down onto the parquet floor. I can see a bit more of the body from here. Whoever it is, they are wearing jeans.

It's not Fiona.

I hurry towards them. And that's when I finally see her, crouched over the body of a man with bright blond hair. Even

365

in the darkness I can tell that it's him. I recognise him from the things I've read online.

Louis Horton-Jones.

He has come, then. He did get my emails after all.

'Fiona! What have you done?'

She stands up and backs away, her eyes fixed on me.

I cry out and lean down over the body. But Jake is still in my arms and I'm worried I'll squash him, so I lay him carefully on the sofa and rush back to Louis.

'Is he all right?' I say, even though I know he's not. I give him a little shake, and something squelches, the sound of something sticky and horrible. My fingers curl with disgust as I place a hand on his cheek and try to lift his head, and that's when I see that he has one hand raised, clasped around something.

A knife handle.

But the blade is not visible, because the entirety of it is inside his neck.

I sit back in horror.

'Oh God,' I say. 'Oh no, please God, no! What have you done?'

'It was self-defence,' Fiona says, her voice low. I can't look at her. 'He was going to kill me. I didn't have a choice.'

'No!' I cry. 'Please God. Not again.'

'I'm sorry.' I can't look at her. 'I'm sorry for everything, Rachel. But he deserved it.'

I close my eyes, but the memories – disconnected fragments – rush in.

It hadn't been a knife that night. Mother had used a hammer.

One of Father's own.

It split his skull nearly in two. We found tiny blood spatters, pieces of his brain and skin and bone, all over the house for weeks after.

'Help me, Rachel,' Mother said, as I raced down the stairs after hearing them shouting at one another. 'Help me drag him into the garden.'

'Mother!' I shouted. 'What have you . . .'

But her eyes blazed at me and I knew not to ask any more questions. I did as I was told, and together we heaved my father's large, lifeless body into the garden.

'I'll bury him later, when the fireworks start,' she said, wiping her hands on her apron. 'He can go in that pond he'd started to dig. You take care of your brother while I sort this out.'

Brian was just two at the time.

'But Mother,' I said, even though I was terrified. 'Why? Why did you . . .'

She had never been violent towards him before, had never even stood up for herself. Not that I'd seen anyway. She was scared of him, or so I thought.

'I've had enough. He's a cheating bastard,' she said, hissing. 'He made a fool out of me. I didn't believe it before, despite all the rumours. Despite the gossip in the village. But I've seen it now, with my own eyes. He's been sleeping with Margery Miller. That little trollop!'

She turned to me. I stared at her, wide-eyed and in shock.

That was my opportunity, I knew. To tell her the truth. But I was too scared of how she might react, so I just stood there like an idiot, and watched as she cried, waiting for her to stop.

I didn't feel any sympathy for her. She was a weak, selfish woman, my mother.

But she wasn't as bad as him.

I missed the fireworks that year. Instead, I was in the garden, helping my mother bury my father in his pond. Brian was fast asleep upstairs. He never knew any of it.

After it was done, she told me I could never leave. That I would have to stay in this house forever, to make sure that no one ever found him.

'They'll lock you up if they do,' she said. 'You're involved, and you're seventeen years old. Not a child.'

Later, when people started to ask, she told the neighbours that she had thrown him out after finding out about his affair with Margery.

'Run off with his fancy piece,' she said, to sympathetic looks in the corner shop. 'Left me to bring up his two kids. Well, good riddance to him.'

But Margery was still there. I used to see her sometimes, in the village, and she'd scurry away. She never asked where my father had gone, but she must have wondered. Perhaps she thought he'd tired of her too. Perhaps she suspected, and was scared of what my mother might do to her if she asked.

Margery was Fiona's great-aunt. I should have taken it as a sign. Why didn't I listen to my instincts?

My mother died when Brian was twenty-two. He was away then, at university. The last few years of her life were difficult, and I had to care for her as well as working.

I thought I'd feel better after she died, but I didn't. I just felt alone. And constantly terrified that the body we buried that night might one day resurface.

That was when I decided to take in a lodger. So that I would never have to be alone in the house. But one by one, they all left me. Elizabeth, the first, who had walked out on her drunk husband to move in with me, said I scared her. That I was overfamiliar. Creepy.

It hurt. I had loved that girl as though she was a sister. I thought we could make our own little family together.

All of those women, I tried to make them into family, but something always went wrong.

And now, Fiona. Fiona is the worst of them all.

'Why did you do this?' I say, sobbing. 'Why did you kill him?'

I look back up, at the spot she was standing on just a moment ago, but she's gone. Vanished.

'Fiona?' I call, into the darkness of my living room. 'Fiona! Where are you?'

I'm terrified.

My hands trembling, I walk to the kitchen and pick up the telephone and call 999. The roads are closed because of the procession, but they tell me they will get to me as soon as possible.

'Please,' I beg down the phone. 'Please come quickly. I can't bear to be here alone.'

FAYE

My heart is racing as I flee the cottage. I can't believe I am running away again, that it has come to this.

That I've ended up in this situation once more.

But this time I don't have the benefit of a head start. People will be looking for me already.

I have only my coat and my handbag, the rest of my cash stashed away inside.

Somehow, I have to find my way back to my little flat in London.

Perhaps I'll be lucky again. Perhaps I'll get away with it. Perhaps I can go back to the simple life that I had before – teaching, sitting in the pub with Jonas, having Sunday lunch with Hannah, my sister who got to live the life I wanted. Because life's a lottery, and not everyone can be a winner.

The green is thick with people, pushing and shoving and trying to get closer to the bonfire.

I wonder what Rachel will do now. I know she has her own secrets. I know how much she loves Jake. Perhaps she won't want to give him up. Perhaps she'll keep him. Perhaps that will be for the best after all.

But there's a niggle in my mind. The niggle that has always

been there, from the very start. The sad look in Fiona's eyes as she told me that Louis had paid her to have the baby.

She pretended she wasn't upset by it, but I watched the way she cradled her bump, and I knew she felt more for that baby than she wanted to admit.

He should never have been taken away from her.

I should never have taken him away from her.

I can't think about Fiona though. I have to focus on getting away, and hoping that they don't track me down.

Rachel doesn't know my real name, and Louis is dead. If I'm careful, and if I'm quick, perhaps I'll be lucky.

I pull the hood of my coat down low over my face, and I squeeze my way past all the people drinking and chatting and *oohing* and *ahhing* at the sight of the procession.

The 'bonfire boys and girls' – as Rachel called them – are on the green itself now. A section has been cordoned off for them to walk down, and they cut through the crowd holding their torches aloft.

I am surrounded by happy families – dads with preschoolers held on their shoulders, grandparents waving sparklers at wide-eyed babies in the crisp night air. The irony of it isn't lost on me – the fact that I will never have this; that I will never experience this for myself.

I have always been on the outside of everything. No one has ever wanted me.

The slow drumbeat from the procession calms me. I keep my footsteps in time with its rhythm. One foot in front of the other, until I am free of this place.

Soon, I reach the edge of the green. The crowds of people

all have their backs to me, turned towards the bonfire. I pause, looking back, as the drumbeat stops and the man on the megaphone begins a countdown from ten.

Then there's a great cheer as the torchbearers throw their torches into the bonfire, setting it ablaze. It takes a few seconds to catch, but the dry, cold night provides the perfect conditions and a crackling sound erupts as the fire takes hold and the flames leap into the air.

Rachel was right. It is a sight to behold.

I turn away from the fire and towards the lane that leads into the village.

I am the only one who notices the blue lights flashing in the distance, growing larger as they speed towards Helston. A trail of them, lighting up the November sky.

Blue lights that I know are coming for me.

SIX MONTHS LATER

RACHEL

I wanted to keep him, of course I did. He reminded me so much of Brian. And it felt like a higher power was giving me another chance at being a mother.

The one I never got to be the first time around.

But that wouldn't have been fair on his real mother. His biological mother, who grew him inside her, and gave birth to him. I would be denying her in the same way that my own mother denied me.

And anyway, it was impossible once the police were involved. There were hours of questions, endless probing and criticism. No one would tell me what was going on, who Fiona really was, or why she stabbed Louis. It was exhausting. They kept me in the police station for what felt like days. There was no respect for my age.

Eventually, they realised that I had nothing to hide. That I was telling them the truth. And that's when they told me that Fiona wasn't Fiona after all. Her name was Faye Miller, and she had kidnapped baby Jake. I told them about the menopause medication I found, zipped under the lining of her suitcase. And they told me they had found her just a few hours after she left the village, and apparently it was all over and she was locked in a cell somewhere, awaiting her fate.

There was one policewoman in particular – PC Andrea Jones. I liked her.

I saw in some of the notes they had written about me that they had wondered whether I might be classed as a 'vulnerable adult'. They seemed to find my proclivity for hygiene and cleanliness cause for concern, rather than simple good sense.

'You're a victim in this too, Rachel,' Andrea said. 'You've been through a really traumatic time.'

I bit my lip. I wasn't used to people being this kind to me.

'Jake is the real victim,' I said.

He was being fostered somewhere, they said. I was devastated – I'd never even got to say a proper goodbye.

'We're working on tracking down his birth mother,' Andrea Jones said to me. 'Don't worry, we'll try our absolute best to get them reunited. It seems there was a lot going on with Mr Horton-Jones' business and personal life that he wanted to keep hidden from the police.'

'Will you let me know when you find her?' I said. 'I know it's not my place but . . .'

'Of course,' she said.

'I should have known he wasn't Fiona's . . . I mean, Faye's . . . but I was so confused . . . he was such a lovely baby, and at first, she was so convincing. I just wanted to help them both.'

She smiled.

'None of this was your fault. Listen to me, Rachel. None of it.'

I nodded, but if I had never emailed Louis to begin with,

376

then he would never have turned up, and Fiona would never have had the chance to kill him.

Brian was right about meddling in other people's business. It never ends well.

I took a sip of the disgusting police station tea. I hadn't the heart to tell Andrea that she was making it all wrong. The porcelain was stained on the inside. I knew just the thing to remove that stain, but I didn't think Andrea would be interested in all that.

'Can I tell you something?' I said, and she looked up from the notebook she was writing in.

'Of course,' she said, smiling again. I liked her smile: the kindness in her eyes. I wondered if she had a child of her own, what kind of mother she was.

'It's about something that happened a long time ago,' I said, hesitating slightly. 'To me.'

'You can trust me,' Andrea said. 'I promise.'

I believed her.

I nodded, closed my eyes and took a deep breath.

'It's about my father,' I began.

I sold the cottage, eventually, once the police had done all their digging – literally and metaphorically – and concluded their investigation.

What broke my heart was that they had to involve Brian. But of course, he couldn't remember a thing. He was only a tot when it happened. When he found out the truth about how he was conceived, he came straight over on a plane from Australia.

We spent hours talking. He told me he had always suspected there was more to our family than he knew about.

'I just had a feeling,' he said. 'Mother was always so strange with me. Doting one minute, and cold and heartless the next.'

I had never cried as much as I cried that day.

But now, things are better.

I have moved into a brand-new flat in the next town along. It's near enough that I don't feel completely cut off from everyone I knew in the village. Nigel has been to visit. I'm still able to be on the bonfire committee, and I've taken a part-time job volunteering at the local library.

I even had a letter from Moira at the Girl Guides, formally apologising for accusing me of hitting Lissa Martin, and asking me if I'd like my position back. Apparently, Lissa had gone on to say the same thing about a number of teachers at her school, and it turns out she had been lying for attention, after all.

I took great pleasure in responding to Moira and telling her that I would be far too busy with my new positions of responsibility to rejoin the Guides.

Last night, Kylie came to visit me. She offered to do my nails again and I made her a cup of Earl Grey.

'I've finished my beautician's training,' she said, as she sat opposite me at my dining table, pushing my cuticles back with a little wooden stick. 'Fully qualified now, aren't I? And I've got a job at that new salon round the corner. So you can come and visit me whenever you like, and I'll sort you out. Mates' rates, Rach.'

I smiled.

'Thank you,' I said. 'I'm . . . pleased to see you looking so well.'

The sleeves of her jumper were slightly rolled up, and as she moved her hands, I saw the scars across her wrists. But they were almost healed, and soon they would fade.

'If it hadn't been for you,' she said, as she noticed me looking, 'then seriously, Rach, God knows where I would be right now. You heard the doctors. If you hadn't found me in time, then I'd be dead. I don't know what the fuck I thought I was playing at.'

'I'm only sorry that you . . .' I began. 'Well, I should never have interfered.'

'You were just looking out for me, Rach,' she said, and I felt my eyes start to prickle. 'I'm sorry I was too much of a twat to see that at the time. You're a good person. Rock solid.'

I rolled my eyes.

'Well, I don't know about—'

'Nah, seriously,' she said, taking my hands in hers and squeezing them. She looked me directly in the eyes. 'Thank you. You saved my life.'

My cheeks felt hot. I gave a short nod, and then she turned back to my manicure. She's found a new suitor now. One who sounds a lot more *suitable*.

It was good to see her, and before she left, we promised to stay in touch. It's taken me a while to get used to having bright red nails, but I suppose it's a little bit of fun, and you're a long time dead, as Brian always says.

I've also joined a writing group. That was Andrea's suggestion. She thought that writing down my story might help me.

379

She suggested all sorts of counsellors and support lines and the rest of it, but I don't want to rake over the past endlessly. What's done is done.

I don't feel lonely any more. I have Daisy, and I keep myself busy, and my flat is neat and tidy and just what I need.

Most importantly of all, there are no stains on the floor, and I don't share it with any ghosts.

RACHEL

I am busy typing up the longhand version of my first chapter on the little laptop that Brian bought me, when the doorbell rings.

I love this flat. I can sit on the small terrace and look out over the street, and watch all the comings and goings. It feels peaceful here, surrounded by people.

Daisy miaows as I stand up, hopping down from her cat tree.

I'm glad I don't have to lock her in any more. Deep down, I knew it was foolish – she was only a cat, after all – but I was always so scared of her digging up Father's grave. But now we live in this lovely cul-de-sac and Brian helped me fit a cat flap in the French window to my terrace, so Daisy can come and go as she pleases.

I answer the door. It's Andrea. I try to remember when I last saw her. It must have been several months ago now.

Faye is awaiting trial for kidnap and murder. There's been a lot of noise in the newspapers, but I've been trying to keep out of it all. Luckily, the reporters don't seem to have worked out where I live yet.

'Hello,' I say, 'this is an unexpected surprise.'

'Sorry not to call ahead,' Andrea says. 'I was just driving past and I thought I'd see if you were in. Have you got a minute?'

'Of course,' I say, standing aside to let her in.

It's a cold January, and she's trussed up like an Eskimo.

'Let me take your coat,' I say. 'Brian hung these pegs up here for me, right by the door. Isn't that good? Just where you need them.'

'Thanks, Rachel,' she says.

'Cup of tea?'

'Lovely.'

We sit side by side in my small living room. I like the way she notices everything. It's all new. Brian's idea – he told me not to take anything from the cottage with me when I moved here.

'You've made this place so cosy,' she says, smiling.

'It suits me just right.'

'I wanted to see how you were doing – but also, we have some news. We tracked down Jake's biological mother. Fiona Ivanov.'

'That was the name that was written in Jake's red book.'

'Yes,' she says. 'She was Louis Horton-Jones' housekeeper. It seems he offered her a large sum of money to have his child, under the condition that she never reveal her identity as Jake's biological mother. She was desperate for the money because her mother was very sick and in need of expensive hospital care. Anyway, we've found her – and she's come back to the UK to collect Jake.'

'Will she be in trouble? Accepting money for surrogacy is a crime, isn't it?'

'Generally speaking, yes, but we're not expecting there to be any charges in this case.'

I close my eyes, picturing little Jake. His chubby cheeks, his huge round eyes.

'I miss him,' I say, unthinking.

'I know you do, Rachel. But this is good news.'

'Why did he do it?' I say angrily. 'Why did he try to buy a baby? It doesn't make any sense. Children are not commodities, things to be traded.'

'We think it was family pressure. He had a ... difficult relationship with his father and stepmother. He felt a lot of responsibility to produce an heir. Someone to pass the family business on to. But his family are very conservative and he wanted it to look legitimate. Hence his confusing relationship with Faye. When that didn't work out, he decided to go for an easier option with his housekeeper. A different kind of exploitation of a vulnerable woman.'

'That's awful.'

'It's all very sad. But the good news is that Fiona was over the moon to be reunited with her son. Also, Jake will eventually be a very wealthy boy. He'll inherit his father's money. Fiona will be able to provide the very best life for him.'

'Well, that's wonderful,' I say, and suddenly I'm crying. I reach for a tissue. 'The best outcome, really.'

'I know it's a lot to take in. But it's thanks to you, Rachel, that this little boy will grow up with the mother who loves him. You should be very proud of yourself. And I know Fiona is very grateful to you. In fact, she wanted you to have this.'

She reaches into her handbag and pulls out an envelope.

'Here. With her thanks.'

I open the envelope and pull out a photograph. Jake is sitting on his mother's knee, smiling for the camera.

He has changed so much in the few months since I last saw him. But he is the same gorgeous boy I held close to my chest that night, his face innocent of the drama of his short life thus far.

I turn the picture over.

There are only a few words written on the back, in simple writing.

Thank you, Rachel
from the bottom of our hearts
♡

EPILOGUE

FAYE

It's not so bad in prison, really.

It's taken me a while to get used to it, but there's a lot of comfort in the routine. I know exactly what to expect each day, and I like that. I've actually written it all out, like a mini timetable, and pinned it above my bed.

I've been offered counselling and all sorts. In fact, I can't remember a time in my life when I've been fussed over more.

I even overheard one of the psychologists call me *fascinating*.

I'm allowed to play the piano, and they suggested I might like to do a degree while I'm here. After all, I'm not going anywhere for a long time.

When I arrived, the other inmates mostly ignored me, and I tried to stay out of their way. It was the same as always – *Invisible Faye*.

I was so lonely.

But then I met Sonia.

She explained to me how things worked: that you had to pick your food options a week in advance – and which were the best choices – and that you had to put in an 'order' for absolutely everything you needed. She told me which guards were the friendliest and which I should avoid. Gave me tips on earning extra money to spend in the canteen.

She's certainly not a friend I'd expected to make. The first time I saw her we were all eating. She's a big woman – almost twice my size, with arms like boulders. I thought she was utterly terrifying, even before I saw her reach over and smash another inmate's face down onto the dining table, without warning, and for no specific reason.

The guards just looked away. They didn't seem to care.

Prison has its own rules, and I'm just starting to get to grips with them.

One night, a few weeks after we became friends, she invited me to her cell. We sat next to each other on her bed, and she gave me some chocolate.

'You don't belong in a place like this, do you, chick? You're like a butterfly in a cage full of elephants – all delicate wings fluttering around, no clue where you're going. If you're not careful, you're going to get trampled on. But I'll protect you.'

She was so kind. Later, she asked me what I was in for.

I told her I'd killed a man, and kidnapped his baby, and she laughed and said, 'Is that right?'

I'm not sure she believed me.

Ever since then, we've been looking out for each other. Sometimes, I do favours for her too. Hiding things in my room, delivering little parcels to people, that kind of thing. It's nothing, really. And it's so nice to have a real friend again.

A *best* friend.

Yesterday, Sonia gave me a small bundle, wrapped in torn

cloth. Not a parcel this time, but something just for me. To keep me safe, she said.

Last night, I unwrapped it when I was alone in my cell.

Inside was a toothbrush. At first, I was confused, and then I saw that the end of the handle had been sharpened into a point.

I wrapped it up again quickly.

I feel powerful with someone like Sonia on my side. Secure.

Even so, I probably won't tell Hannah about her when she comes in for her visit today.

She's still so upset about what happened with Louis.

Last time she visited, she told me what the police had uncovered: that Louis had been laundering vast sums of money through his father's gyms for the past few years.

'He's part of an organised crime group, Faye!' she said. 'I can't believe we had him round for lunch, that we didn't realise. We should have protected you. We let you down and I'm sorry.'

After everything he put me through, the news didn't really surprise me, but she was horrified that I'd ever been involved with someone so dangerous.

She was so upset about it.

Hannah would never believe that someone in here – someone like Sonia – would want to be friends with someone like me.

Yes, it's definitely best I don't tell Hannah about Sonia.

She'd only worry.

ACKNOWLEDGEMENTS

I had such fun writing this book, and I'm indebted to everyone who has had a hand in my writing career. First and foremost, thank you to my brilliant agent Caroline Hardman as always and for everything. And to my editors at Quercus: Cassie Browne and Kat Burdon, who are so wise and perceptive, thank you for helping me make my writing so much stronger. I genuinely enjoy receiving editorial feedback from you – it's so reassuring to know I have you on my 'team' and working with you really feels like a collaboration.

Thank you to all the people who have worked on this book behind-the-scenes at Quercus: Ella Patel, Ellie Nightingale, David Murphy, Frances Doyle and Amy Knight. And a huge thanks to Lisa Brewster, for yet another incredible cover.

Thank you to all my friends in the crime and psychological suspense writing community – it's an honour to be considered one of your peers, and one of the greatest joys of this job are the other writers I have met and become friends with. I'm biased but writers really are the most interesting and supportive people you could hope for as colleagues!

A huge thanks to my family, but especially to Ol who is my tireless sounding board when it comes to plot conundrums, and who listens so patiently and provides such brilliant ideas when my creative brain is spent. Special thanks to Daphne for telling everybody we meet 'my mummy is a writer'. I will never forget you telling a flight attendant about my books, as we queued for the toilet (on a 5am flight, when I certainly wasn't feeling my best!), listing all the titles perfectly and suggesting she look them up on her phone after we land. I'm as proud of you as you are of me, Pidge.

But finally, the biggest, hugest thanks to everyone who has read my previous books! It's honestly the most wonderful feeling to hear that I'm an 'auto-buy author' for some of you now – and your messages and social media mentions really keep me going when writing feels like a long, lonely slog in the dark. Thank you especially for all your reviews – I know they take time to write, but please keep them coming. I read as many of them as I can, and I so appreciate them.

As always, you can find me on social media @charduck or at my website: charlotteduckworth.com. I would love to hear from you!

I so hope you enjoyed *The Wrong Mother*. I'm immensely fond of Rachel, and I think this book might be my favourite yet (OK, yes, I do always say that! 😆).

Charlotte x

The perfect husband . . . or a perfect lie?

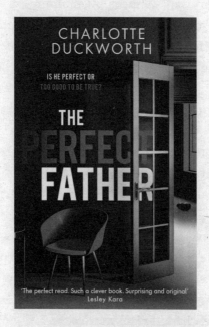

'Compulsively readable with an ending
you will not see coming'
Woman & Home

Out now in paperback, eBook and audio

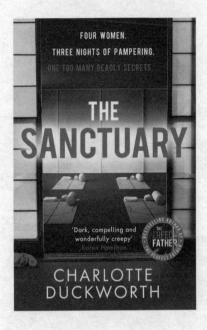

How far would you go to get what you want?

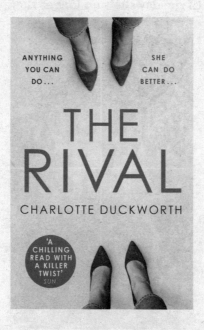

'A taut, chilling read with a killer twist at the end'
Sun

Out now in paperback, eBook and audio

You can't stop watching her.
Until the day she's no longer there . . .

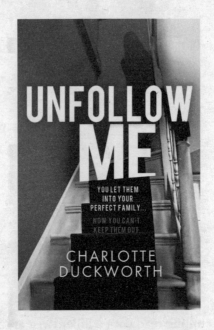

'Brilliant and insidious'
Lucy Clarke

Out now in paperback, eBook and audio

QUERCUS